MICROPHONES

AND
Murder

**The Podcasting Sisters Mystery Series
by Erin Huss**

MICROPHONES AND MURDER (#1)

PODCASTING *Sisters* MYSTERIES

MICROPHONES AND *Murder*

ERIN HUSS

HENERY PRESS

Copyright

MICROPHONES AND MURDER
A Podcasting Sisters Mystery
Part of the Henery Press Mystery Collection

First Edition | February 2020

Henery Press, LLC
www.henerypress.com

Trade Paperback ISBN-13: 978-1-63511-563-5
Digital epub ISBN-13: 978-1-63511-564-2
Kindle ISBN-13: 978-1-63511-565-9
Hardcover ISBN-13: 978-1-63511-566-6

Printed in the United States of America

To Debby Holt for restoring my confidence

ACKNOWLEDGMENTS

To my agents Ella Marie Shupe and Sharon Belcastro—your faith in my work and perseverance means everything to me. Thank you!

To Heather McCoubery, Kathryn R. Biel, and Debby Holt for the beta read, blurb help, and proof reading.

To everyone at Henery Press—I am grateful to be part of the Hen House. This has been a dream!

And, most importantly, thank you to Jed, Natalie, Noah, Emma, Ryder, and Fisher. I love you all.

SEASON ONE: WHERE'S AMELIA CLARK?

New True Crime Series Coming October 10!
Missing or Murdered

"Halleluiah we're here!" Camry drummed a celebratory tune on the dashboard. "And so begins the story of two sisters, setting out on a journey to solve a ten-year-old, cold-as-ice, minimal-evidence-provided, make-or-break-your-career, missing-person case. This moment has to be documented. Say cheese." She held up her phone and took a picture of us using a big-eyed Snapchat filter. "Why aren't you smiling, Liv? Aren't you excited?"

"I'll be more excited once we get settled." I unbuckled my seatbelt and peered out the window. Hazel's home looked like it was plucked from a Thomas Kinkaid painting. A two-story white farm-style house with teal shutters, dormer windows, a wraparound porch, and a beveled walkway lined with roses. This was the type of home where most people would imagine a happy family gathered around a dining room table, stuffed stockings on the mantel, kids playing catch in the backyard—the type of home where nothing bad ever happens.

But I was not most people.

When you spend your waking hours thinking, researching, and talking about murder and missing-person cases, your view on the world shifts. People are monsters. Monsters disguised as the handyman, the boyfriend, or the friendly neighbor in the cozy farm-style house at the end of the street.

Okay, I realize not *all* humans are monsters. Most are well-intended, law-abiding citizens. But I can't help myself. I'm a true crime podcaster, or I'm trying to be. But, as far as I knew, Hazel's house was just as idyllic as it appeared.

At least I hoped it was, because it was about to be my home for the next six months.

Sitting in a rocking chair on the porch was Hazel. Or so I assumed. We had never met. She's my stepsister, Camry's, great aunt on her father's side. I pictured Hazel as Sophia from the *Golden Girls*. In reality, she looked like every stock image of Mrs. Claus I'd ever seen.

"You're finally here!" Hazel tramped down the stairs with her arms open. "I've been looking forward to this for weeks."

Camry slammed the car door shut. "Aunt Hazel, it's been too long."

The two hugged while I unloaded the car.

"Look how gorgeous you are." Hazel held Camry at arm's length. "I see so much of your dad in you. God bless his soul." She made the sign of the cross.

So did Camry.

My arms were full.

"Come meet my sister, Liv Olsen," said Camry.

Hazel casted her eyes in my direction. "Oh you sweet thing, I thought you were one of the neighborhood kids helping with the luggage. Come here." She pulled me in for a hug. My head landed at her chest. When you're five feet tall, you spend a lot of time in boobs.

"Thank you for opening your home to us," I said, once released. "I can't tell you how much it means to me." I guess I could have told her, but I'd probably cry. Free boarding eliminated an entire section of my itemized budget for the show.

"Pffft, that's what family is for!" Hazel grabbed a suitcase. "I could not be more excited about your radio show."

"It's a podcast," I said.

Hazel paid no notice and wheeled the suitcase down the beveled walkway with her arm interlocked with Camry's. I grabbed the last of our bags and stood at the curb, gazing up at the house.

I can't believe I'm here.

I'm in Santa Maria.

I'm doing it.

Yikes!

Holy crap!

Oh my gosh.

Oh. My. Gosh. I'm doing this. I'm here. I'm investigating a decade old missing-person case. I've quit my job. Invested all my money. Never mind I have no idea how to actually create a podcast from scratch on my own—

I can't feel my legs.

"Liv, are you coming?" Camry hollered from the doorway and waved for me to come in. "Hurry up!"

One foot in front of the other, I told myself.

One foot in front of the other…

The inside of Hazel's house matched the front. To my left was a den with a brick fireplace, velvet armchairs, a floral sofa, and a grandfather clock. The carpet was teal, the walls were papered in a cherry blossom print, and there was a picture on every available surface—old photos in brown hues, modern school pictures of gapped-tooth children, Hazel with a gray-haired man I assumed to be her husband. Another one of Hazel and her husband on a cruise. Then Hazel and her husband in front of the Eiffel Tower. Then Hazel and her husband at a cemetery wearing all black and standing behind a cherry wood coffin with a splay of daisies on top. Two younger women with dark brown hair and Hazel's narrow jawline were standing beside them. Their noses were red, tissues were clutched in their hands, and their arms were wrapped around each other. The next picture was of Hazel and her husband in front of this home, standing behind a young boy with a mop of brown hair, sad blue eyes, a suitcase in hand, and a stuffed sea lion tucked under his arm.

You could learn a lot from family pictures.

The rest of the house was homey. A straight staircase, cottage windows, and a comfy looking couch in the family room. The dining room was to my right, the table was set, and in the kitchen was a buffet-style spread waiting for us—and fifty of our closest friends.

Oh my word. That's a lot of food.

Camry and I shared a look. We had stopped for dinner in Santa Barbara, but I wasn't about to turn down a meal. Not when Hazel went through so much trouble.

We left our luggage by the door, and I filled my plate with tri-tip, barbecued bread, macaroni salad, beans with bits of bacon tossed in, salsa, and a green salad. I sat at the table and gave my intestines a quick pep talk.

Hazel came from behind and filled my cup with lemon water. "Have you ever had real Santa Maria Style BBQ, Liv?"

"No, but I've read all about it." If you googled Santa Maria, California the first thing to come up would be Santa Maria Style BBQ, the second would be wine, the third strawberries, the fourth a guide to the local beaches (there are many), and the fifth would be a missing-person report for twenty-three-year-old Amelia Clark who was last seen October 10, 2008—which is what brought me here.

I took a bite of bread. *Oh my.* The crunch of buttery garlic filled my mouth. "This is amazing."

"These beans are delicious, too," said Camry with a mouthful. "And I don't even like beans."

"Special family recipe." Hazel winked.

Camry was right. The beans were the best thing I'd ever tasted. Until I dipped the bread into them. Then *that* was the best thing I'd ever eaten.

Hazel took a seat across from us with a plate piled with all the fixings. "I'm going to make pancakes for breakfast tomorrow morning, and I thought you might like to try my homemade spaghetti tomorrow night. For lunch, we'll do something simple, like salami sandwiches or macaroni salad. I'll write out the daily menu for you." She pointed to the chalkboard hung on the wall.

"You don't have to feed us," Camry said between bites. "Liv has a detailed budget. She even has a line item for toilet paper."

"I have toilet paper," Hazel said. "Is there a certain brand you need? I think mine is double-quilted let me check." She started to stand, and I stopped her.

"What Camry meant was that we don't want you to spend money on us. We have plenty set aside for food and necessities."

"I would never let a house guest of mine *pay* for food or toilet paper." She appeared hurt by the very notion. "If you want to stay at my house I get to feed you. That's part of the deal."

It's official. I'm in love with Mrs. Claus.

"Sounds like a good deal," I said.

Hazel settled down. "Now that we've got that nonsense out of the way, tell me more about this radio show."

"Podcast," said Camry.

Hazel ignored her. "When is it coming out?"

"We're going to release the first episode on October 10, the anniversary of Amelia's disappearance," I said.

"That gives you less than two weeks." Hazel waved a piece of bread around while she talked. "You can do a show in two weeks?"

"I've done as much work as I can from home already. We should be fine." *I think. I hope.*

"Camry told me you used to work for a fancy radio station in San Diego."

"Podcast," I said. "And, yes, I worked for *Cold in America*." I stuffed bread in my mouth, hoping the subject would be dropped. Talking about my old job gave me heart palpitations.

It didn't, however, have any effect on Camry's organs. "*Cold in America* is only the *biggest* true crime podcast in the *world*, hosted by the queen of podcasting herself, Mara Lancer."

"Wow," Hazel said in awe. I could tell she was genuinely impressed, which caused my heart to hiccup. "And you quit that job to come here?"

"She sure did." Camry flung an arm around my shoulders and gave me a squeeze. "The old detective on Amelia Clark's case sent all the information to *Cold in America*, hoping Mara would do a season on it. Liv read the entire case file and thought it would make an interesting show. She pitched a spinoff called *Missing or*

Murdered to Mara with Liv as the host."

"And what did Mara say?" Hazel asked.

"No." Camry removed her arm from around my shoulders. "Mara said there wasn't enough information available, but Liv here thought differently and quit her job."

Hiccup.

"Bought all the equipment with her own money."

Hiccup.

"Draining all her savings. Gave up an apartment with a killer view and came here. Basically, her entire future rides on the success of this podcast."

Hiccup.

Hiccup.

Hazel dropped her fork. "You must be really good at what you do."

Camry nodded. "Mara said Liv was the best engineer she'd ever worked with."

Oh geez.

What Camry failed to mention was that while, yes, Mara did say I was the best *mix*-engineer she'd ever worked with, she also said that I lacked the *oomph* required to host and executive produce a podcast under the *CIA* umbrella.

Talk about a punch to the ego.

But after much soul-searching, I realized she was right. I was a think-things-through, well-organized, wash-my-bra-daily, nonassertive-oomphless person. I was also a redhead. People expect more oomph from redheads.

Camry didn't understand. She was born with oomph. Her mother was married to my father. I was seventeen and about to move out when the two got together. My brother was twenty-two and already in the police academy. Camry was twelve. Twelve-year-olds were annoying.

Twenty-two-year-olds were slightly less annoying.

Camry was Irish on her father's side and black on her mother's (she hated the term African-American. *What are you? Angelo-*

Saxon-American then? she'd say). She had raven hair, bright hazel-brown eyes, flawless skin, lush lashes, and dimples. She was more of the life-of-the-party, wake-up-ready-for-the-runway, loud-assertive type of person. She also lived by the rule: what's a hamper? Which should make sharing a room for the next six months interesting.

Hazel scooted off to the kitchen and returned with more food. "Have you talked to Richard and Janet Clark yet?"

"Not in person," I said. "We're going to stop by their bakery tomorrow."

"Richard will be there. You'll like him. He's a nice man. But you won't see Janet." Hazel took a sip of water. "Speaking of Janet. If you're looking for a scandalous story for your show, I've got a whopper for you."

I eyed my audio equipment sitting by the front door, debating if I should grab my recorder. My hands were covered in grease. If the story was worth using, I'd interview Hazel later, I decided.

Hazel dabbed her mouth with the corner of the napkin. "I had asked Janet if she'd like to be on the Christmas parade committee, you know, to be polite since she's never had friends. This was shortly before Amelia went missing, and do you know what she said to me?"

Hazel paused until Camry and I said, "What did she say?" in unison.

"She said no! Just like that 'no.' Excuse my language but, what the frog?"

I stifled a giggle.

Camry didn't.

"It rubbed a lot of people the wrong way. Then, of course, when we heard about Amelia's disappearance, I tried to bring the Clark's dinner, but do you know what she said?"

"No?" said Camry.

"She said no! Not that I'm judging. Grief looks different on every person. And there's no grief worse than losing a child." She crossed herself. "All I'm saying is she should have allowed the community to help her. We were all worried about Amelia."

"Did you know her?" I asked.

"Not well. She worked in the same building where my husband, John, got his weekly dialysis. Pretty girl. A little too thin toward the end, but she had a nice face. Rest her soul." Hazel crossed herself. "As a matter of fact, Amelia disappeared the same day John passed." She crossed herself again, and I wondered if there was a crossing limit.

"Did you see the YouTube video?" I asked.

Hazel cut her meat while shaking her head. "No. But it's not right. Why would you take a video of a person and post it online without their permission? It's awful."

"It's hilarious," Camry muttered while loading her fork. I kicked her under the table. "What? It *was* funny. Why do you think it went viral so quickly?"

I blew out a breath, my lips making an involuntary raspberry noise, and directed my attention back to Hazel. "So, about the video. You didn't see it, but did you hear about it prior to Amelia's disappearance?"

Hazel held up a finger, signaling for me to wait until she's finished chewing the food in her mouth. "Yes." She paused to swallow. "Of course, I heard about the *incident*. Everyone was talking about it. Poor thing, she must have been humiliated. Channel Two did a whole story on it the day before she went missing."

"The day *before*? Are you serious?" I'd spent hours scouring the Internet for information on Amelia, and I never came across any news reports published before her disappearance. I made a mental note to contact Channel Two tomorrow. Maybe they knew the true identity of HJZoomer22—the username of the person who posted the video. Neither Camry nor I have had any luck. HJZoomer22 created the account on October 3, 2008, uploaded the video of Amelia, and hasn't posted a thing since.

"When we heard Amelia was missing," Hazel continued, "most people thought she took off because she had been publicly humiliated. And who would have blamed her? Then they found the car with all her stuff in it..." her voice trailed off. "People don't leave town without their wallet. They just don't. That's when the community came together to help find her."

This I could use.

The parade story? Probably not. I didn't want to cast doubt on the Clark's character unless the story called for it.

"I'd like to interview you," I decided. "Even if you didn't know Amelia well, I could use the perspective of someone who was around during that time. I want the show to unfold naturally, that's why I'm not recording all episodes before release." Which is what Mara does. "I want the listeners to feel like they're taking this journey with me."

"With *us* you mean," said Camry.

"Sure, with us. But I'm the host of the show."

"And I'm your peon." Camry stabbed a piece of meat with her fork.

"For the last time, you're not my *peon*. You're here to help with audio and research. Which is *exactly* what I said you'd be doing when you asked if you could help with this podcast."

"Producer sounds a lot nicer."

Camry made no mention of producer until we were three hours into our trip and it was too late to turn around. The problem with making Camry a producer was she was unpredictable, had a tendency not to listen, and was outspoken. The reason I said yes was because of her investigation skills. If you give her Internet access she'll find anything about anyone within minutes.

Here, she could use this superpower for good. At home, she used her powers for evil. Like stalking her ex-boyfriend's new girlfriends, hacking email accounts, and changing grades. Which is how she got herself kicked out of college and ended up a permanent occupant of our parents' guest room.

"Oh!" Hazel gasped so loud I feared she'd inhaled a chunk of meat, until she said, "I know the perfect person to help you with your radio show."

"Podcast," Camry said.

Hazel ignored her. "You have a cousin who is an Internet star," she said to Camry. "Let me make a phone call." Hazel beelined for the kitchen before we could stop her.

"What do you think she means by Internet star?" I asked Camry.

"I wouldn't know. I'm just the peon."

EPISODE ONE

Gone Cold

The next morning, I woke to the scent of sweet buttercream and bacon. Morning rays peeked in through the curtains and filled the room with soft light. Hazel's guest suite reminded me of *Anne of Green Gables*. The walls were papered in the same blossom print as downstairs. Sheer green drapes adorned the window with an antique writers table below it. The twin beds were on opposite sides of the room with white lace bedspreads and wrought-iron frames. I imagined it as the grandchildren's room, where cousins gathered to play, tell secrets, and jump from bed to bed.

Camry woke with a grunt and pulled the comforter over her head. "It's too early to be conscious."

"If the sun is up we should be, too. We've got a full day ahead of us." I got up, made the bed and got dressed in a pair of skinny jeans, a white tee and my Converse wedges. I have a pair in every color. Today, I was wearing green to match my eyes, and I was on my way to find my oomph.

Camry rolled upright and picked the sleep off her eyelashes. She was wearing yesterday's tank top and underwear. "What time did you go to sleep?"

"Not that long ago." I stifled a yawn. "Up late watching the video again."

"How many times have you watched that thing?"

Answer: a lot.

I've watched "Aluminum Woman Goes Mad" (the YouTube video of Amelia) so many times it's burned into my subconscious. I could see it in my dreams. The dark room. The round tables covered in white cloth with blue overlays. Amelia, thin and frazzled, in a silver dress (that, yes, looked a bit aluminum-ish). It was the annual Direct Dental's Gala—where the managers from each branch would get dressed up, eat dinner, and talk floss. Amelia was the assistant *to* the manager. I'm not sure why she was even there, I'd yet to get a hold of her old boss.

Direct Dental's CEO, Mike Cromer, was standing on the stage talking about teeth and the recession. "Poor people still need to brush," was his opening line. Amelia walked in late and found a seat at the back table. A waiter approached and placed a plate down in front of her. Amelia stopped the waiter before he could leave, saying something to him, and then he removed her plate. My best guess was that she asked for the vegetarian platter. Was Amelia a vegetarian? I didn't know. But why else would you ask for a different meal?

The waiter returned shortly with another plate. Amelia took a bite, using her left hand to maneuver the fork, and quickly summoned the waiter back. She pointed to the plate and the waiter did a sort of half bow, as if saying he's sorry. It was too dark to read their lips, but I think her food was cold. The waiter grabbed the plate and returned shortly with another. But Amelia didn't notice, and grabbed her bag and jolted upright, banging her head on the bottom of the plate. Food flew. People gasped. Mike Cromer stopped mid-sentence. Amelia tripped and fell forward, accidently punching a man in the crotch. The man collapsed to the floor (I'd since learned that man was the CFO. Pretty sure nothing good comes from nut-punching the man who signs your checks).

The next forty-five seconds is why the video had over ten million views.

Everyone was up and out of their seats, staring at her. When the waiter offered Amelia a hand, she yelled something inaudible and jerked away. This is when security got involved. Two men in suits each grabbed an arm. Amelia appeared panicked even *manic*. A man yelled, "way to represent the company!" which prompted Amelia to scream, "Then consider this my two weeks' notice!" She slunk her arms out of the security guard's grasp and ran away like she was being chased, when in reality, no one had moved—aside from the CFO who was rolling around on the floor holding his crotch.

This video is why I was drawn to the story. Back in 2008, YouTube was still new and a video with over 600,000 views in less than three days was considered viral.

Today a video is viral if it hits five million in a short period of time. People seeking Internet fame upload over 300 million hours of footage every minute on YouTube, hoping for a viral hit.

Amelia achieved this on accident and a week later she was gone. If this doesn't speak to my generation then I don't know what does.

"You know what I think," Camry said. She was now up, digging through her duffle bag. "I think she was on drugs. Not the hard stuff, like cocaine or meth. I'm thinking opioids. The way she jumps up reminds me of someone who needs a quick fix."

"Can't you swallow opioids? Why would she have to leave the table?"

"I dunno," she said from inside the sweater she was pulling over her head. "Maybe she was on her way out for a cigarette? Do we know if she smoked?"

"She doesn't strike me as a smoker. But these are the sorts of questions her friends and family can answer for us. It could have been a panic attack or an emotional breakdown?"

"She's too thin and too neurotic in that video to be sober."

"Thin and sober people can still be neurotic." I used my foot to push Camry's shirt, pants, bra, and dirty mismatched socks over to her side of the room.

Camry stared at me. "You make a good point."

"Just because I don't dump my underwear on the floor doesn't make me neurotic." I grabbed my toiletry bag and scooted off to the bathroom.

Camry followed with her toothbrush in hand. "Last night I sent another message to HJZoomer22 on YouTube." She plopped herself on the toilet seat.

I twisted off the cap to my facial cleansing pads. "What did you say?"

"I said exactly what you told me to. That I work for the podcast series *Missing or Murdered*, and we'd like to speak to him about the video."

"Good."

"And that he was basically lower than scum for posting it in the first place. I also said that he was a prime suspect on our list."

"You what?" I accidentally knocked the container of cleansing pads to the floor.

"Kidding! Calm down. I'm not a complete idiot." She swiped a pad off the tile and rubbed it all over her face. "Ugh. I'm *so* tired. What time is it? Like five a.m.?"

"It's seven thirty and it smells like Hazel is already up and cooking." Surprisingly, I was hungry. Starving even.

Which was good, because when Camry and I made our way downstairs we found a Vegas worthy buffet waiting for us.

"Morning," Hazel sang from behind the griddle with a gingham print apron on. "You girls sleep good?"

"I slept amazing." Camry tossed a grape into her mouth.

"I knew it! The gal on the infomercial said a good night's sleep is guaranteed or your money back." Hazel gave us each a plate of fresh-from-the-griddle pancakes.

I took a seat at the table and drizzled my pancakes in warm maple syrup. "What are your plans today, Hazel?" I asked.

Before she could answer, the lights around the room flickered on and off several times.

Camry hid under her plate. "What's happening?"

"It's the doorbell, silly." Hazel licked pancake batter off her finger. "I forgot the door was still locked. Hold on a sec." She rushed out of the room.

"You think putting a glass plate over your head will protect you from flashing lights?" I said to Camry.

She stuck her tongue out at me.

Hazel returned, following her was a tall guy in board shorts with a dark hoodie pulled over his head.

Camry flattened her bed hair down and batted her big eyes. "And who is this?" she crooned.

"You remember my grandson, Oliver?" said Hazel. "Your cousin."

"Cousin?" Camry squeaked. "Oh, yeah, of course. My cousin. It's been a long time." She tried to play it cool, but her face was bright red and I was dying inside. The "remember when you hit on your cousin" story would for sure be told around the Thanksgiving table for the next decade.

The cousin didn't respond to Camry. Instead, he approached the table and extended a hand out to me. "I'm Oliver."

"I'm Liv. Nice to meet you." I slipped my hand into his. Oliver's skin was crackly and callused but warm. He had a strong scent of ocean. So strong, it overpowered the buttermilk pancakes in front of me. "Are you the Internet star grandson?"

"According to my grandma, yes." Oliver pushed his hood back, revealing a mop of dark curly hair that covered his ears. I recognized him as the blue-eyed little boy from the picture—the one with the sea lion tucked under his arm. He had an accent I couldn't quite place until Hazel tugged on his sleeve and signed in ASL. Then I got it. Oliver was deaf.

"I don't remember you being hard of hearing last time we met!" Camry yelled.

"It's a more recent development," Oliver said and signed. "And you can say 'deaf,' it's not offensive."

"Oh, okay. It's nice to see you again! I think the last time I saw you was at your grandpa's funeral!"

"He can read lips. No matter how loud you talk he still can't hear you," Hazel said, waving a spatula at her. "But we can, so stop yelling. You're hurting my ears."

"Right. Got it." Camry shoved another grape into her mouth and took a seat at the table.

"You guys are doing a radio show?" Oliver asked as he worked his way through the buffet, scooping eggs, bacon, strawberries, and pancakes onto his plate.

"It's a podcast," I said and signed at the same time. I took four years of American Sign Language in high school and three in college. Then I became an audio mixer.

Oliver took a seat at the table with his plate. *"How do you know ASL?"* he signed.

"I took it in school," I signed back, slowly. I was a bit rusty.

"What's your name sign?"

"I don't have one."

Only a person in the deaf community can give you a name sign. Typically it has something to do with a physical trait.

"Do you come here for breakfast every morning?" I signed.

Oliver pointed his fork toward the window. *"I live down the street."*

"You're grandma must love having you close."

"Yes. She likes to feed people."

"I see that."

Camry waved her napkin to get our attention. "Some of us don't know sign language and are feeling left out. Can you speak as you sign, please?"

"Oliver has Meniere's Disease," Hazel said out of the blue. "It affects the inner ear."

"They didn't ask for my medical history, grandma," he said.

"No we didn't," I said and signed. "But I'm dying to know why you're an Internet star."

"I have a YouTube channel." He shrugged like it was no big deal.

"That's *seriously* how you make a living?" Camry asked.

"He does technology things." Hazel placed a cup of fresh squeezed orange juice in front of each of us. "He's real good at it, too," she signed as she talked with such fluidity you could tell it had become second nature to her. "He installed Wi-Fi in my *whole* house. Took him less than ten minutes and now you can use the Internet in the bathroom. Imagine that."

"I'm basically a genius," said Oliver.

"And modest," I added.

"You don't have to be modest if you're a genius."

"Is that written in the genius instruction manual?"

Oliver nodded. "Yes, because I wrote the instruction manual."

"Ahh. It's nice to see you all getting along so well," Hazel said. She was back behind the griddle flipping pancakes.

How many is she going to make? Oliver had three. I had two. Camry had one. I didn't want to be rude, but my stomach could only hold so much.

As if reading my mind, Oliver tapped my shoulder. *"She takes food to churches in the area for the homeless."*

"Ahhh, gotcha." Phew.

"I told the girls you could help them with their radio show," Hazel said and signed while cooking. She's talented.

"It's a podcast," said Camry. "And that's a great idea. Liv could use another assistant. Just don't ask to be a producer."

Our first stop of the day was at former Detective Leon Ramsey's, home. He lived in a fifty-five-plus community not far from Hazel's. Leon's wife, Opal, and a Golden Retriever with a bad hip named, Minnie, greeted us with a hug and a wet nose to the crotch (from Minnie not Opal).

The Ramsey's home was a cozy doublewide. Family pictures were proudly displayed around the living room. There was a collection of porcelain figurines in a large hutch next to a grandfather clock that chimed noon as soon as we arrived. Opal and Minnie escorted us to a closed-in porch where I meet Leon Ramsey for the first time.

Leon was older than I expected. His hair sparse. His skin pale. His eyes sagging. From our phone conversations, I knew he had been under the weather but was still, in his own words, "sharp as a tack." He was sitting in a chair with a quilt over his lap. Camry clipped a lavaliere mic to his shirt, right under his mouth. We'd had practiced clipping the mic on, taking it off, and recording with my portable equipment this morning. I wanted to look professional even if I was learning as I went.

Minnie parked herself at our feet while Opal excused herself to go fetch something from the kitchen. Camry and I simultaneously heaved a sigh of relief when that "something" was a box marked *Amelia Clark* and nothing edible. We were still recovering from breakfast.

After a quick test to be sure our microphones were on and recording, it was time to start. My stomach did a roller coaster lurch and I paused to give myself a quick pep-talk. I was nervous, but only because I had so much riding on this venture—as did Amelia.

You can do this, Liv.

I rolled my shoulders, sat up straighter, and spoke clearly. "Can you tell us who you are, a little bit about your background, and how you became involved in the Amelia Clark case?"

Leon pulled in a breath. "My name is Detective Ramsey. I worked homicide for thirty years and was the first detective assigned to the Amelia Clark case in October of 2008. It's the only case file of mine that's still open and I want it solved before I die."

From our phone conversation, I'd say he had another twenty years left on this planet.

Looking at him, I was not so sure he had twenty minutes.

"How long were you on the case?" I asked, already knowing the answer. Leon had covered this the first time we spoke on the phone, back when I was gathering information to pitch the story to Mara.

"I officially worked it six years until my wife forced me to retire," he said. "But I've never actually stopped working it."

"Can you walk us through the timeline? From the day Amelia was reported missing to when the official investigation began?"

Leon slipped on a pair of readers and grabbed one of many notebooks from the box and flipped to the first page. The notes were written in shorthand and near impossible for me to read. "Her father, Richard Clark, reported her missing on the fourteenth of October. A police officer was dispatched to Amelia's apartment to perform a well check. There was no obvious sign of a struggle, and it was thought that she had skipped town until talk of the video had blown over." Leon peered over his glasses and spoke from memory. "One week later, on the twenty-first of October, her car was found parked near a hiking trail off Bradley Road. Inside, we found her wallet with hundred dollars in crisp twenties, cell phone, keys, and forensics found small traces of blood on the steering wheel and the underside of the driver's seat. This is when an investigation was launched."

"Was any other DNA recovered from the vehicle?" I asked.

"The vehicle was swabbed, but we weren't able to find any, no."

I referred to my list of questions. "I want to ask more about the video, but before I do, can you tell us about the search on the twenty-second of October? I read about it online."

Leon told us about the mass search from memory. Orcutt Hollow is a three-mile-long trail for novice hikers not far from Hazel's house. Twenty volunteers showed up, along with two cadaver dogs. The search lasted two days and nothing was found. "There's a list of those who volunteered for the search in the box," he said. "It'll be a good reference for you. Have you contacted the Santa Maria PD for her file?"

"*Yes...*" I said, unsure of why he was asking. Leon and I had talked about this on the phone last week. I had told him about how I requested to see her case file and a detective by the name of Leah LeClare called me back and said it was an open investigation and not available for the press.

When I reminded Leon of this conversation, he acted as if it was the first time he'd heard this. "It's been sitting at the bottom of the homicide files for years. They need the public's help!" Which is verbatim what he had said last week. "Yes! This damn case was hard right from the go of it," Leon said, answering a question I hadn't asked. "But I never gave up."

I began to worry that Leon was not as *sharp* as he claimed to be.

"Amelia didn't own a credit card and rarely used her debit card," he said, looking far more animated than he did when we first arrived. "There wasn't much payment history to show us where she'd been the days or weeks prior. The last recorded transaction was on the tenth. Amelia withdrew three-hundred dollars from an ATM off Bradley Road at 6:13 p.m. We were able to pull footage from the security camera, and that's the last reported sighting of her." Leon dug around in the box until he found the Missing Person Poster.

And there she was.

Amelia "Millie" Clark, last seen October 3, 2008.

Hair: Blonde.

Eyes: Blue

Height: 5'6"

Weight: 105 lbs.

Last seen wearing a denim mini skirt, black leggings, black heels, a white shirt and a black vest.

Certainly not hiking attire.

Amelia had upturned eyes, a diamond-shaped face, a narrow nose, full and unsmiling lips, and shoulder-length straight hair. She was beautiful.

Leon slapped his leg. "I think she's alive!"

Errr...I was caught off guard. When we had spoken on the phone, he said she was most likely dead. "What makes you think she's still alive?" I asked, working hard to keep my voice from reaching a *holy-hell* octave, because I was having a minor panic attack inside. His flip-flopping and memory lapses were scary.

Scary because he was the most reliable source I had.

"It's a hunch," he said.

"A hunch?" I worked hard to keep my face flat. "Why do you

think she'd stay hidden all these years?"

"That is the question." Leon tapped his temple. "You don't run away and hide unless there's something or someone to hide from. Or unless someone is forcing you to stay hidden. And I don't think she'd run away because of a silly YouTube video."

Now I was intrigued. "Then what do you think happened to her?"

"That's for you to find out." Leon pulled another notebook from the box. This one was filled with interviews he'd conducted— Amelia's co-workers at Direct Dental, neighbors, and friends.

Camry flipped through each page and snapped pictures.

Leon stopped her. "Take all of it home."

"Are you sure?" The box was filled with a decade's worth of work. As much as I wanted to dive in, I was anxious to handle the precious cargo.

Also, I couldn't read his handwriting.

At all.

"I'm positive." He pushed the box toward me using the end of a cane.

"Why is this name highlighted?" Camry pointed to *Carlos Hermosa* written in the margin.

Leon's eyebrows shot up to his forehead. "Now there's an episode for you. A suspect was never officially named but...the place is...he's the one to..." he paused to take a breath and...

"Leon?"

EPISODE TWO

Mr. CinnaMann

Leon Ramsey died.

The last words out of his mouth were, "Now there's an episode for you. A suspect was never officially named but...the place is...he's the one to...go to..." Gone.

Was Carlos Hermosa a suspect?

Or were these two separate thoughts? A suspect was never named. He was the one to...go to...*where?* Where! I'll never know.

Out of respect for Opal and Minnie—who sat dutifully at her owner's side while I frantically searched for a pulse—Camry and I left with the box in tow, allowing them time to process and grieve alone.

On our way out, Opal confided in us that Leon had been diagnosed with lung cancer six months ago. It's no wonder he was in a hurry to get the case solved.

He never said anything to me about being sick and I felt awful.

The situation was distressing.

Not distressing because the success of *Missing or Murdered* counted on Leon's knowledge of the case (even though it did).

But because it brought back the same hollowing feelings I felt when I watched my mother lose her seven-year battle with ovarian cancer. You don't recover from a parent's death. You just learn to live with the pain. Sometimes you even forget about it for a short while. Then something happens to remind you of the massive hole in your heart and the raw, all-consuming grief returns with a vengeance.

When this *something* happened, I worked.

It was the best distraction.

Without Leon, my best bet was to talk to Richard and Janet Clark.

Which is precisely where I was going.

"Slow down! You're going to get us killed!" Camry held tight to the grab handle as I whipped my little Ford Focus onto Bradley Road.

It was three forty-five and CinnaMann's closed at four p.m.

"Does he even know we're coming?" Camry asked, still holding tight.

"No," I said, concentrating on the road. People here drove the actual speed limit and it was maddening. "I sent him a Facebook message yesterday saying we'd come in today, but he hasn't read it yet."

"Then let's go in the morn—Squirrel!"

I swerved to the right lane, narrowly missing the runaway rodent. "Bakeries are busy in the morning; I want to catch him before he leaves for the day."

"What if he isn't there—stop sign!"

I came to a screeching halt. "According to Yelp reviews he's always there."

"Are you sure we should be doing this right now? I'm freaking out. You're freaking out. We should freak out in private."

"I'm not freaking out," I lied.

I was absolutely freaking out.

I made a quick right into The Orcutt Plaza lot, sailed over the speed bumps, and found a parking spot. CinnaMann's Bakery was tucked between a dance studio and a dry cleaner. Painted on the window was the familiar caricature of a chef holding a tray of steaming cinnamon rolls. The same chef that was on their Facebook page.

Amelia's parents, Janet and Richard Clark, owned

CinnaMann's. I'd only seen pictures of the two online. Richard looked exactly like someone who owned a bakery. Kind of like the Pillsbury Doughboy with a gray handlebar mustache. Janet looked exactly like someone who had lost her only child—frail, hollow eyes, long face, blonde hair down to her waist. It was surreal being so close to something I knew so much about yet had never seen in person. Like spotting a celebrity at the mall.

"Are we recording this?" Camry removed her seatbelt.

"Give me a lavalier mic and bring the rest in, discretely. I don't know if he wants to be recorded."

Camry's fingers worked quickly to untangle the lavalier cord she'd shoved into the bag at Leon's. "Got it!" She held up the mic and frowned. "You look *really* nervous. Are you nervous? 'Cause you look it."

"What? No. I'm upset and sad and..." She was right. I was nervous. But I didn't know I was nervous until she said I looked nervous and now I was hell-a nervous.

Calm down, Liv.

Deep breath.

You've got this.

I didn't know why I was even nervous.

I'd dug deep into the Clark's past (74 percent of murders are committed by a person close to the victim, seemed a good place to start). The only thing to show up was a civil suit settled out of court in the nineties and hundreds of Yelp reviews talking about what a "kind-hearted" and "charismatic" person Richard Clark was. He and I had even conversed over Facebook messenger.

Me: *My name is Liv Olsen, I am a podcaster from San Diego. I'm interested in highlighting your daughter's 2008 disappearance in our podcast series. I believe we can shed new light on the case.*

CinnaMann's Bakery (two weeks later): *What's the name of the podcast?*

Me: *It's a new podcast titled,* Missing or Murdered.

CinnaMann's Bakery (three weeks later): *Let me check with*

my wife.

Me (one week later): *Hi there! Checking in. Did you have a chance to speak with your wife?*

CinnaMann's Bakery (a week later): *We're fine. Thank you for your interest.*

Me (immediately): *My pleasure. We will be traveling up to Santa Maria in the next few weeks.*

CinnaMann's Bakery (one week later): *Be sure to stop by the bakery when you're here.*

Me: *I will, thank you.*

Me (yesterday): *We're in town and plan to stop by tomorrow afternoon.*

Now it was time to meet CinnaMann in person. I wanted so badly to do right by Amelia. To do right by Leon. Just do this thing right!

Guess this was where *oomph* came in to play.

And better I find some, fast.

I unbuckled my seatbelt and turned to Camry. "Let's do this."

The chef caricature on the window of CinnaMann's was faded and peeling along the edges. Someone had scratched "JP loves HJ" into the leg and I wondered why Richard hadn't replaced it. Inside, the bakery was smaller than I imagined. This wasn't a sit-down-and-leisurely-sip-your-coffee type of joint. So much of the space was taken up by the kitchen, leaving little room for customers to maneuver. The walls were bare white with scuffed baseboards. The flooring was checkered and scratched. The menu was a changeable letter board hung slightly off centered above the display case. But the air was delicious: a mixture of filtered coffee and mouth-watering pastries.

Who needs ambiance anyway?

Behind the counter was a high-school-aged girl cleaning out the display case. She stood and greeted us with a you-seriously-are-showing-up-five-minutes-before-we-close smile. "Welcome to CinnaMann's," she said. "We have two cinnamon pull-apart loafs left." She held up a tray of gooey bread, dripping in a cinnamon and sugar glaze.

I had zero appetite.

"Those look yummy," I said. "But we're here to speak to Richard Clark. Is he available?"

The girl, *Val* per the tag pinned to her apron, put the tray down. "Sure, who are you?"

"Amelia Clark."

I felt an almighty heave of horror.

Did I say Amelia Clark?

Val's smile froze in place.

Camry pushed past me. "Hi there, I'm Camry Lewis and this is Liv Olsen. We're from the mega, soon-to-be-hit podcast series *Missing or Murdered*. We'd like to speak to Richard about his daughter, Amelia Clark. Can you tell him we're here, please? He's expecting us."

Val's eyes went from Camry to me and back again. "*Sure*," she said, drawing out each letter. "Hold on."

Val disappeared through a pair of swinging doors.

I turned to Camry in a panic. "I can't...why...how...I was thinking about Amelia and the name popped out of my mouth. I don't know why I did that. I'm so frazzled about Leon. We should have waited until tomorrow—"

Camry slapped me across the face. "Get a grip, woman, he's coming."

Okay, I got this.

Richard Clark pushed through the double-swinging doors. He was thinner than in the pictures I'd seen of him online. Older. Grayer. Had on a chef's coat streaked with flour and icing.

"Can I help you?" He had a smooth, charming voice and a million-dollar smile.

I held out a hand. "Hello Mr. Clark. I'm *Liv Olsen*," I said carefully. Not making that catastrophic mistake twice. "Nice to finally meet you in person."

"You too." Richard shook my hand, but his face was void of recollection.

"I'm the one doing the podcast about Amelia's disappearance," I said.

Still nothing.

"We spoke on Facebook?" I tried.

There was an awkward silence until Camry added, "*Missing or Murdered* is the name of the series." She pulled a business card from her bag.

Richard's face went puce. "I thought you weren't doing it."

I was taken aback. "When we talked online you said you were fine with it."

"No, I said 'we're fine' as in we're fine, we don't need you to do it."

Oh.

This isn't good.

"I'm sorry for the miscommunication. I took your response as you were fine with the series."

Richard squinted down at me as if I were a moldy leftover. Val was crouched behind the display case, cleaning, except her eyes were on us and she'd been wiping the same spot for several minutes. "Well, we aren't," he said and thrust the business card into my hand. "Janet and I discussed it at length and decided that we don't want anyone jeopardizing Amelia's case."

"We would never jeopardize anything," I said in a rush. "What we'll do is garner public interest. Someone here knows what happened, and by putting Amelia in the limelight, that someone is more likely to talk."

Richard remained unmoved.

Dammit.

I couldn't believe this was happening. No Leon. No Richard. No podcast. No justice for Amelia. No perfect record for Leon. Financial ruin for me. There was a lot riding on this.

I summoned all the oomph and professionalism I could muster. Mostly asking myself: *What would Mara do?*

Answer: Mara wouldn't have said her name was Amelia. She would have made sure the success of her series wasn't hinged on a man who was on his deathbed. She wouldn't be here because there wasn't enough material for a series.

Okay, scratch that.

What would Liv do?

Answer: Liv would apologize profusely and return home with her metaphorical tail between her legs.

Okay, scratch that.

What would a professional do?

Answer: "I can't begin to understand what you and Mrs. Clark have gone through," I said, keeping my voice steady. "Our intention is only to help. I've worked on *Cold in America* for the last seven years, the most popular true crime podcast series in the world. I know what I'm doing and promise to craft the story with the utmost respect for both Amelia and your family. We've already begun production. If you're not interested in recording, I respect your decision." I wanted to tell him we couldn't press forward without his blessing, but I had a feeling he'd take that as an opportunity to say no, again.

"You've already started the podcast?" You could almost see the wheels in his head turning.

"We have." Which was technically true. I had the intro recorded, the avatar was on our hosting site, website was up, social media pages were live, and the two-hour interview with Leon was recorded. We were *in* this.

Richard's shoulders fell. "What do you need from me?"

I felt faint with relief. "Can I ask you a few questions?"

"Yeah, okay, sure. Come on back." He pushed through the double-swing doors.

Camry and I shared a look. She mouthed *what the frog?*

My sentiments exactly.

We followed Richard through the kitchen. There was a teenage boy mopping the floor and another scrubbing an oven. The counters were clear. The trash was piled by the back door and country music blasted from a small radio. Richard led us out the exit to an alleyway where we found a small round table and chairs.

Richard sat down, dropping like a man who has spent much of the day on his feet. The chairs were stiff and wobbly. I forgot I was mic'd until the pack in my back pocket hit the metal with a *thud*.

"If you're going to do this, I need to be informed of what information you find and what you're going to use. I can't have information leaked that only the detectives know. It *will* jeopardize her case," Richard said. His words were sharp and to the point. Like a papa bear protecting his young. But there was also a charm about him. I could see how under less stressful (and awkward) encounters he could be quite pleasant.

"We can certainly discuss new findings with you and Mrs. Clark," I said.

"Leave Janet out of this. She doesn't like talking about Amelia."

Understandable. "Would you be open to us recording our conversations to use in the series?" I asked.

"No."

I kept my mic on anyway and readjusted in my seat, suddenly remembering Camry. "This is Camry Lewis, she's helping with the podcast."

Richard nodded.

Camry nodded.

I nodded because I was nervous.

"What do you want to know?" asked Richard.

"First, I hate to inform you, but Detective Leon Ramsey passed away earlier today," I said.

Richard pursed his lips, as if deciding how he should feel.

"Leon is the one who contacted me," I said. "He was passionate about Amelia's case, even after retirement, and wanted it solved."

Richard was unresponsive, not even a "that's a shame" or "I'm sorry to hear that."

I recalled an interview I'd read online. It was published in *The Santa Maria Tribune* the day before the Orcutt Hollow search. Richard had poked at Leon, calling him "an amateur." I wondered if

Richard blamed Leon for the case going cold? I'll ask once I'm able to coax more than one-word answers from him, I decided.

"I'd love to get to know more about who Amelia was," I said, figuring it a good place to start. "Her hobbies. Personality. Who did she hang out with? A story or two from her childhood. Whatever you'd like listeners to know."

"Amelia was a nice kid," Richard said. "She was athletic. Played sports all through school."

I waited for him to continue but he didn't. "Did she have other hobbies?"

"She painted. The chef on the window is her work. She did that in high school."

This warmed my heart. I made a mental note to take a picture of the window to post on our website. "She was very talented," I said.

"Yes."

"Can you tell us about the week she disappeared?"

"Janet and I were at a convention in San Francisco all week and returned late Friday evening. We called her several times. Went by her apartment. When we were unable to get a hold of her for several days, we called the police to file a report." His voice was monotonic. You could tell this was a story he'd had to repeat hundreds of times before. "A week later they found her car with all her stuff inside. She'd been having a hard time and we thought she had taken off. But the police found blood on the seat and steering wheel and opened an investigation."

"Did you see the YouTube video?" I asked.

"Yes."

I rephrased. "*What* do you think of the video?"

"People around town said she had a mental breakdown, some said she was anorexic."

"What do *you* think happened?"

"I think anyone who posts a video of a person with the intent to make fun of them deserves to be shot."

Wow. Okay. I could tell he meant it. Which brought me to the next question. "Have the police told you who posted the video?"

"No."

"Have you tried to find out yourself?"

"No."

"Have you talked to Detective LeClare recently?"

"Yes."

Richard had a barbed wire, ten-foot high, impenetrable wall constructed around him. I hoped that, as episodes were released, and we were able to create more buzz, he'd be more open to talking because this was painful.

"Do you know a man named Carlos Hermosa?" I asked.

"Yes."

I rephrased. "*Who* is Carlos Hermosa?"

"He was her neighbor."

"So he was your neighbor, too?" I asked, confused. I thought Amelia lived at home.

"No, Amelia lived at Santa Maria Way Apartments."

"How long had she been on her own?" I leaned across the table, better positioning the mic hidden in my shirt. Not that I would use this interview in the show without Richard's permission, but so I could reference it later for information.

"About three months."

EPISODE THREE

A Runner

Carlos Hermosa could be a white rabbit leading us to a dead end, *or* he could hold all the answers. Either way, he was the only lead we had.

So down the rabbit hole we went.

Amelia's old apartment was located in your typical eighties inspired apartment building. Ordinary. Bland. Nondescript.

Which made describing it hard.

"Santa Maria Way Apartments is a two-story building with a grass courtyard," I said into the recorder. Camry and I were standing out front near a bus stop. "Each apartment has a patio attached and..." I pinched the bridge of my nose. "What do you call a building with those plank things on the side?" I asked Camry.

She looked at me, then at the building, then at her phone. "Let's ask the Internet. 'What are those plank things on the side of the building called'?" she said out loud as she typed. "And...according to Google they are called clapboard. It's a clapboard building." Camry turned her phone to show me.

"That's a log house."

"It's not a log house. Look closer." She zoomed in and, yeah, she was right, it was a clapboard building.

"Sorry." I cleared my throat and continue. "A beige clapboard building, weathered, dull. I feel like a good analogy would work here." My brain was fried. "Dull like...like..."

"Like a twenty-minute description of a beige clapboard building everyone will fifteen-second skip through?"

"You're not helpful. I'm world building."

"I understand what you're doing," Camry said with an exaggerated roll of her eyes. "You're attempting to narrate like Mara does on *Cold in America* with all her pointless analogies. '*The car hops like a fat pigeon about to take flight,*' or '*the lake glistens like a freshly washed babies butt.*'"

For the record, Mara had never used the pigeon analogy.

The butt, yes.

"No one cares what the apartment building looks like," Camry said. "They want to know about the surrounding area. Is it sketchy? Could its location play a role in her disappearance? I'd say something like—" She slowly turned around, taking in a 360 view. "—the apartment is located on a busy street, near a freeway off-ramp, situated between the town's drive-in theater and a gas station. Across the street sits a private Christian School. Schools out for the day. You can see a handful of soccer practices being held on the PE field. The cheers of children are mixed in with the cacophony of cars zooming by. Or whatever you want. You're the boss."

For a moment, I stood there and stared at my kid stepsister, not sure if I was in awe or irked. Likely the former. Definitely the former. I lifted the recorder to my mouth. "Amelia's apartment is located on Santa Maria Way, situated between the town's drive-in theater and a gas station."

I kept the recorder on while we searched for unit 42B—Amelia's old apartment. The original management company went under in 2010, and her property manager died in 2015. Our sole purpose for this visit was to get a visual of where Amelia spent her last days and to snap pictures for the website—if we happened to run into Carlos Hermosa—perfect. But over ten years later, there was a slim chance he still lived there.

Apartment 42B was the furthest unit from the street. A neighborhood of modest homes sat on the other side of the property line wall. I could see the top of a man's head walking slowly across and heard the roar of a lawnmower. The aroma of freshly cut grass filled the air, and I couldn't help but wonder how the homeowners felt about having an apartment complex as their backyard neighbors.

Unit 42B shared at least two walls and had an apartment directly below. Leon said there was no sign of a struggle in her home, but it was worth noting that if something would have happened here, it seemed unlikely there'd be no witnesses.

Of course, at the time, Carlos Hermosa was in one of those four units.

Which one? I had no idea. And Richard was of no help.

Down a short walkway was apartment 42B's covered parking space—less than twenty feet from her front door. I snapped a few pictures, took video of the walkway, and recorded description I'll likely never use, but it was better to have too much material than not enough. And if today was an indication of how this case would go, I may need to dedicate an entire episode *to* world building.

"We need to find more people to interview or this investigation is going nowhere," I said to Camry. "We need high school friends. A prom date. Anyone she played sports with. Childhood neighbor. Someone who can give us insight into who Amelia was and her frame of mind the weeks leading up to her disappearance." I'd sent a Facebook message to the Righetti High School Class of 2003 group, but had yet to get a response.

"Oh! Oh! Oh! I got it!" Camry flapped her hands like a fat pigeon attempting to take flight (I may need to use that analogy in an episode). "I know the best place to find more people to interview. A Facebook mom's group. My mom is part of one in San Diego." Camry had her phone out, her fingers flying across the screen. "You can sell your old stuff, ask for advice, post current events, ask questions about lactating and crap like that. You know, mom stuff."

It took a minute for the brilliantness of her idea to sink in. "Holy hell, that's genius! Everyone who grew up with Amelia and went to school with her is in their early- to mid-thirties now. They're probably moms."

"And old people love Facebook!"

"I wouldn't call early- to mid-thirties old." Especially since I was nearing thirty myself.

"Found it," said Camry, almost signing. "*California Central Coast Mom's Group*, they have over sixteen thousand members. By the way, I'm using your Facebook account."

"That's...wait, what? Why don't you use your own?"

"I don't have Facebook and your profile pic is of you and Taylor."

Taylor was my niece. She was eight. In the picture she was an hour old. I hadn't updated my profile in years. I used Facebook for research only and...*wait a second*. "How'd you access my Facebook account?"

"'Cause you have the same password for *everything*," she said as if it were obvious.

"How do you know my password?"

"Not important...request submitted. They won't approve it until I've agreed to the rules." She scrolled. "There are a lot of rules. Over fifty. No mommy shaming. Self-promoting is limited to once a month. Admins reserve the right to delete posts. No posting about deleted posts. Sale items...yada...yada...yada...Geez, moms have a lot of rules. Okay, submitted and...I guess it takes a minute to be accepted." She pouted. "I like instant gratification."

Don't we all? "Let's get back to Hazel's and attempt to organize Leon's notes."

"And eat. I'm starving."

"Really? After everything that's happened today, I don't think I could eat."

"Yeah, you wouldn't."

"What's that supposed to mean?"

"I dunno, I just felt like saying it."

As we turned to leave, a woman in pink scrubs pounded up the stairs to apartment 42B. Her arm was wrapped around a brown grocery bag, which she balanced on her hip while she unlocked the door.

Camry and I shared a look, both thinking the same thing.

Up the stairs we went. One-by-one. Camry knocked while I switched on the recorder. The door opened and the pink scrub-wearing woman answered. Per the name embroidered above the breast pocket, this was Susan.

I greeted her with an exaggerated smile. "My name is Liv Olsen, and this is Camry Lewis. We're doing a podcast series on the disappearance of Amelia Clark, the woman who used to live in this apartment." I pulled a business card from my pocket and handed it to her. If I were lucky, she'd allow us in to have a look around. If I were unlucky, she'd call the cops.

Susan looked as if she'd just swallowed a fly. "Who disappeared?"

"Her name was Amelia Clark, she lived here in 2008," I said.

Susan scratched the back of her head. "Never heard of her...wait! Is that the YouTube chick who took off?"

"Yes," I said. "She used to live in your apartment."

"Seriously? The manager never told me *that*." Susan grimaced and looked over her shoulder, as if making sure Amelia wasn't standing behind her. "You should probably talk to my downstairs neighbor, Carlos. He's lived here forever. He might have known her."

My breath hitched in my chest. "Carlos Hermosa does still live here?"

"Yeah." Susan checked her nail beds. "He's a total jerk."

Camry and I said goodbye and flew down the stairs to apartment 41A. I could hardly believe my luck. What are the odds?

Carlos' patio was filled with sun worn toys that spilled out into the walkway, and I jumped over a sand bucket. Camry pounded on the door with a little too much vigor, but her knocks were muted by the television.

I rang the bell, twice.

No answer.

I leaned over the patio. The glass slider was open, and the screen was closed.

I cupped my mouth. "Hello! Anyone home!"

The television muted. "Get the damn door!" yelled a woman.

A man grunted. A kid screamed. The door opened. It was a guy who looked about as weathered as the patio toys. Balding, potbelly, wrinkled around the eyes, a tank top so tight I could see the indent from his belly button, dark sleeve tattoos on his right arm of a skull, an eagle, the names Presley and Ensley written in block lettering, and on the upper bicep was a pineapple. It was the only tattoo in color.

I guessed this was Carlos.

"We aren't church going people" he said and swung the door shut.

I rang the bell. The door reopened. Carlos was not amused.

"We're not proselytizing," I said in a hurry. "We're looking for Carlos Hermosa. Are you him?"

"Maybe."

"Your neighbor upstairs told us to come talk to—"

"She called management!" He stepped outside in his bare feet and looked up. "Why don't you come downstairs and deal with it yourself!"

"Wow, hey now." I stepped in front of Carlos.

"You say something to me?" Susan poked her head over the railing.

Carlos pointed up to her. "If you got a problem you can come tell me directly to my face."

Camry reached for Carlos' arm and he flinched back. "Don't put your hands on me."

Well, this escalated quickly.

"She didn't say anything," I said.

Carlos ignored me.

"You leave the toys in front of my stairwell and it's a tripping hazard." Susan's entire upper torso was now hanging over the side of the railing, and I feared she would tumble over.

"Why don't you watch where you're going?"

"Learn to control your kids!"

"That's it!" Carlos clapped his hands. I had no idea what clapping meant, but neither Camry nor I were physically able to break up this fight. Especially Camry, who was now taking video with her phone.

I shoved the recorder under my arm, stuck my fingers into my mouth and let out a high-pitched whistle. This got their attention.

"Cool it, both of you!" I yelled. "We are not here from management; we're podcasters doing a series on Amelia Clark."

Carlos stumbled backwards. "Did you say Amelia Clark?"

The upstairs door slammed shut. *Guess we're done with Susan.*

"Yes, we've been told you knew her," I said.

Carlos took a step closer and peered down at me. I tried not to shrink. "You're doing a podcast about Millie?"

Camry was still recording video.

"So you did know Amelia then," I said.

"Yeah, I knew her. Knew her enough to know she went by Millie not Amelia." Like Richard, his words were sharp. Unlike Richard, he was not charming.

"Would you be willing to sit down and speak with us? Now, or whenever is convenient for you."

Carlos spit into the flowerbed and wiped his mouth with the backside of his hand. "What's the name of this show?"

"It's called *Missing or Murdered*," I said.

Carlos pulled his phone from the front pocket of his jeans. He tapped the screen with his pointer finger until he found what he was looking for. "Apple has never heard of ya."

"That's because this is our first season. But we're fully dedicated to this project."

"How dedicated are you?" he asked, like he'd just initiated a challenge.

I held the recorder up higher.

"I quit my job, sold most of my belongings, borrowed money from family, and came here indefinitely. That's how dedicated," I said. "Speaking of which, I'm recording this conversation."

Carlos jerked his head. "Why? I told the police everything in 2008. And I retell them every few years when they take interest in the case again. I ain't got nothing more to say about it."

"See, the problem is the police won't release the case file. So I don't know what you told them," I said. "And those listening to this won't know either."

Carlos was stoned faced. Not a flinch of an eye, not a flair of a nostril. "Millie was my neighbor. We were friendly. Last I saw her was the Monday before she disappeared. We met for lunch during my break."

"Where did you work?" I asked.

"Construction."

"What was the name of the company?"

"I don't remember."

"Where did you two have lunch?"

"I don't remember."

"What street was it off of?"

"Not sure."

Great. The first person I interviewed today died. The second gave one-word answers. The third had selective amnesia.

I need to work on my interviewing skills.

"Look, Carlos," I said, trying to reason. "Your name has come up during our investigation and this is an opportunity for you to clear up any misunderstanding."

"There's nothing to clear up. I don't know anything. Never have."

I didn't believe him—but, oddly enough, I didn't completely distrust him either.

Honestly, I had no idea what to make of Carlos.

"What was Amelia's mood when you two had lunch?" I asked.

"Some prick with a camera posted a humiliating video of her.

How do you think she was doing?"

"I imagine she felt embarrassed," I said.

"So why ask if you already know?"

"Because I *don't* know. It's a guess. I want a first-hand account from someone who was with her during that time."

"She was embarrassed," he said.

"Can you tell us what Amelia was like? Her personality. Interests?" I asked.

"She was funny. Strong. Impulsive. Artistic. Liked to decorate. A runner. Stubborn."

A runner? This was new.

"Where would she run and how often?" I asked.

"She'd run a few times a day, mostly up and down Santa Maria Way."

"A day?" Camry choked out.

"Yeah, she was training for a New Year's Day marathon."

"But still, a couple of times a day?" Camry said, gawking. "That's nuts."

I shot her a look.

"What?" she said defensively. "It *is* nuts."

"It's how she dealt with stress," Carlos said. "Nothing *nuts* about it." He took a step back and spit into the flowerbed again. "Does CinnaMann know you're doing this?"

"We spoke with him earlier today," I said.

The door to Carlos' apartment opened and a cute brown-eyed toddler in a Moana costume poked her head out. "Daddy, can we play now?"

"Give me a second, princess." He smiled down at his daughter. It was the first time I'd seen his teeth.

The little girl fell to the floor and kicked her legs. "I want to play now!"

"Whatever you want, princess." He scooped his daughter off the ground and walked inside. "If I were you, I'd drop this before people start getting hurt," he said and slammed the door shut.

Yikes.

Guess we're done.

I was riding high on adrenaline but waited until we were in the car before I said, "Can you believe what just happened?"

Camry let out a yelp. "You were a rock star, Liv."

I pulled my seat belt on. "Wow, okay. Hold on. Let's take a moment to think about what we have."

"What we have is a suspect."

I gave Camry a look. "We must maintain journalistic objectivity for this podcast to be a success."

"Yeah, yeah, yeah. That guy lives on a short fuse, lived directly beneath Amelia, and he basically threatened to kill us."

"Let's not be overdramatic. He said we should stop before people get hurt." Which I suppose was a threat, the more I thought about it.

Hiccup.

"Which is basically the same thing. Also, he knows something."

This I agreed with. Carlos Hermosa knew more than he was letting on. Did I think he killed Amelia? Or kidnapped her? Or...whatever happened. I wasn't sure.

Camry buckled in. "And can we talk about Amelia running a few times a day? No wonder she was so thin."

Richard said she was athletic. Carlos said she ran. This information coincided with her car being at a hiking trail, but why hike late at night in a mini skirt? Unless...

"What if she didn't disappear on the tenth?" I was thinking out loud. "What if she disappeared early on the eleventh? She parked her car to run the Orcutt Hollow trail and didn't return."

"Why would she go for a run without her phone?"

"She had an old flip phone, it didn't have music or a fitness app. What would be the point? Think about it, if you were going for a run what would you bring?"

"My *iPhone*, headphones, a barf bag, defibrillator, insurance card, my car...cause I'm not running."

"She probably had an iPod and didn't want to lug around

anything else." I cocked a thumb to the box sitting on the backseat. "When we go through Leon's notes let's see if there's a list of items found in her apartment. Specifically looking for an iPod."

Camry reached into the back seat, pulled a notebook from the box and flipped it open. "I hope he has a decoding device in there as well because this all looks like drunk writing."

I glanced over and, yeah, she was right. It was written in illegible shorthand. And I had about a week to make sense of it.

EPISODE FOUR

The Warning

We were back at Hazel's before sundown. After dinner, I set up a studio in the guest room closet, slid the door closed, and spent the next seven hours recording narrative and editing. I could no longer feel my legs, but it was worth it. The first episode of *Missing or Murdered* was done. I started with the intro music. An arrangement I mixed myself using audio clips from the YouTube video, a news report and an orchestral hybrid adventure melody I had purchased on Stock Music.

At the twenty-second mark, I introduced Amelia Clark, talked about the YouTube video, her case and why I chose to investigate. I talked about Leon, how he reached out to *Cold in America* but got me instead, and inserted snippets of our phone conversations I'd recorded when I was still in San Diego. I spoke about my quest for *oomph,* and gave a description of Santa Maria. At thirty-five minutes, I inserted part of Leon's interview and ended it with me saying, "I don't feel a pulse!"

I have a hyper critical ear, so of course I thought the whole thing sounded terrible. Which was one step above crap. Which were my exact sentiments after every episode of *CIA* I'd worked on. Episodes that have been downloaded hundreds of millions of times. Episodes that went on to win awards like the Peabody and the Scripps Howard.

Oh hell.

My heart hiccupped.

Why did I quit my job?

I could have continued to work on *Cold in America* and produced *Missing or Murdered* on the side. I could have traveled up to Santa Maria on the weekends to conduct interviews. I could have produced an entire episode *before* I presented the idea to Mara.

Stupid move.

A move fueled by pride. The need to prove myself. Why did I have to prove myself to anyone?

So what, my boss called me oomph-less? She also called me one of the best mix engineers she'd ever worked with. But *nooooo*, I had to hang my hat on the "oomph" remark and do something impulsive and completely out of character like quit my job. And what did I have to show for it?

Answer: A single episode and not enough material to produce three more. No sponsor or any source of income. And I may have inadvertently killed the only person willing to offer insight into the case.

Okay, I realized I didn't kill Leon. But the stress of doing a podcast couldn't have been easy on him. I could hear the struggle in his voice when I listened to the interview, and I felt *awful* about it.

Truth was, the situation would feel a lot less dire if I weren't deliriously exhausted and sitting in a closet amongst dress-up clothes, boxes of naked Barbie's, stuffed animals, and a creepy looking porcelain doll.

I slid open the door and stretched my sore back. It was nearly three in the morning and I was physically and emotionally spent. Camry was sitting cross-legged on her bed, surrounded by Leon's notebooks, with her computer on her lap, iPad and phone beside her, face trained intently on her laptop screen.

I sat at the desk under the window, sinking into the chair slowly. Most of my limbs had fallen asleep. "What are you working on?"

"I'm reading a thread on the mom's group," she said without

lifting her eyes. "A woman posted a picture of a bad manicure she got at a local salon. Then the salon owner came on and blasted this woman, saying she's trying to sabotage the businesses. Then admin deleted the post. Then the salon owner reposted, and the thread continues. I have to keep up before admin deletes it again. It's like a reality show, only better."

"Did you look at Leon's notes?" I tried not to sound as annoyed as I felt. Camry had every right to have fun. It was late. I was tired and wallowing in despair.

"You okay?" asked Camry. "You look like you're going to pass out. Are you going to pass out? 'Cause you look it."

"No, just tired," I said. "Did you find anything new?"

"A lot actually." She tore her eyes away from the computer screen and referred to her iPad. "Leon mentions Carlos fifty-two times so far, but I'm only through four books. The short of it, from what I can decipher, is they suspected Carlos knew more than he was letting on. They brought him in on October 22 and questioned him for eight hours. He told them exactly what he told us. In one notebook Leon writes that Carlos willingly submitted a DNA sample to the police. Which he thinks is telling."

Very. It was unlikely Carlos would submit DNA without a court order if he were responsible for Amelia's disappearance. It didn't mean that he wasn't involved in some other way, or that he didn't know what happened, though. It just meant that he was confident *his* DNA wasn't in her car.

"I also did some digging into Carlos' past," Camry said. "He has no record, a 675 credit score, works for a property management company, has three credit cards with zero balances, two baby mommas with zero marriages, fifty grand in a savings account and a Facebook page but no other social media accounts."

"That's a lot of money sitting in the…wait, why do you have his financial information?"

"You can tell a lot about a person from their credit score. I think he's saving for a house."

"Do I want to know how you found this out?"

"Probably not," she said. "I'm looking for his email address so I can get more insight."

"Camry, no hacking into email accounts," I said. "It's illegal."

Camry rolled her eyes. "It's not illegal, it's frowned upon."

"Frowned upon? Is that why you were kicked out of Stanford?"

"*No*, I was kicked out of Stanford because I hacked Phil's new girlfriend's account and sent an email to a professor."

"An email saying she would perform sexual favors for an A," I reminded her.

Camry waved her hand as if shooing away a fly. "Details are not relevant to what we're talking about."

"Fine. Anything else?"

"As a matter of fact, yes." She plucked a stack of pictures from the box. "I found photos of Amelia's car. There were Christmas decorations on her passenger side seat. A plastic Santa head, an open box of candy canes, and some other cheap looking festive garb. All with tags on them. Weird, right? It was the beginning of October."

That is weird. "Let me see them."

She handed over the pictures. All were small 4x6, which wasn't conducive for investigation purposes. Unless you had superhuman vision—which I don't. "Can we blow these up without distorting the quality?" I asked, flipping through the stack.

Camry shrugged. "Probably not."

She was probably right.

I squinted at the images, willing new information to jump out at me. The first picture was of the blood found on the steering wheel. There was a dark red smear, about a quarter of an inch long, across the leather stitching. The next picture was a close-up of the second spot of blood found. From what Leon had described, I thought the blood was directly under the driver's side seat—hidden. But this spot was about an inch long and on the front part of the cloth seat. Not sure how or why this was relevant, but it seemed like something I should mention on air.

The third picture was of the inside of Amelia's car. On the

passenger seat were the Christmas decorations. I agreed with Camry, it was odd that Amelia would buy candy canes and plastic Santa heads at the beginning of October, but what grabbed my attention was the fact that all the decorations were stuffed into a plastic CVS bag. In 2008, Californian's weren't required to bring their own reusable bags to the store like they are now. So the chances were good that Amelia actually purchased these items at CVS. And since they were on her seat, chances were even better that she went to CVS right before she went missing.

Also, it proved that she planned to be around during Christmas.

If I tilted my head to the side, I could almost see the top of a receipt sticking out of the bag as well.

"Can you see how many CVS stores are in Santa Maria?" I asked Camry. "Starting with the stores closest to her apartment. I'm sure Leon already checked, but maybe there's an employee who saw her and would be willing to speak to us."

"Aye, aye." Camry gave me a captain salute and started typing.

I had no idea how she has so much energy...*oh, never mind.* There was an empty Red Bull on the ground.

I placed the pictures back in the box. "Did you post on the mom's group?"

"Yep, but no replies yet."

Dang it.

"However," Camry said, "the *Missing or Murdered* Facebook page is up to a thousand likes now. Woohoo!" She did jazz hands. "We're practically Internet famous. Speaking of which, I checked out Oliver's YouTube channel. He's, like, a legit YouTuber and I'm just throwing this out there: I know he's, like, older than me, but if he's my grandpa's, brother's grandson then..."

"He's still your cousin," I said.

She pouted. "A shame because he's hot. And I mean that in a total none incestual kind of way."

"Obviously."

"Guess how many subscribers he has?"

"I don't know...ten million," I said.

"I hate when you do that!"

"Do what?"

"When I ask you to guess something and you over guess making the number now seem insignificant."

"When have I ever—" I was interrupted by a crash. Instinctually, I covered my face but not before I was blasted with tiny shards of glass.

Confused, I gazed up. The window above the desk had a hole big enough for a toddler to stand in. Camry was up on her knees on the bed with her mouth open.

We glanced around the room and find an...*apple*?

What the hell?

Camry and I rushed to the window, careful not to step on glass. No one was outside. Not a screech of a tire. Not the sound of feet against the pavement. Only the stillness of the night and the hum of a street lamp.

"Liv, you're bleeding." Camry pointed to my face.

I touched my cheek and marveled down at the blood coating my fingers. "Grab my recorder!"

"But there's blood dripping from your face."

"I don't care. It's in the closet plugged into my laptop. Hurry, hurry!" I was barefoot. Camry had socks on and was fueled by a Red Bull.

She danced through the glass to retrieve the recorder and handed it to me. I wiped the blood from my eye using the backside of my hand and pressed Record. "An apple just flew through the window, breaking it and spraying glass across the room." I held the recorder up to Camry's mouth. "Say 'you're bleeding' again."

"You're bleeding," she said robotically.

"No, say 'Liv, you're bleeding' more concerned, like you did before."

"Oh, okay." She cracked her neck. "Liv! You're bleeding!"

Dramatic, but better.

The door swung open and there stood Hazel in a long paisley-printed nightgown with curlers in her hair and a bat in her hands. "Oh my word, what happened?"

"Liv's bleeding!"

"Oh you sweet thing." Hazel grabbed my hand and pulled me down the hall into the bathroom. I tiptoed around the glass, still recounting the event into my recorder.

This was huge!

Not only would it make for an exciting episode and an even better teaser trailer. It meant we struck a nerve. Someone here knows what happened to Amelia, and that someone wanted to scare us out of town.

Hazel pulled an impressive first aid kit from under the sink and applied an alcohol compress to the cut above my cheek. I winced.

"Hold still, you're a mess." Hazel's nose was an inch from mine. Camry joined her. I went cross-eyed staring at the two.

"You think she needs stitches?" asked Camry.

"No, but she could use a good waxing," said Hazel.

"You're right. Eyebrows, lip, chin."

"You two know I'm conscious, right? And I'm recording this?" I stood and went to the mirror. There were two superficial cuts on my forehead. The one above my eyelid looked deep, and there was a gash going from my chin to ear. And, yeah, I could use a good wax.

When did I get chin hair?

Why do I have chin hair?

Hazel forced me back on the toilet and ripped open a package of gauze using her teeth. "How did this happen?"

Camry passed Hazel a tube of Neosporin. "Someone threw an apple through the window."

"Oh no, you sweet thing." She dabbed at my forehead with a cotton swab. "It probably fell from a tree."

"Do you have an apple tree?" I held the recorder up to Hazel's mouth.

"Pffft. Of course I have an apple tree. Honestly. Who do you think I am? All my pies are made with fresh Granny Smith apples straight from my tree in the backyard. That Nancy Paloza down the street uses canned. Can you imagine?"

"What a poser," Camry said and gave Hazel a cotton swab.

"Granny Smith apples are green, this one is red," I said. "Also, an apple from the backyard is not likely to travel around the house and in through the front upstairs window."

"That's because someone threw it!" Camry was suddenly in hysterics. The Red Bull must have worn off. "If Liv wasn't twisted around in her chair the apple would have smacked her in the head. She could have died."

"I doubt it would have killed me," I said. "But just in case, can you say that again?" I held the recorder up to her mouth.

"It could have killed you!"

"Now, now, now, girls. Calm down." Hazel placed a butterfly bandage above my eye. "It was probably an accident. Who would go and do something like that on purpose, huh?"

"*Carlos*," Camry coughed into her palm.

"We don't know anything," I said. "We talked to several people today, and Camry posted about the podcast on a Facebook page with over fifteen thousand members. Plenty of people know we're in town."

"*Carlos*," Camry coughed again.

"Stop that." I tossed a washcloth at her. "We don't know anything."

"Carlos said to stop the podcast before people start getting hurt." Camry gestured to me helplessly. "Have you *seen* your face? You're hurt."

This was true. But I still wasn't convinced it was Carlos. There were too many locals who knew about the podcast now. Plus, Carlos didn't seem like the type to throw fruit.

Hazel continued to put me back together. Pouring—what felt like acid—into my gashes then covering them in soothing ointment and gauze.

Eventually, the adrenaline drained from my body and my sanity returned.

Holy hell.

I grabbed hold of Hazel's arm. "I'm sorry about the window. I'll clean the mess and pay for the repair."

"Never you mind all that." Hazel placed the last bandage on my face and smoothed it down with her finger. She had a grandmother's touch.

"We can stay at a hotel if you're uncomfortable?" I offered.

"Don't you dare. It's only a piece of fruit. Plus—" A smile crept across her face. "—I think it's all rather exciting."

Glad she thinks so.

We were back in the guest room. It was windy outside, and because there was no glass in the window, it was windy inside. The floor was peppered in leaves and pine needles from the front yard trees. I picked the apple up by the stem. "It's more oval than round, with moles, and it doesn't have the waxy feel of a store-bought apple," I said into the recorder.

Hazel looked closer. "Honey crisp is my guess. They grow decent around here. But this is one ugly apple. Like some kind of mutant."

"Any of your neighbors have a honey crisp apple tree?" I asked Hazel.

"Not on this street. Weird thing to throw through a window."

"Agreed," I said. "A bit risky, too. An apple might not necessarily break the glass. A brick or a rock would do the job."

"Seriously?" Camry said. "You two are spending way too much time examining a freaking piece of fruit and too little time calling the police."

Good point.

An hour later we (as in the police officer called to take the report, Camry, Hazel and myself) stood together on the driveway looking up at the window. "Hazel's driveway is long and curved, no chance someone threw the apple and ran away before Camry and I looked out. Which meant whoever threw it, hid until the coast was clear.

Or maybe they're still hiding," I said into the recorder.

"I thoroughly searched the area," said the cop, a young guy with dark sideburns and a dimple chin.

Camry patted his shoulder. "Don't worry about it, she's world building."

"For the podcast?" asked the Officer.

"Exactly." Camry held up a Ziploc with the apple in it. "Here's your evidence. You can run fingerprints on fruit. I googled it. They're doing it in England."

The police officer took the bag and examined the apple. "Not sure the department will cover the cost of running prints on fruit."

"You need to give it to Detective LeClare," I said. "She's the one working the Amelia Clark disappearance, and obviously whoever threw that apple is involved."

"Yeah," added Camry. "And tell her we want to speak to her."

In my periphery I could see Oliver running down the driveway. He had a wetsuit on his lower extremities and a hoodie on the upper.

I checked my watch: five forty-five a.m. Surfing time.

"You okay?" Oliver slouched down so he and Hazel were face-to-face. "I was about to leave when I saw the cop car."

"I'm fine," Hazel said and signed. "It was a little mishap."

Camry tapped Oliver's shoulder to get his attention. "It wasn't a mishap." She whirled her hands around while she talked. It looked like she was attempting to sign "Jingle Bells." "It was assault with a fruity weapon."

Oliver looked to me for clarification.

"*A person threw an apple through the window,*" I signed.

Oliver took a step closer. "You're hurt!" He grabbed my face between his hands and examined my cuts.

"It's fine. Good thing I'm not taller, the apple would have smacked me right in the head." I laughed.

Oliver didn't. He traced the bandage on my forehead with his fingertip and stared intently. His eyes were a deep, sea color blue with specs of green and white, striking against his dark hair.

"I'm going to head out," said the cop.

For a second, I forgot he was there.

"The cop is speaking to me," I said to Oliver.

Oliver's eyes dropped and his face went red. He took a step back and bumped into Camry. Then stumbled into the cop. Then stepped on Hazel's foot and used her shoulder to steady himself.

I smiled inwardly.

What can I say? I have that effect on men.

Okay, I typically didn't but, you know, there was a first for everything.

EPISODE FIVE

Planted

"Hazel's grandson helped us board up the window. Now we wait and see if the detective contacts us," I said to my brother, David. The phone was sandwiched between my ear and shoulder while I pushed the cart behind Camry. We were at Target. We'd come to buy antacids but got sucked into the bargain bin area. "I offered to stay at a hotel, but Hazel wouldn't hear anything of it."

David was at work. I could hear the station chatter in the background. He was recently promoted to detective. A huge relief. I didn't like him on patrol. It's a dangerous world out there and people are monsters. "Sure, it could have been someone trying to scare you off, or they were attempting to get your attention, saw the light on, threw the apple, didn't anticipate the apple going through the window, got scared and took off."

He made a good point. I hadn't thought of that.

Camry held up a hat with *I'm not short. I'm travel sized* printed on the front. "You need this," she mouthed.

I shook my head no.

Camry threw the hat in the cart.

I placed it back on the rack.

"Liv, now I'm worried," said David. "Can't you investigate from home?"

"What? No! I'm fine. We're fine. It was just an apple." Aimed right at my head.

"An apple this time. Next it could be a brick, or a keyed car, or you're run off the road by a maniac, or taken hostage, or even murdered. People are crazy." David didn't have to listen to true crime podcasts because he lived it. "Give me the address where you're staying. I'm sending you pepper spray. No arguments about it." David took his role as protective older brother serious.

It wasn't like pepper spray was going to protect me from flying fruit (or a flying brick), but I gave him the address anyway. We hung up with the promise I'd be careful.

Camry held up a spiral notepad with a unicorn on the cover. "I feel like I need this."

"For what?"

"I don't know. Notes?"

"How much?"

"A dollar?"

"Eh, whatever. It's your money"

She tossed it into the cart. "Also, how cute are these tissues?" She held up travel-sized Kleenex with owls printed on them.

"It's up to you."

Camry tossed them in.

"Did David say anything about me?" she asked while looking through the gift labels. "Like, did he ask if I got hurt or if I was okay?"

"Of course." That was a lie. He didn't ask about her. But I didn't want to hurt her feelings. David had never paid much attention to Camry. Not because he didn't care about her, and not because her mother married our father *less* than a year after our mom died, and not because she's so much younger than him, but because...*well*...scratch that. Those *are* the reasons why he didn't pay much attention to her.

"What did he say about me?" Camry asked.

Oh geez. I sucked at lying. "He wants to make sure we're safe."

"Oh." She shrugged like she's doesn't care, but I caught a smile spreading across her face. At our parents' wedding, Camry had given a toast about how excited she was to *finally* have siblings.

I feared neither David nor I lived up to the hype.

Camry tossed a pink tumbler into the cart along with a scarf, a package of mechanical pencils, and an eraser in the shape of an elephant.

"Okay, I think you're covered. Let's go find the antacids before you spend any more money." I had to get control of the fire raging in my throat before I could concentrate on anything else. Hazel had made homemade maple-bacon glazed donuts this morning and served them with fresh fruit, cheesy eggs, sausage, and indigestion.

We followed the signs to the laxatives, antacids and nausea medicine aisle. I could use all three. Camry consulted the back of a Pepcid AC box. "I've never had such bad heartburn in all my life."

"How can we ask Hazel to stop feeding us so much without being rude?"

Camry grabbed one of every antacid and dropped them in the cart. "I don't know, maybe there's a card for that?" I followed her three aisles over to the greeting card section. "Let's see, 'thank you religious.' 'Thank you funny.' 'Thank you sentimental.' 'Thank you sympathy.'" There's no *thank you but for the love of all that is holy put away the deep fryer*. Hallmark should really look into that."

I laughed. "I don't think there's a tactful way to refuse her food. We have to suck it up and eat." I grabbed a bottle of Tums. "Can we take this and other antacids at the same time?"

"Let me see." Camry studied the back of the bottle. "Oh, I just remembered."

"What?"

"That I'm not a pharmacist. Let's go ask."

We got in line at the pharmacy. The acid was blistering in my esophagus and I couldn't wait any longer and popped two Tums into my mouth.

"I saw that," someone loudly whispered into my ear.

Startled, I whirled around. It was Oliver. He released a lopsided smile. Sometime between this morning and now, Oliver had cut his hair. Goodbye mop of dark curls. *Hell-o* coiffed mane.

Wow. Good thing he isn't my cousin.

I playfully smacked him on the arm. "You scared me."

Oliver feigned pain. "So violent," he said and signed.

"Don't mess with a woman who has heartburn."

"I see my grandma is feeding you well."

"She's trying to kill us by way of consumption." Camry ran her finger across her neck. Which isn't the sign for kill, but got the point across. "Oh, I forgot."

"That you're not an ASL interpreter," I said.

"No, that I need toothpaste. Be right back." She dashed off, stopping first at an end cap to check out the selection of discounted lip glosses.

I turned to Oliver. "What brings you to Target on this fine day?" I asked and signed.

He held up a package of HDMI cables. "For the security cameras I'm installing at my grandma's house."

I moved up in line. Oliver moved with me.

"I feel terrible. I told her we'd stay at a hotel, and I offered to pay for the window. She won't hear of it. Please let me pay for the security cameras."

"The system's five-hundred dollars."

I nearly passed out. "What I meant to say was, *help*. Let me help cover the cost by buying those cables...assuming they're under a hundred bucks."

Oliver placed a hand on my shoulder. "Don't worry. It's not a problem," he said without signing. "She doesn't know I'm installing them. It's mostly for my own peace of mind. I'm wondering if this is all worth it though?"

He lost me. "If the cameras are worth it, because I'm sure you can find a cheaper system on eBay."

"No, the podcast you and Camry are trying to do. Is it worth getting hurt over?"

"No one got hurt."

He gave me a look.

"Okay, I got a few scratches, but if I thought we were in serious life-threatening danger I'd send Camry home and go to a hotel."

We moved up in line.

Oliver ran a hand through his newly coiffed mane. "I don't think you realize that this is big time, real world stuff you're getting involved in. It's not a joke or a game, or something to be taken lightly."

"Excuse me?" I liked messy haired Oliver better.

"I think you're in over your head here. Maybe you two should think about doing a different project."

"Over my head? I'm in over my head? You think I'm in over my head?" When I'm upset, I'll repeat the offending remark over and over until I can come up with a good retort. "I'm in over my head?" Sometimes it takes a while.

"Next!" said the pharmacist tech.

"They're calling me up," I signed. *"Goodbye."*

I left Oliver and pushed my cart up to the counter, seething. The pharmacist tech, Penny (per her name tag), drummed her lacquered nails on the register while I slammed the antacids on the counter, mumbling to myself, *"Over my head? I'm a podcaster. He makes YouTube videos. Where's the camaraderie?"*

"Excuse me?" asked Penny

"Sorry, I'm talking to myself." I dropped the last of the medication on the antacid pyramid I'd built on the counter. "Which of these combinations would be best to battle the worst heartburn known to man?"

"Let me ask the pharmacist." Penny went to talk to the man counting pills behind the partition.

Do I think this is a joke?

Does he see me laughing?!

Camry appeared at my side with a box of Direct Dental Toothpaste, lip gloss, and a nail file. "Where'd Oliver go?"

"To buy an over-priced security system," I said and left it at that.

"Awe. Do you miss him?" She dug her elbow into my rib.

"No."

"Yes you do. My sister has the hots for my cousin," she sang and now everyone was staring at us.

"No, I don't," I said loud enough for all to hear. "And maybe we don't say that sentence in public."

"Good idea."

Penny returned and plucked two boxes from the pyramid. "He says you can take these and the Tums." Of course, they're the most expensive brands. Whatever. At this point I'd swallow a cactus if it would help.

Okay, maybe not a cactus.

Penny rang us up. "Did I hear you say podcast?"

Camry slid a can of mints across the counter. "Yes, we're doing a podcast about a local girl, Amelia Clark, who disappeared in 2008."

Penny twisted her face. "I knew Millie. We worked together at Direct Dental."

Camry and I both froze in place.

Penny?

My mind spun this name around.

Penny?

Aha!

"Are you Penny McDonald?" I asked.

I'd found a Penny McDonald when I searched 'Direct Dental employees 2008' on LinkedIn. I'd sent her a message, but she never responded. This Penny didn't look like the LinkedIn Penny. LinkedIn Penny was a slender blonde with long hair, sparkling blue eyes, and a smooth complexion. This Penny was round and blemished and her eyes didn't sparkle. But I could see the resemblance.

"No. I'm Penny *Green*," she said. "Sure, I was once Penny McDonald. I was originally Penny Scott. Once I was Penny Lin, but we don't need to get into that right now." She snorted a laugh.

That was lot of Pennys to keep track of.

"I sent you a message on LinkedIn," I said.

"Oh, yeah? Like, I don't ever go on there anymore," she said with a shrug. "What's the point when you got a job, right?"

"Can I speak to you about Amelia? Do you have a break coming up? We'll wait for however long. It doesn't matter. Whatever you want." I knew I sounded eager and a bit too desperate—but that's only because I was eager and a bit too desperate.

Penny checked the clock on the wall behind her. "I'm off in three hours."

"Perfect. Where should we meet?" I handed her a business card with all my information on it.

"In the back near the dumpsters. It's where employees have to park." Penny scanned the last of our medicine. "That'll be seventy-three dollars."

Ouch. That put a ding in my budget. However, we didn't have to buy our own toilet paper anymore, and I did score an interview out of it.

Worth it.

To pass the time, Camry and I drove to the Orcutt Hollow where Amelia's car was found. The trail starts at the end of a residential street at the very south point of Santa Maria. In 2008, this was an unofficial hiking trail. A few years ago, the property was purchased by a third party and donated to the city. Now, Santa Maria Parks and Rec ran it. They've since paved a parking lot and put in mile markers—which is wonderful for the residents here, but terrible for us because it completely changed the landscape.

"Based on this—" Camry held up the picture of Amelia's car—a white Toyota Camry. "—she was parked right—" She spun around with her arm outstretched, finger pointed. "—there."

"Are you sure?" She was pointing at a fire hydrant.

"Positive. Look at the background. It's the same brown hills."

She was right.

In the picture, Amelia's car was parked at the curb. There were wild grown shrubs and a dead tree beside her vehicle and the same brown hills off in the distance. Now, there was a fire hydrant, manicured bushes, and a row of newly built homes.

"This bothers me," I said into the recorder. "On the tenth of October, which was a Friday night, Amelia was dressed like she was going out. A skirt, heels, and black leggings underneath, which must have been the style in 2008. You don't dress up like that unless you're going to meet friends, or even going on a date. Then she takes out three hundred dollars, which is a lot of cash to carry. Then her car is found *here*. I think it was a plant."

"It's not a plant," Camry said. "It's a fire hydrant."

I gave her a look, not in the mood for jokes.

"Sorry," she said and backed away.

"A plant as in, someone put her car here to make it look like she went hiking and disappeared."

"What if she went hiking the next morning and *did* disappear? Like you said."

"I'm not so sure about that theory anymore. Leon said the cadaver dogs didn't pick up her scent on the trail. Also, it's a small town. Someone would have seen her Friday night if she went out." I blew out a breath and took in my surroundings. "Where did you go, Amelia?" I whispered to myself.

Camry and I walked the three-mile hiking trail. She took video and I recorded audio of us huffing and puffing. It wasn't an arduous trek; we were just out of shape. The ground was rocky and the dirt was soft. A dangerous combination for anyone wanting to run. We reached the end and sat on a tree trunk. The view was breathtaking. Rolling hills that seemed to go on forever. Horses galloping in the distance. Small farmhouses peppered throughout the landscape and a vineyard took up an entire hillside.

"I'm not buying it," I said to Camry. "She didn't disappear here. If she were training for a marathon, why would she run this measly three-mile trail? This isn't much of a workout for in-shape people, and it's a terrible surface to run on. There aren't trees or foliage for an attacker to hide in."

"But we don't know what this place looked like in 2008," Camry said.

She made a good point. "But I doubt Parks and Rec would maintain two hundred acres, nor do I think they'd chop down trees around here. It is a possibility, though. Can you—"

"Call Parks and Rec to get information about Orcutt Hollow," Camry finished for me. "Got it."

"And what about—"

"Asking a park ranger to give us an interview," she finished for me. "Got it."

"Then—"

"Can I give myself a bonus for being the best damn peon you've ever had," she said. "Got it."

"I was going to say, we should stop by the ATM Amelia was last seen at." I pulled Camry in for a side hug. "But you are a damn good peon."

EPISODE SIX

The Body

"Orcutt Bank is located a parking lot away from CinnaMann's," I said into the recorder. "There's one exit out of the bank parking area. From there Amelia could have cut through the main parking lot to Bradley Road, which leads to Orcutt Hollow, or she could have pulled onto Clark Ave, which leads to the freeway."

"It's funny that we're researching Amelia Clark while *on* Clark Ave." Camry leaned against the hood of my car and tossed a Tum into her mouth. According to the bottle you can have up to fourteen a day.

I wasn't sure if that meant fourteen at one time, or throughout the day. Either way, I'd already eaten my allotted amount.

"I think most towns have a Clark Ave." I stood at the ATM and looked around to see what Amelia could have seen. "McDonald's, pet groomers, dry cleaner, CinnaMann's, and a dance studio," I said into the recorder.

"Don't you think it's weird she was last seen in the same shopping center her dad's bakery is located?" asked Camry.

"This shopping center appears to be the hub for the area. Plus CinnaMann's closes at four, and Richard and Janet were out of town. Unless she stopped by the bakery to check on things. Which is a possibility I suppose."

"Did he say what time they got back Friday night?"

"No, I don't think so."

"We should ask him. They're still open." Camry held her watch out for me to see. "It's ten till four and we have an hour before we need to meet Penny."

"Might as well."

A different girl was working behind the counter, and her relief was palpable when she realized we were not there to buy anything. The display case had already been cleared and cleaned.

Mr. Clark greeted us with open arms, far more welcoming than our first encounter. This was the Richard Clark everyone talked about. Before we could ask about Amelia, we were invited back to the kitchen.

"It took me ten years to perfect the recipe. Amelia was my taste tester," he told us during the tour. Which didn't take long, the bakery was small. There were two rooms. One was the prep area with a mixer that was taller than me. The second room was for the ovens and cooling racks. Richard walked us through the delicate step-by-step process of how to make the CinnaMann's cinnamon rolls. It was quite the ordeal. I had no idea. Growing up, my cinnamon rolls came from a tube.

I made the mistake of saying as much to Mr. Clark, and before I could say no, there was a piping hot cinnamon roll in front of me. And this was no Pillsbury cinnamon roll. CinnaMann's rolls were seven inches tall and three inches in diameter. They came with raisins, or no raisins, nuts or no nuts. You could get it drizzled with caramel or chocolate. "The works" came with hazelnuts, chocolate, caramel, buttercream frosting, and rolled in brown sugar—in other words, it was heartburn on a plate.

This was what Mr. CinnaMann presented to us.

"Guaranteed, this will be the best bun you'll ever taste." He handed Camry and me each a fork and stood by, awaiting our reaction.

This is going to hurt.

Camry was first to take a bite. Her brow glistened under the bright lighting as the fork landed in her mouth.

"Mmmmm," she said with wide, watering eyes.

I shoved a forkful into my mouth. Buttery soft dough, glazed sugar, and savory cinnamon. It was delicious.

Until I swallowed.

My stomach attempted to reject this sweet turn of events. And it wasn't the cinnamon roll's fault. It was the acid eating away at my intestines. But I powered through, taking large bites to end the agony sooner, because that's what good podcasters do.

Who needs stomach lining anyway?

Richard next invited us to his office, which didn't involve eating so I was happy. His office was really just a waist-high counter near the ovens. Pictures were taped near the computer. Most were of the store. One from opening day: Richard with a pair of large scissors about to cut the ribbon. I assumed the dirty blonde child at his side was Amelia. The others were of Richard with various individuals I assumed to be customers with cinnamon rolls and other baked goods in hand. There were six rows of "Thank You, Sponsor" plaques from soccer, softball, baseball, and volleyball teams hung on the wall.

On the desk was a framed picture of Janet, Richard and Amelia. Amelia was standing between her parents in a purple cap and gown with a yellow *Excellence in Academics* sash draped around her neck. According to my research, she never graduated from college so this must have been her high school graduation.

Janet appeared uncomfortable. Her pose reminded me of an old Victorian photograph. Face void of emotion, hand wrapped around her middle, head tilted, and eyes trained on the camera in an almost disturbing way. Could have been a poorly timed photo—but then why display it?

Richard and Amelia both had mega-watt smiles and arms flung around each other. It was almost as if Janet was photoshopped in.

"Would you mind?" I held up my phone and pointed to the picture.

Richard nodded his approval, and I snapped a pic for the website.

"Amelia was very pretty," I said to Richard, still studying the picture. She looked better here than she did in the video. At least fifteen pounds heavier. The fuller face looked more natural on her frame. Not that she appeared overweight. She appeared healthier. Happier.

"She looked like my mother; that's who we named her after," Richard said, peering over my shoulder. "Which is why most people called her Millie, to differentiate between the two. I liked her full name better, so we called her Amelia."

"Is your mother still alive?" I asked.

"No, she died about a year before Amelia went missing. The two were very close."

I felt a pang of sadness for Mr. Clark. Both of the Amelias in his life were gone.

Richard pulled out a stool and had a seat. "You two come up with anything new?" He was so relaxed and much more amicable than he was during our first meeting. I didn't know what changed over the last twenty-four hours, but his cooperation would make our investigation easier.

On the walk over, I thought about if we should mention the apple through the window incident. I assumed he'd ask what happened to my face. I looked like I got in a fight with a rosebush—and the bush won, but he'd yet to mention it. "We had a visitor last night," I started. "Someone threw an apple through the window of the house we're staying at and broke it."

Mr. Clark's eyebrows shot up. "Who would do that?"

"Someone wanting us out of town," said Camry. "Or an immature kid with good aim."

Mr. Clark took a moment to digest this information. "What time?"

"It was early in the morning, around three a.m."

He rubbed his chin. "My guess would be a kid."

"Have you ever had anyone vandalize your home or the bakery?" I thought back to the initials carved in the chef on the window. Though, that hardly qualified as vandalism.

"No, everyone's been supportive," he said with a shrug.

"Another question: After Amelia went missing, do you know if surveillance was collected from any of the stores in the shopping center?" I asked.

"Just the bank. I don't think anyone else had cameras back then."

"Not even McDonald's?" asked Camry.

He shook his head no.

Shoot.

"What time did you and Mrs. Clark get home Friday evening?" I asked.

Richard drummed his fingers on the counter while he thought. "Between eight and nine. Why?"

"We're putting a timeline together. If she was at the bank across the parking lot at six fifteen p.m., would she have stopped by the bakery to check on things if she knew you two were still out of town?"

"No. She didn't show a whole lot of interest in the bakery after she graduated high school. She wanted to do her own thing."

"Do you think she would have exited Clark toward the freeway, or Bradley toward the hiking trail?" I asked.

"Orcutt Hollow is up Bradley, so that's my guess," he said.

I took my notebook from my bag and peeked at the list of questions I'd jotted down last night. "Did Amelia ever mention going to lunch with Carlos Hermosa?"

"Ramsey asked me the same question, but I don't know. She hung out with him quite a bit before she left."

She left?

I swept a stray hair off my face to buy time. He distinctly said, *before she left.* Could easily have been a slip of words *or* a slip of the tongue.

"Where did she go?" I asked.

He tapped his forehead as if saying *duh.* "I meant before she disappeared."

Huh. I bit at my lip, deciding if I should press the issue or continue.

I decided on the latter. "Do you know why she used cash instead of a debit or credit card?"

He grunted. "You know kids. They think they've got it all figured out. Amelia was desperate to make it on her own and she thought using cash would help her save money. When really she should have built her credit up."

"Did they find an iPod in her apartment?"

"They didn't say. She had one, though. Janet and I gave it to her the Christmas before she left."

She left.

There it was again.

Now I'm pressing it.

"You keep saying 'before she left.' Do you think she left on her own will? Because Detective Ramsey said the same thing before he died."

Mr. Clark frowned. "We say 'left' because it's better than the alternative."

Oh.

"Do you think if we stop by the house Mrs. Clark would be more open to speaking with us?" I asked.

Richard was shaking his head before I even finished. "Janet's never been one to discuss private matters with other people, and she doesn't like talking about what *could* have happened to Amelia."

I made a mental note to still try. From the graduation picture and Hazel's parade story, I got the sense there was something off about Mrs. Clark, and I'd like to see what that something was myself.

"Is there anyone else you can think of who we should reach out to? Friends? Family? Ex-boyfriends? Teachers she was close to?" I asked.

Richard scratched his chin. "How about the people she used to work with?"

"We're on our way to talk to one of them now."

"That would be my best bet. Let me know what you come up with." He walked us out. "Hold on a sec," he said, suddenly remembering. "Let me grab a cinnamon roll for the road."

Heaven help me.

Before we met Penny, I stopped at the gas station to fill up my car. Camry ran inside to use the restroom while I waited by the pump, watching the dollar amount go up...and up...and up...and *up.*

Gas is too damn expensive.

Good thing Hazel was taking care of toilet paper and food, otherwise we'd be walking around town. I could almost hear Camry's snarky commentary if that were the case. Being that she would take a defibrillator with her if forced to run, I couldn't imagine she would be too happy to tour Santa Maria by foot.

Gas was still pumping, and I couldn't look at the price any longer. I leaned back against my car and scrolled through emails on my phone. Most were spam. There was a bridal shower evite from a former co-worker at *Cold in America*, and a—

"Liv!" Camry sprinted across the fuel lanes, dodging the truck pulling in, and rammed into the trunk of my car.

"What is wrong with you?" I asked.

"There...is...a...body..." She paused to catch her breath. "They found a body."

"Who is *they*? And what are you talking about?" I was so confused. She went inside to pee.

"It's on..." Camry cocked her thumb toward the Food Mart. "There's a television...the news..." She sucked in a breath. "Come on!"

I returned the fuel nozzle to the pump, spilling gas on my shoe in the process, and followed Camry inside. Mounted to the wall behind the register was a television turned to the local news station. Across the bottom of the screen in big bold letters it said, "Decomposed Human Body Found at Santa Maria Park." Video was playing of yellow crime scene tape flapping in the wind with CSI working in the distance.

"Can you turn it up, please?" I asked the man sitting behind the register. He was playing on his phone and chewing on a toothpick, completely unaware of our presence.

I rang the bell on the counter.

The man looked up at me at me as if I appeared out of thin air.

"Can you turn up the television, please?"

It took a painful amount of time for him to process my request. Too long. I spotted a remote control held together by duct tape near the register and snatched it up. Sometimes you just got to do things yourself.

I turned up the volume.

"Authorities are investigating after decomposed human remains were found at Waller Park earlier today," said the news anchor, a young woman with a helmet of blonde hair. "The discovery was made just after ten a.m. by a city worker there to fix a sprinkler."

They cut to a man with a gray mustache. "Yeah, uh, I was digging up some old pipe when I noticed what looked like a piece of clothing. Then the more I dug the more I realized it...uh...yeah...it was attached to a body."

They cut back to the news anchor. "EMS responded and pronounced the individual deceased at the scene. Authorities have not been able to identify the victim. Next up, a four-ounce strawberry is for sale by a local farmer. Ken has the full report after the break. Stay tuned."

For a while, Camry and I stood there in silence, both thinking the same thing, but neither one of us willing to say it out loud.

"Why would you need the EMS to pronounce a decomposed body dead?" Camry finally asked.

So, okay, I guess we weren't thinking the same thing.

"You, uh, done with my TV?" The man behind the counter asked.

I nodded my head slowly and placed the remote into his palm. "Where is Waller Park?" I asked him.

"Not too far." He pushed his eyebrows together. "Why?"

Why?

Clearly, he was not paying attention.

"Do you think it's..." Camry started to say.

I blew out a breath. "Not sure. It takes eight to ten years for a body to decompose if it's buried with no embalming or coffin." *I kind of hate that I know this.*

Now the man behind the counter was giving us a funny look.

"I'm a true crime podcaster," I told him. "We're here doing an investigation into the disappearance of Amelia Clark."

He still gave us the same look, which was my cue to leave.

"What do we do now?" Camry asked as we walked back to my car.

The truth was, I had no idea.

We didn't have any contacts at the police station, or the news station, or *any* kind of station for that matter. I had doubt that I'd find out the identity of the body before anyone else did. If it were Amelia, they'd notify Richard and Janet before the name was released. I would assume he'd let me know, since we appeared to be on better terms now.

There wasn't a whole lot we could do except go see what Penny had to say.

EPISODE SEVEN

Who is Blake Kirkland?

Penny was waiting for us by the dumpsters in black scrubs, her hair swept into a claw clip, hands clutching two Target bags. It was too windy outside to conduct our interview, so we piled into my car. She sat in the passenger seat and eyed the Tums container sitting in the cup holder.

"Is this the one you just bought?" She gave the bottle a shake. What's left rattled around.

"We don't mess around with our antacids," said Camry from the back seat. She had on her scarf and was sipping water out of her new tumbler.

"Be careful you don't OD," said Penny.

"Can you OD on Tums?" asked Camry.

"Technically, you can OD on anything," said Penny.

"Like food?" Camry held up the bag from CinnaMann's. "Would you like to take home two fresh cinnamon rolls?"

"Are those from CinnaMann's?" Penny snatched the bag and stuck her nose in to take a whiff. "Mmmmm, these are totally my favorite. I haven't been there in years, but I used to go all the time."

I was done talking about food. Between chocking down the cinnamon roll, and the news of a decomposed body in Waller Park, my appetite may never return. "Should we start?"

Penny took one more whiff then wiggled around in her seat to get comfortable. "What do you want to know?"

Because of our close proximity, I was able to use the recorder. I placed it on the center console and made sure it was on. "Start off with your name and how you knew Amelia."

"My name is Penny Green. I'm a pharmacist tech at Target, and I sell Flynnwood Beauty products. I brought you both samples." She gave Camry and I plastic portion cups filled with green goo. "This is aloe rub for your feet and hands." Next she pulled a blue tube from her bag. "This is our number one selling product. It's a colon cleanse."

Camry grabbed the tube from Penny and read the instructions. "Where do you stick it?"

"You mix it with water and drink it, silly." Penny had a high-pitched hyena laugh that could shatter glass. "The special blend of herbs and vitamins will release the toxins in your body, reduce bloating and it's only forty-nine-ninety-nine."

As appealing as fifty-dollar diarrhea sounded, we weren't there to talk colons.

"Did you sell Flynwood Beauty while you worked at Direct Dental?" I asked, attempting to segue.

"No, no. This is a new company. It's only been around since 2015. I started last month, and I've already hit level four manager status."

I'm sure that meant something.

I gave up on segues. "How did you know Amelia?"

Penny tucked a strand of hair behind her ear. "Millie and I grew up together, but she was a few grades younger than me so it's not like we hung out then. I didn't really get to know her until I started working at Direct Dental. I was the receptionist and she was the manager's assistant. She'd cover for me when I went on breaks or if I called in sick and vice-a-versa."

"Did you two ever spend time together outside of work?"

"Sure, a few times," she said. "But it was mostly in a group with other work people."

"Did you ever go to her apartment?" I asked, thinking about Carlos.

"No, she didn't get her own place until...gosh...I guess it was about a month before the video. She was really into interior design. She read a lot of those home décor magazines."

Carlos also said Amelia enjoyed decorating. These insights into Amelia's life and her personality would help the listeners connect more with her.

And the more they connected, the more they'd care.

The more they cared, the higher chance we had of finding out what happened.

"Did Amelia ever talk about Carlos Hermosa?" I asked.

"She didn't *talk* about him, but I know they were friends." Penny rolled her eyes and launched into a fifteen-minute rant about Carlos Hermosa. Turned out Penny and Carlos were the same age, went to school together from kindergarten through high school, and they grew up across the street from each other. In short, Penny knew Carlos well, and she wasn't a fan. "He was a total troublemaker," she said. "And he'd bring these guys over who would break into our cars, and they'd deal drugs on the corner. Carlos spent like six months on house arrest when he was in high school."

Camry and I shared a look and she scrunched her nose. She had dug into Carlos' past and didn't find a criminal record—and Camry is especially thorough when it comes to Internet stalking. But if all illegal activity happened before Carlos turned eighteen, then those records would have been sealed and Camry would have had no way of seeing them.

"He's just bad news," Penny continued. "I don't even know why or how they became friends."

"If Amelia didn't talk about Carlos, then how do you know they were friends?" I asked.

"He brought her lunch once. It was about a week before she was fired, and they ate together in the break room." She picked imaginary lint off her pants. "I overheard some of their conversation when I was heating up my food. They were flirty. I remember she had a salad with pineapple in it, and she was trying to get him to eat it, but he said he doesn't eat fruit. Then she told him he was a pineapple because he was sweet on the inside and prickly on the outside." She looked off in the distance. "I totally forgot about that conversation until now."

I thought back to our interaction with Carlos and the pineapple tattoo on his upper bicep—the only tattoo in color.

"Did she ever talk about drugs?" Camry asked.

"No, but she definitely didn't look good before she disappeared. Her hair was thin, and her face was thin, and her body was thin. She was basically just thin all over. Millie wasn't the type to open up about deep stuff, so I don't know if she was struggling with drugs or if she was anorexic—like some people around town have said. I figured she'd lost so much weight because of stress." Without warning, Penny started to cry. I was caught off guard by the sudden outburst of emotion. "I just don't know what happened to her!" She sniffled. "I had to quit my job because I just...I couldn't do it. Her name was on everything and it ate me up."

Camry gave her an owl Kleenex and Penny blew her nose.

"I'm so sorry," I said.

"It's horrible! And because of..." Penny stared down at the recorder and snapped her mouth shut.

I sensed her reservation and added, "I can change your name if it makes you feel more comfortable." Not that it wouldn't take three seconds for listeners to figure out her true identity.

Assuming we had listeners.

"Cornelia," said Penny.

"I'm sorry?"

"You can change my name to Cornelia. It's my favorite girl's name."

"Okay, Cornelia, go ahead," I said.

Penny/Cornelia sighed. "I know who posted the video," she said so low I wasn't sure I heard her right.

"You're HJZoomer22?" Camry blurted out.

"No! Of course not!" Penny ripped the tissue into confetti. "Blake Kirkland, he worked for Direct Dental doing marketing, he's the one who posted it. I told him not to, but he did it anyway."

I worked hard to keep my voice and face neutral. "Why do you think he posted it?"

"I've asked myself this a million times. I just don't know. He was recording the Gala and captured everything on video."

"Did Blake know her?"

"I don't think so."

"Did you tell this to the police?" I asked

Penny gave a feeble nod of her head. "A detective came to Direct Dental and interviewed a few of us right after they found her car."

"Was it Detective Ramsey?"

"That sounds familiar." Penny sniffled. "Another detective named La-something called me a few days ago. I'm supposed to go down and give another statement tomorrow."

This gave me pause. I wondered what else Penny knows that would interest the detective.

"Did Detective LeClare say why she wanted to speak to you?" I asked.

Penny used what was left of the tissue to wipe her nose. "She didn't say. I'm guessing it's because I worked with Millie. Not sure what else I can offer. Last time I saw Millie was the day she left Direct Dental. HR called her in and, like, ten minutes later she was escorted out."

"What about Blake Kirkland?" I asked. "Have you spoken to him recently? Did he give a statement?"

"He took off after Millie disappeared." Penny wiped her cheeks using the backside of her hand. "I heard he went to Oregon and OD'd on pain meds. The guilt killed him."

"Guilt from posting the video?" I asked.

"Yes. He took the video, then Millie disappeared. He thought it was his fault. Ate him up."

What a sad way to go. That is, assuming what Penny said was true. She could have made this all up just to give us a sales pitch.

But my gut told me there was truth to what she said.

Maybe not truth to all of it.

But truth to some of it.

Which gave me an idea.

"Does Waller Park mean anything to you?" I asked, watching her reaction carefully.

Penny gave a slight shrug of her shoulders. "Sure. I take my kids there to feed the ducks all the time."

She wasn't rattled by my question.

Or she was an excellent actress.

Either way, I had nothing and it was time to move on.

"Do you remember who else the detectives interviewed at Direct Dental?" I asked.

Her tears dried and only smudged mascara remained. "I know they interviewed me. They interviewed our boss, Kelly Barnard. And, obviously, they interviewed Jeremy." *Annndd,* cue the tears. "He was away when she went missing and had no idea what was happening until he got back and there was a detective waiting for him at his desk. People totally thought he must have known. He broke down right there in front of everyone. It was awful. So awful."

"Who is Jeremy?"

Penny chuckled through her tears, as if I just told a joke.

"No, really, who is Jeremy?" Now I was dying to know.

Penny looked from Camry to me, and back again. "You don't know who Jeremy Wang is?"

"No, I don't."

Penny shifted around in her seat to square me. "You seriously don't know who Jeremy Wang is?"

"Tell us already!" Camry was sitting on the edge of the seat.

I cut my eyes to give her a warning, but she wouldn't look at me.

"I'm sorry about that," I said to Penny. "We only started the investigation, and I haven't heard about Jeremy Wang yet. Any information would be helpful."

Penny gave us a skeptical look. "Jeremy is Millie's ex-boyfriend. He worked in accounting at Direct Dental."

It took a minute for my brain to compute this.

...

Still computing.

...

Computed: Holy hell!

"Do you know why they broke up?" I asked in a rush.

Penny nodded her head, playing with the tattered tissue in her hands. "I was the only person in the office who knew they were together. Direct Dental used to transfer people who were dating. But Jeremy said he was ready to take their relationship to the next level and Millie wasn't. So he dumped her. She didn't say anything, but you could tell she was totally heartbroken. That's why I thought she'd lost weight."

"When did this happen?" Camry asked. She was practically sitting on the center console.

"About two months before Millie went missing."

Camry and I shared a look. She was already on her phone, searching for a Jeremy Wang.

I twisted around to square Penny and crisscrossed my legs. "Okay, I need you to start from the very beginning and tell me absolutely everything you can remember about Amelia and Jeremy Wang's relationship."

EPISODE EIGHT

The Boyfriend

"It's like the podcast gods are shining down on us today," Camry said from the passenger seat. "The true identity of HJZoomer22 *and* a mysterious boyfriend." She drummed the dashboard. "What a huge break!"

Yes and no. Before I could give thanks to the podcast gods, there was still a little thing called *facts*. I had to confirm Blake Kirkland was a real person and that he did post the video of Amelia. I also had to figure out why no one had mentioned Jeremy Wang before today.

Not Leon. Not Richard. Not Carlos. Not any news media outlet. Not anyone. There had never been one mention of Jeremy Wang, an ex-boyfriend, or any former romantic flings.

Jeremy was either an elaborate lie created by Penny so she could sell us a colon cleanse, or he was taken off the suspect list early on and of little consequence to the case. But if Penny was right, and Jeremy broke off the relationship because of Amelia's inability to commit, then that made him a suspect in my book. They broke up. Amelia got her own apartment. She got close with her new neighbor, Carlos. Carlos visited her at work. Jeremy become jealous and...

It was certainly worth looking into.

I turned right on Clark Ave. and got stuck behind a produce truck going twenty in a forty-five zone. It was nearly dusk and I had hours of material to edit. "When we get back to Hazel's, I'll get started on episode two. You try to find more information on the body found at the park and Jeremy—ouch!"

Camry smacked me on the back of the head and frantically pointed out the window. "*Pullover, pullover, pullover, pullover.*"

I did as instructed, afraid she was about to vomit, and pulled into the parking lot of a strip mall that looked more like the set of an old western movie. "What's wrong?" I asked.

Camry grabbed my head and directed my attention up. On the second floor, in bold hard-to-miss print was a sign: *Jeremy Wang, CPA.*

"Well I'll be damned," I said. "Do you think it's the same Jeremy Wang?"

Camry already had her phone out. "Yes!" She turned the screen to show me a picture from Yelp. It was a thirty-something-year-old man with a crooked smile, pearly teeth, dark hair in a side part, hazel eyes and, when I zoomed in, there was a faint scar in the middle of his left eyebrow.

"He's the right the age."

"Says here that he has an office in Santa Maria," Camry read. "But he primarily works out of his office in Las Vegas."

"Does it say when he's in town?"

"According to his website, he'll be in tomorrow" she said, a self-satisfied smile spread across her face. "Told ya the podcast gods are happy with us."

Perhaps they were.

We raced home and spent the rest of the night researching Jeremy. I looked through Leon's notebooks. Camry scoured the Internet. By the time the sun rose, we were practically experts on all things Jeremy Wang.

"Let's compile everything that we know into one list so I can write a better narrative on Jeremy." I sat up in my bed and opened my laptop. I was wearing yesterday's clothes, only because I never slept. Between Jeremy and the body at Waller Park (which had produced no new information) my mind had not shut down.

Camry's on the other hand...well, her brain shut down shortly after three a.m.

"Come on." I clapped my hands. "Time to wake up."

"No," she moaned from under the covers. "I'm still sleeping."

"Too bad." I tossed a pillow at her.

She threw the covers off of her head, sending the dirty clothes that were piled on her bed to the floor. "I hate you."

"No you don't. Now, get up. Let's do this."

"*Fine*," she grunted and rolled up right, her eyes still closed.

"I'll start." I grabbed my notebook. "We know Jeremy is a certified public accountant and manages wealthy people's money in both California and Nevada."

Camry patted around her bed until she found her iPad hidden beneath a blanket. "We also know he worked for Direct Dental until 2009."

"He grew up in Santa Barbara, attended UCSB, and was once quoted in the university paper saying...shoot. I forget. What did he say?"

Camry picked the goop out of her eyes and consulted her iPad "He said, 'It's a nice change,' when asked about a summer rainstorm in 2002."

Not exactly a smoking gun, but we knew Jeremy didn't mind the rain. Which felt more relevant at two a.m.

"Jeremy opened his Las Vegas office nine years ago," Camry read from her own notes. "He comes to the Santa Maria office twice a month. Which I find weird. Why does he have two locations so far apart?"

"He still has family here," I said.

"I guess that makes sense," she said, not sounding totally convinced. "Jeremy has not had a single speeding or parking ticket in the last seven years, nor has he ever been arrested or sued."

"How do you know that?"

"It's a matter of public record. Also, he has a 780 credit score."

"Do I want to know how you found that out?"

"Nope."

"You're killing me." But I added this information to my list anyway and glanced at my notes. "Jeremy married Doris Fundoogle one month ago in Vegas."

"And we assume she willingly took his last name," Camry added.

"It doesn't look like Jeremy has kids. He has a private Instagram account, and a Facebook page for his business that he updates regularly with *Wall Street Journal* articles."

Camry swept her hair up into a bun and used a pencil to keep it in place. "According to the waitress I talked to when I called the Wang's family restaurant, Jeremy drives a brand-new black Audi SUV, and helps with the bookkeeping. The waitress, who is also Jeremy's cousin, had no knowledge of Jeremy and Amelia's relationship. However, she was eight when Amelia went missing— so there's that."

"That seems odd to me. Think about it, if my ex-boyfriend went missing shortly after we broke up, I'm sure my family would talk about it for years to come. That's a big thing. You'd think she would have at least *heard* of Amelia before, or heard the story of her cousin's girlfriend who disappeared. Unless it's a family secret."

"You're wrong. If you had an ex-boyfriend who went missing, we'd mostly be talking about the fact that you actually had a boyfriend."

I threw another pillow at her and she bat it away with her iPad.

"Stop screwing around, Liv," she huffed out in a nasally voice. "Don't you know how serious this is? Don't you know that we're not *allowed* to have fun? My entire future is riding on this podcast! Do you want this to end in my professional and financial ruin?"

"You do a terrible Liv impression."

"I'm working on it." She crossed her legs. "Okay, what more information do we have?"

"I went through Leon's notebook. He wrote that Jeremy was in Austin for work from October 8 until October 11. Then, according to the notes, Jeremy went straight from Austin to Phoenix and was there until October 20." Leon also wrote a few other things about Jeremy that we couldn't decipher because hiring a graphologist to interpret his handwriting was not in my budget. As it turned out, the notebooks were mostly Leon's ramblings, pages and pages of him attempting to work through the case on paper and getting nowhere. The more frustrated he became, the sloppier his writing got.

"He also wrote that Jeremy 'sobbed uncontrollably' throughout the entire first interview and called Amelia 'the love of his life' multiple times," I added. Which I found odd. If Amelia was the great love of his life, then why wasn't he listed amongst those who searched for her at Orcutt Hollow? You'd think he'd be the first person to volunteer to find her.

"According to Yelp, *Jeremy Wang, CPA*'s hours of operation today are from nine to five and he has 4.7 out of 5 stars," Camry read from her iPad. "And Yelpers call him Tax Man."

Which brought our cast of characters to: Mr. CinnaMann (Richard), Mrs. CinnaMann (Janet), Aluminum Woman (Amelia), Tax Man (Jeremy), Pineapple Man (Carlos), and The Colon Cleanser (the nickname Camry gave to Penny). This was beginning to sound like a bad murder-mystery party.

Next, I typed up a list of questions for Jeremy (I had many). His office opened at nine a.m., and I wanted to be prepared. The professional approach would have been to email him and set up a convenient time to talk. This was a podcast. It didn't matter where the other person was located, so long as they had access to Skype. But with him being in town only twice a month, I decided to use the barge-in-and-hope-for-the-best approach, not wanting to miss the opportunity to see this mysterious boyfriend in person.

We pulled into the parking lot of *Jeremy Wang, CPA* at exactly eight forty-five a.m. and waited.

Or stalked.

Whatever you want to call it.

Camry rummaged through her bag and produced one of Leon's notebooks. "He mentions Blake Kirkland on December 17, 2008, but all it says is 'find Blake Kirkland' and nothing else."

"I didn't see Blake's name in any of the books I looked through," I said.

"I sent messages to more Direct Dental employees on LinkedIn," said Camry. "Using your account."

"Naturally."

"No replies."

"Naturally."

I wrapped my hands around a mug of hot chocolate. Hazel's special recipe, which consisted of half-and-half, vanilla syrup, five scoops of chocolate mix, and love. My cholesterol may never recover from this trip.

Camry flipped to a new page. "Leon wrote the number for Portland PD in the margins."

I polished off the last of my drink. "Does it say who he spoke to?"

"No, and the rest of his notes are snippets from conversations he had with Richard." Camry took a bite of a blueberry muffin. Crumbs trickled down her sweater and onto the seat. "I don't think they got along."

"I guessed that. Does it say why?" I used my hand to sweep her crumbs into my empty mug.

"Let's see...on January 18, 2009, Richard called Leon a...I can't make out this word."

I looked to where she was pointing. "Douche?"

"Or dummy?"

"Probably douche."

"Probably. Oh look, Richard called the next day to smooth things over."

"That's nice."

"Sure, but—It's nine o'clock!" Camry shoved the notebook into her bag, licked her fingertips clean, and sat up straight. We stared up at the office. The blinds were still drawn, and the *Closed* sign wasn't flipped. No Jeremy Wang.

9:10: Blinds still closed.

9:20: We fought over who had to check if the door was locked.

9:21: Camry confirmed that was locked.

9:33: No sign of life.

9:45: I called his office phone, and it went straight to voicemail.

10:15: Camry took a power nap.

10:45: My eyelids drooped.

11:00: We polished off a bottle of Tums.

11:15: I tried to peek in through the window with no luck.

11:20: I blasted the A/C and Central Coast Country.

11:25: Camry switched it to a rap station.

11:26: We decided on no music.

12:52: Camry smacked me on the shoulder and pointed out the window. A black Audi without license plates pulled into a parking space.

Camry and I ducked down and waited until we heard the car door close before we risked looking up. It was Jeremy Wang all right. He had on dark slacks and a blue dress shirt with the top two buttons undone. With a cell phone pressed to his ear, he rushed up the stairs, locking his car over his shoulder using the fob.

I clipped on a microphone, grabbed my recorder, another lavaliere mic, and checked to be sure everything was on. "Let's do this," I said to Camry.

Bells tied to the door handle announced our arrival. The lobby was long and narrow with large bay windows and green drapery. Framed pictures were leaned up against an empty receptionist desk and the couch was wrapped in plastic. There were two doors to our right. One labeled "bathroom" the other not labeled but open. Inside, Jeremy was reclined in an office chair with his feet propped up on the windowsill, and back to us, still on the phone. He must not have heard the bells.

"Not yet," he said. "Trust me...it could be a good thing...right, let me check." Jeremy spun around in his chair and jumped back, dropping his phone on the floor.

"Hi," I said with a wave of my hand. "I'm sorry to interrupt you."

"No, no, it's fine." Jeremy clutched the edge of the desk and blew out a breath. "I didn't hear you come in. Hold on one second." He bent down and grabbed his phone. "Dori, let me call you back...Okay...I love you. Bye." He slid the cell into his shirt pocket and walked around the desk to unwrap the armchairs. "Sorry about the mess. I'm redecorating. Take a seat."

Camry and I sat down slowly. I, at the very least, thought he'd ask who we were before offering us a seat. "Did you know we were coming?" I asked.

"No, but I welcome walk-ins." He sat behind the desk and wheeled his chair closer. "How can I help you?"

"My name is Liv Olsen, and this is Camry Lewis. We're podcasters working on a series about the disappearance of Amelia Clark."

"On Millie?" Jeremy grabbed a pen and leaned back. "What kind of podcast?"

"It's a true crime investigation. We'd love to talk to you if you have time."

He clicked his pen. "Is this like a school project?"

"No, it's more like a job project."

"Like your full-time job?" he asked, sounding skeptical.

"Yes. Do you have time to talk?"

Lucky for us, he did.

Jeremy agreed to an interview and Camry clipped a lavaliere microphone to his shirt and stripped him of the pen he was obsessively clicking.

I was not expecting Jeremy to be so compliant. Nor was I expecting him to be so welcoming. He appeared to be a nice guy.

But looks could be deceiving.

Camry gave me the list of questions I'd typed out. All fifty-seven of them. I started with number one. "Can you tell us your name, who you are, and how you knew Amelia?"

"My name is Jeremy Wang. I'm a certified public accountant, and I dated Millie from July of 2007 until August of 2008." He then launched into the story of how he and Amelia met without me having to ask—almost like he'd been provided a list of questions prior to our interview. Or perhaps it was the natural progression of the conversation and I was reading too much into it.

Jeremy rocked in his chair, looking off into the distance while he spoke. The accounting job at the Santa Maria Direct Dental office was his first paying job after graduation. It was a small branch. Only fifteen employees. And he had met Amelia on his first day when he passed her cubical on the way to the bathroom.

"She was chewing the end of a pen, working on an Excel spreadsheet for her boss," he said. "She had on a black dress and her hair was twisted into a bun using one of those claw type clips." The memory brought a smile to his face.

Jeremy thought Amelia was cute but shy. After a month of employment, and two hundred trips to the bathroom, the two finally had a conversation beyond the casual "hey, how's it going."

"We talked about *Grey's Anatomy*," he said. "I told her that I'd never seen the show before, and she got really animated and told me the entire plot about McSteamy and McDreamy and all the other characters. When she's passionate about something, she talks with her hands and stumbles over her words." He laughed and swiped a pen from his desk, studying the Ballpoint logo before continuing. "It was cute," he said, pain flickered across his face.

It was on a Thursday, recalled Jeremy, that he finally asked her out. The company had an anti-fraternization policy, which he didn't think was going to be a problem. "It was one date, and it wasn't like I planned on getting serious with anyone. I was only twenty-three years old."

Jeremy was still living an hour away in Santa Barbara, and they met for tacos at a restaurant there. Later that night, while walking on the beach, the two shared their first kiss and, "I knew then I was in trouble."

"How so?" I asked.

"Amelia was not..." he paused to search for the right words. "She was closed off. And she didn't like crowds. We rarely left my apartment the entire time we were dating. If you can call nights spent at home eating pizza and having sex dating."

For the record, I do.

"Why do you think she was closed off?" I asked.

Jeremy bit at his bottom lip and shrugged but offered no answer.

"Why did you break up?" I asked, not wanting to rely solely on Penny's side of things.

Jeremy pulled his mouth to a line and clicked the pen against his temple, as if deciding how to answer. "I was ready to tell Direct Dental about our relationship and she wasn't."

"What would have happened if they found out?" I asked.

"They'd transfer me to a different branch."

"Which branch?"

"Santa Barbara."

I shook my head, trying to understand. "But you lived in Santa Barbara. Wouldn't it have been convenient for both of you, since she spent so much time there anyway?"

"Yes."

Huh. Odd. "How'd she take the break up?" I asked.

Jeremy refused to meet my gaze. "It was heart wrenching for both of us. But what was I supposed to do? I couldn't be cooped up in my apartment with her forever."

"I have a question," Camry chimed in. I'd almost forgotten she was here. "Did she not want to tell Direct Dental so you could stay with her in the office?"

"We didn't spend much time together at work," he said.

Camry leaned forward. I unclipped my mic and held it up to her mouth. "But if she was shy and closed up, like you said, maybe having you close was comforting to her? Just a thought."

Jeremy shook his head. "She wasn't the type to allow someone to protect her. She's more the type to throw herself in front of a moving train to protect someone else. And she's a runner. She'd run from problems."

I clipped the mic back on my shirt. "What did she need protecting from?"

"Isn't that why you're here?" he asked, his eyes meeting mine.

Goosebumps erupted down my arms.

"It's been over ten years," Jeremy said. "Someone has to figure out what happened."

"Did you take her?" *Might as well ask since I'm here.*

"No! But think about it. They found two spots of blood in the car, but they recovered no other DNA." He slammed his fist to his chest. "*I* had been in that car recently. Her *parents* had been in her car recently. There's no way they thoroughly searched that thing and came up with zero DNA. They found the blood, tested it, and that's it."

He raised an interesting point, *but* I said, "Detective Ramsey told me they swabbed the whole car."

"Then why didn't they find my DNA in there?"

"The car could have been cleaned before it was dumped," I suggested. "But the person who dumped it missed the blood stains because they were too small. Also, why were you in her car if you two had broken up?"

Jeremy clicked the pen again. The *click-clack* would be hell to edit, but it appeared to be a nervous habit of his. Which begged the question: What was there to be nervous about?

"A little over a week before Millie disappeared, she drove me home from work when my car wouldn't start," Jeremy said.

Without warning, Camry ripped the mic from my shirt, dragging me with it. I grabbed hold of the back of her chair to keep from falling over. "Why would she drive you all the way to Santa Barbara if you two were broken up?" Camry asked.

"To be nice," he answered.

"Yeah, but she was heartbroken, and by your own account, she ran from her problems. Why would she want to put herself in a situation with you if you broke her heart and she was still recovering?"

I yanked the mic from Camry's tight grasp and clipped it to my shirt. "I'm sorry about that."

"Don't be sorry. It's a good question," Jeremy said. "It had been almost two months since we broke up, it wasn't like it was a fresh wound."

"It takes longer than two months to get over a heartbreak like that," Camry said.

"We were on friendly terms." Jeremy shifted in his seat, clearly uncomfortable.

"Ex-lovers can't be friends," Camry retorted.

Camry spoke from experience. Her last boyfriend, Phil, dumped her with no warning on their one-year anniversary. It took six months before she could talk about him without bursting into tears—and she still can't look at pictures of when they were together. She was heartbroken. I could tell that listening to Jeremy's description of his and Amelia's relationship was bringing those emotions back to the surface for her. Problem was, Jeremy wasn't Phil and Camry wasn't Amelia. She was making this personal, and while I did feel bad for Camry, I was sending her mental messages to shut her mouth.

We had to remain impartial and allow our guests to tell their story without our interference. Camry was treating this like an interrogation.

"Ex-lovers *can* be friends," Jeremy said.

"Not that soon afterward," Camry said. "An hour alone in the car would have been hard for both of you."

Jeremy studied Camry while I nudged her with my foot. She pretended not to notice and stared straight ahead. We sat in silence for several awkward seconds that felt more like hours. I was about to apologize once again, but Jeremy broke the silence first.

"She wanted to talk about getting back together." He paused to clear his throat. "She missed me, and I missed her and..."

I waited for the rest of the story, but it didn't come. "And what?" I asked cautiously.

Camry gasped. "You hooked up! The two of you hooked up right before she disappeared, but then you didn't take her back."

I looked to Jeremy for confirmation, but he didn't answer.

Which answered the question.

"Loving Amelia Clark was hard. As much as I wanted to, I couldn't go down that path again. Nothing had changed, and I didn't want to get hurt more than I already was. She was the great love of my life and—" He snapped his mouth shut. "Can you not use that last statement?"

"Why not?" I asked.

"Because he has a wife now," Camry said. "She probably wouldn't like that."

Oh.

Right.

The wife.

She probably wouldn't.

Jeremy dropped his pen. "How'd you know I was married?"

"It's a matter of public record," Camry said.

"Oh," is all Jeremy could say.

"We've been doing research on everyone involved," I said.

Jeremy nodded his head slowly. "That's a good idea."

"Does your wife know about Amelia?" I asked.

"Yes, she does," he said.

I consulted my list. "Why do you have an office in Vegas and in Santa Maria?"

"To help keep an eye on family," he said.

"I thought your family lived in Santa Barbara?"

"I have family all over the Central Coast."

Fair enough. Moving on. "Was the night you two hooked up the last time you saw Amelia?"

"I saw her the day after the gala incident. She was crawling through the lobby, trying to sneak past the receptionist."

"Wasn't Penny the receptionist?"

"Yes, she was also the office gossip. Millie was avoiding her. She didn't want to talk about the gala."

"Did *you* talk to her about the gala?"

"I tried to, but she ran off. I left about an hour later to fly to Austin for business."

"And you were in Austin for a week, then flew straight to Phoenix, right?" I asked.

"No. I was in Austin from the fourth until the eleventh. Then I came back for two days and flew to Phoenix to visit friends."

Wait a second. "You were here in Santa Maria for two days?"

"Yes."

"Detective Ramsey said you flew from Austin to Phoenix."

"That's because he didn't listen." Jeremy rolled his chair closer and slammed his pointer finger on the desk. "I told him exactly where I was, who I was with, and when I was there. I even provided phone numbers and flight information for him to check, but he never did. Never."

"How do you know he didn't?" I asked.

"I *know* he didn't."

Just like Carlos, I had no idea what to make of Jeremy Wang's demeanor. I sensed his frustration. I sensed the pure affection he had for Amelia. I sensed the reservation in his words, and I had the strangest feeling that he was hiding something from us.

But what?

I checked my questions. "Do you know Carlos Hermosa?"

"No."

"Detective Ramsey didn't ask you about him?"

"No."

"The name doesn't sound familiar at all?"

"No."

"Amelia never mentioned him?"

"She lived with her parents during the time we were dating."

I referred back to my questions. "Have you ever been to Waller Park?"

Jeremy scrunched his brows together. "I don't think so. Millie would go running there sometimes."

My stomach did a summersault, and Camry and I shared a look.

"W-why do you care about Waller Park?" Jeremy asked.

I cleared my throat. "A decomposed body was found there yesterday by a city worker. We haven't been able to come up with more information."

Jeremy leaned back. "I think I heard about that. They haven't identified the body yet, though."

"Do you think it could be Amelia?" I asked cautiously.

"I don't know." He didn't appear bothered by the possibility that Amelia's body had been found, which gave me two thoughts.

One: it had been so long that he had already come to terms with the fact that Amelia was dead.

Two: he wasn't worried that the body was Amelia because he knew where she was. And she wasn't at Waller Park.

I blew out a breath and checked my list of questions. "What did you make of the YouTube video?"

Jeremy frowned. "The entire video looked like an accident blown out of proportion."

"Did she ever drink or experiment with narcotics?" I asked.

"No," he said without pause. "She didn't like the way alcohol made her feel, and to my knowledge she never touched a drug."

There went Camry's theory.

"What about her weight loss? Everyone we've talked to has made a comment about how thin she was."

"I think the stress of our break-up, coupled with training for a marathon, caused her to lose weight."

"Did you know a guy by the name of Blake Kirkland?" I asked.

Jeremy's cheeks went red. "I know of him. He took off before I could meet him in person. Coward. He sent me a letter apologizing for sharing the video, talking about how guilty he felt. But he obviously didn't feel that bad if he didn't take it down. I hate that video. That's not Millie, and it kills me that's how everyone will remember her."

"Can you tell us who the real Millie was?" I asked. Through all my research I still didn't know who Amelia Clark was. I had glimpses of an athletic, pretty girl who had a bad night, but no idea *who* she really was.

"Millie Clark had a self-deprecating sense of humor. She took pride in her work, was artistic, a terrible cook but a good baker, and she snored." His mouth curved into a smile. "She claimed she didn't, but I can assure you she did, especially when she was really tired. She was a vegetarian, and she was scared of chickens, wouldn't go near them, or talk about them. She was a human calculator, could do math in her head even better than I can. Was particularly good with statistics. She had the best laugh—it was this loud, boisterous, contagious giggle. I couldn't get enough. She had a tender heart. She put other people's needs before her own." Tears welled up in his eyes. "She liked her TV shows. She'd talked about the characters like they were real. If a commercial came on and the announcer said, 'Are you unhappy with your long-distance plan?' she'd answer him. Always. She'd force me to sit and watch *Grey's Anatomy* with her. I hated it, but I watched it solely because she enjoyed it so much. I still watch it to this day for the same reason."

The lobby door jingled. Jeremy blinked the tears from his eyes, and Camry handed him an owl tissue. "I'm sorry," he said. "I got carried away and forgot a client is coming in."

I choked back my own emotions and reminded myself that no matter how touching of a soliloquy that was, Jeremy very well could be the reason Amelia was gone.

"I appreciate your help." I gave him a business card. "If you think of anything else please don't hesitate to call."

Jeremy walked us out. A young couple was waiting in the lobby.

"What's your goal for this podcast?" Jeremy asked us at the door. "Is it like *Cold in America* where you tell the story and hope the public takes it from there? Or are you actively looking for Amelia?"

Good question.

It would be unprofessional to suggest I was qualified or even capable of solving a missing-person case.

Even if that was my goal.

"I want to tell Amelia's story in hopes someone with information will come forward," I said. "If anything, we can show people that Amelia was more than Aluminum Woman."

Jeremy smiled. "I'd like that."

EPISODE NINE

Morning Knolls

I was aching to get home and listen to Jeremy's interview, but there was still work to be done. I decided to test my luck and try Janet (just in case the podcast gods were still on my side). The Clarks lived in an area of Santa Maria called Morning Knolls—a modest neighborhood with modest homes and modest street names.

Siri announced our arrival, and I had to double-check the address: 343 Humble Drive.

Yep, this is it.

For someone who wanted to "make it on her own," Amelia didn't stray far. I could see the top of her apartment building from the street.

Located at the end of a cul-de-sac, the Clark house was smaller than I pictured it would be. A single-story stucco home with blue fascia, brick columns, and a patch of bright green grass out front. To the right was a vacant house, and to the left was a vacant lot. Morning Knolls was established in the late eighties but there's a pattern. Occupied house, vacant lot, occupied house, vacant house, vacant house, occupied house.

"Why are there so many empty lots and houses around here?" I asked Camry.

"I don't know. Let's ask Google." She consulted her phone. "Google has no idea. Seems like a nice place to live. If suburban America is your thing."

Suburban America is a lot of people's thing.

"It doesn't look like Janet is home," said Camry.

No it didn't. The garage was closed. No car in the driveway. Blinds drawn. "We should at least knock," I said.

I hid the microphone inside my shirt. Through the side window, I could see the glow of the television. "Someone must be home," I said.

Camry knocked. "You nervous? 'Cause you look it? Are you nervous?"

"Stop asking me if I'm nervous, it makes me nervous." *Great, now I'm nervous.*

Which didn't matter since there was no answer.

So we knocked again.

And again.

And again.

"Someone is home. Richard is at the bakery, so it has to be Janet," I said.

"Maybe she's watching us," said Camry and shifted her eyes from side to side.

We searched the entryway for cameras and didn't find one.

I cupped my hands and peeked through the window. There was a dusty piano with a large photo of Millie as a child hung on the wall in the family room. The frame was gold and had cobwebs hanging off of it. Amelia looked to be around seven years old in the picture. Her smile was gap-toothed, her bangs teased, her hair braided into two pigtails, and there was a duck pond in the distance. I couldn't see the couch from the window, or the television, or any sign of life.

"Give me a business card," I said to Camry.

Camry pulled out a card and I scribed on the back. *Mrs. Clark, we'd love to speak with you. It does not have to be recorded. Thank you, Liv Olsen.*

I tucked the card under the welcome mat.

"You use the word 'love' a lot," Camry said as we walked down the driveway.

"No I don't."

"You say, 'I'd *love* to interview you,' or 'I'd *love* to meet with you.' I'd love...love...love."

Okay. Maybe I do.

I made a mental note to stop it.

We got in the car. "What now?" asked Camry.

"You can find more information on Blake Kirkland while I edit the second episode. Let's try calling the newspaper again to see if they'll give us anything on the body. I need to email contacts and listen to Jeremy's interview." I buckled in and started the engine. There were so many things to do, and such a short time to do them. A cloning machine would be helpful right about now.

"I say we go out!" Camry acted like this was the best idea she'd ever had.

"What? No."

"I would *love* if you went out with me."

"No."

"Come on we've never just hung."

"No."

"Please," she said, and clasped her hands together. "It will rejuvenate us. You think Santa Maria has a night life?"

"I think I have a ton of work to do, plus I'd lo...I *want* to do that interview with Hazel."

"We'll do it first thing in the morning while she's cooking breakfast. I promise not to go to bed until I find more information on Blake Kirkland. Come on. Let's see what Santa Maria has to offer. Get to know the locals."

"No."

"Please."

"No."

"Please."

"No."

"Please."

We did this for a while, until I gave in.

Mostly because Camry had been working hard, and I knew the

interview with Jeremy brought up a lot of suppressed emotions. I also knew she needed fun in order to stay motivated. "Fine. What did you have in mind?"

"Hold on, I'm asking the mom's group."

EPISODE TEN

"Lost" Footage

While no one was willing to speak to us about Amelia Clark, over one hundred moms weighed in on what Camry and I should do on a Friday night.

Movie at the Mall.

Santa Maria Racetrack.

Haggerman Field to watch a softball game.

Every third comment involved wine.

Neither Camry nor I liked wine.

Until we received a Facebook message from a local winery. They wanted to give us complimentary VIP treatment for the night. Cowboy-limo ride included.

Then we liked wine just fine.

VIP sounded fancy. I didn't pack fancy. What I had was a pair of dark jeans, a white lace tank top, a blue blazer and black Converse wedges. I let my hair fall below my shoulders in a pile of red curls and slipped my portable recorder into my pant pocket. Camry must have thought clubbing was on the agenda because she had on a short black romper, leaving nothing to the imagination, her makeup was worthy of its own YouTube tutorial, and her hair was pulled into a high bun.

We invited Hazel to join us. Even though she had already started on our six-course dinner, she happily abandoned her post and got ready. She reappeared looking quite fab in a pair of black gaucho pants, a scoop necked red top and sheer scarf.

Standing next to Camry and Hazel, I felt like the frump of the trio.

Turned out a cowboy limo was really a Suburban. Which was fine by me, the last time I rode in a limo was for my mother's funeral. There's nothing quite so somber as following a hearse. Watching your father and grown bother in tears, and...

Nope. No. No. No. There is no need to tromp down that memory lane.

Tonight, we would let our hair down, sip wine and...do whatever else it is you do at a wine tasting.

The Grotto De'Vino was located in Old Orcutt—about four miles from CinnaMann's Bakery. It had the same old western vibe as the rest of the town. The parking lot was packed and...*great*. Oliver was waiting out front.

"What's he doing here?"

"I invited him." Hazel applied a layer of red lipstick and smacked her lips. "Doesn't he look dashing with his new hair cut? It was my idea."

"Yeah, dashing all right," I muttered.

Actually, I was glad he was there. It had taken me two days, but I finally came up with a good retort to his "in over your head" comment.

And it was a good one.

Oliver was wearing a white collared shirt tucked into a pair of dark jeans, and he was chatting candidly with the guy working the valet booth. Hazel grabbed him by the arm to let him know we're here.

He turned and smiled. "You ladies look beautiful tonight."

"Thanks. Let's go in," I said. My retort was not suitable for Hazel's ears and would have to wait until we were alone.

Also, I had to look up the ASL signs for "moron."

Oliver held the door open for us and we stepped inside. A man in a suit appeared out of nowhere. "Good evening, Ms. Olsen and guests. Please, follow me."

He recognized me?

Wow.

I couldn't help but feel important.

We glided through the reception area into a softly lit room with candles in alcoves, wine barrels stacked against one wall, and linen-covered tables. There was a woman sitting atop a barstool in the corner with her guitar, crooning Adele hits. We were escorted to a u-shaped booth in the back. It was cozy. It was romantic. It was VIP.

We slid into the booth. Camry first. Hazel followed. I was next. Oliver last.

Is there a graceful way to enter a u-shaped booth?

"This place is so fancy," Hazel said in awe as she looked around. "I've lived here all my life and have never been wine tasting at...I forget, where are we?"

"The Grotto De'Vino," answered a woman in a shift dress and cowboy boots. "I'm Sandy the owner, and you must be Liv?" She reached a hand out to me. "I recognize you from your profile picture."

Right. Camry was using my Facebook account.

Which suddenly felt like a very bad idea.

"Hi Sandy." Camry waved. "I'm the one you spoke to online. I'm Liv's sister, Camry Lewis, and this is my Aunt Hazel and cousin Oliver."

"Awe, a family affair. I love it!" Sandy clasped her hands over her heart. "I'm thrilled you took me up on my invitation to come tonight. We're a family-owned business, been here over fifty years. And can I just say that I think this podcast you're doing is a wonderful idea. I grew up in the house behind Millie and would love to see her brought home safely."

Out of the corner of my eye I noticed Oliver was on his phone swiping through YouTube comments. I touched his shoulder so he knew what was going on.

He looked up at Sandy and smiled. "Hello."

"Hello," she said back.

"Do you still live in Morning Knolls?" I asked and signed. She was caught off guard by my use of ASL, but quickly put two and two together.

"No! My parents sold their house in 2010!"

"You really don't have to yell," said Oliver.

"So-rr-y!" Sandy made the sign for "thank you."

"We were at Morning Knolls this afternoon. Do you know why there are so many vacant lots and empty houses?" I asked as I signed.

"Yes! It's because of the con-tam-in-ated soil!" She made an "x" with her pointer fingers. "The oil company bought back a lot of the hou-ses! It was a big lawsuit!"

Oliver returned his attention to the phone in his hand.

"Hold on a second." I pulled the recorder from my back pocket. "I'd lo...*like* to hear more if you have a moment?"

She had a moment.

Twenty of them to be exact.

Camry, Hazel and Oliver sat by while Sandy explained (loudly and enunciating each syllable) the 2006 lawsuit against the oil company filed by her parents and seven other families who lived on the same street.

According to Sandy, none of the families were informed of possible ground contamination from past oil production in the area when they purchased their home. Of the eight families involved, there were three cases of leukemia, two hypothyroidism, one thyroid cancer, and one brain tumor. All diagnosed in their late teens/early twenties. All grew up in Morning Knolls, playing in the dirty soil, growing vegetable gardens and fruit trees, mud fights, running through the sprinklers—just being kids without any inclination that the sand filling their sandboxes was poisonous.

Sandy's brother was diagnosed with leukemia at twelve and again at twenty-three. He died in 2009. According to Sandy, the oil company eventually paid punitive damages, bought the homes, cleaned the bad soil, and managed to do so without going to court and with very little press.

"And you lived one street over from the Clarks?" I asked.

Sandy had since taken a seat. "Their backyard backed up to ours! They had several houses on their street with bad soil as well. That was a different lawsuit!"

"Do you know if the Clarks' was tested?"

"After the lawsuits, the oil company offered to test everyone. But I don't know if the Clarks ever did!"

"What year did the oil company start buying houses?"

"In 2010!" She held up ten fingers, even though Oliver had completely checked out of this conversation.

I made a mental note to ask Richard about the oil company and thanked Sandy for her time.

"My pleasure! Should we get started?" Sandy stood and placed a menu in front of each of us. Which was great, because I was starving. Except the only thing on there was wine. "I'll first need to see IDs." She specifically looked at me.

I gave my license to Oliver so he could give it to her. He read it before passing it on, which was quite rude. I had my *real* weight on there. "You're twenty-seven!" he said loud enough for the whole town to hear. "I thought you were nineteen until Hazel said we were going wine tasting then I figured you were twenty-one."

"Nope, I'm twenty-seven. Well acquainted with the 'real world.'" I hooked my fingers into quotes.

Oliver made a fist, placed it on his chest and rotated it clockwise. The sign for sorry. It felt more sincere in ASL. *"I thought you were two kids doing an amateur podcast because they're popular right now. I had no idea you were so old."*

"Thanks. I'm younger than you." I was guessing. He looked around early- to mid-thirties.

"You know what I mean."

Yes, I did.

"I'm a professional sound engineer. I know what I'm doing." Which was kind of true. *"I have a lot riding on this."* Which was

very true.

Oliver shifted around and put his arm on the back of the booth. I caught a whiff of his cologne. A citrus, leathery combination with a hint of ocean and, without warning, my stomach fluttered—traitor.

"I misjudged the situation and I'm sorry. Forgive me?" he said without signing.

"I suppose." Like I had a choice when he was batting those baby blues and flashing his dimpled right cheek at me.

Sandy passed our licenses back down the line.

"We'll bring your first tasting by shortly," she said. "If you have any questions please let me know, and feel free to record whatever you'd like in here! Thank you again for coming in," she said this directly to Camry.

Oliver tapped my shoulder. "*I couldn't read her lips. What did she say to Camry?*"

"*She said, 'Thank you for coming in.' Why?*"

"*She's hiding something.*"

"*Who? Sandy?*"

"*No Camry.*"

"*How do you know?*"

"*I can tell by her face.*"

Camry banged the table. "No secret language."

"It's not secret, it's ASL," Hazel said and signed. "You should learn."

"What are you hiding?" I said to Camry.

"*Pffft*, what? I'm not hiding anything, why would you say that?"

"Because I can tell," said Oliver. "Your nostrils flare when you're not being truthful."

She covered her nose. "So you lose your hearing and gain super powers like Daredevil?"

"Daredevil lost his sight not hearing," Hazel added.

Camry held up her palms. "Sorry, I am not proficient in DC comic books."

"Daredevil is Marvel, dear." Hazel tapped Camry's hand.

We all looked at Hazel.

"What?" She shrugged. "I like comic books. Who doesn't?"

"Really?" Camry dropped her chin into her palm. "Which superhero is your favorite? I personally enjoy Thor."

"No, no, no." I waved my hand. "Spill it."

"Fine," she said with an exaggerated sigh. "I may have given myself the title of producer of advertising and media relationships when I asked what we should do tonight. Hoping a local business would offer their services for free, which they did! *So we'll mention them on the podcast or put it on our website.*" She spit the last sentence out so fast I almost didn't hear her right.

Almost.

I nearly leapt over the table. "I am not going to promote any local business!"

"Calm down," she drew out the words and rolled her eyes. "This is a great way to supplement your income until you get an advertiser."

"I can't supplement my income with wine." I was furious.

"No!" Now Camry was furious. "But other businesses will hear about this and want to advertise. What's it going to hurt if you mention it on *your* podcast or put it on *your* website?"

"Because I have no clue who hurt Amelia! It could be the owner of this winery, or the owner of a local restaurant, or the person who runs the floral shop. The point is we have no idea. If I take money from a local business, and that person ends up being involved, I ruin the credibility of the podcast. I paid for a hosting site, and they find sponsors. Chances are we won't have a sponsor until a few episodes have been released. That's how it works!"

Camry opened her mouth, about to say what, I'll never know; Sandy cut her off when she returned with wine glasses. She placed a sheet in front of us. Everyone began to read but I was too mad to look.

"We're going to start with the white." She set the glasses down.

I downed the wine. Tasted like sour grape juice. *Next.*

"So, um, actually we're going to examine it first," said Sandy.

Oh. I thought the point of this was to taste the wine?

Whatever.

"I'll pour you another." Sandy snapped her fingers and the man to her side poured a small amount into my glass. I examined it through the glass. It was cream in color and smelled like grapes. *Next.*

My knowledge grew as the night went on. By the time we reached the reds, I was practically a sommelier-*er*.

"This smells like winter and puppies!" I held up my glass. "Cheers!"

Everyone tapped their glasses to mine. I sipped it oh-so-eloquently except I felt it dribble down my chin. "This glass has a hole in it."

"Why don't you have a cracker?" Oliver pushed the tray my way. "Like all of them."

"You're so kind." I took one and attempted a bite, but I missed my mouth. The darn table was wobbly. I tried again and made it that time. *Yayz me.* I felt quite pride of myself...*I mean... prouderered...prouderer...prided?*

"Oh you sweet thing, you must not drink often," Hazel said.

I stared at her fuzzy face and said, "Huh?"

She patted my hand. "Have another cracker."

"No thanks." I pushed the tray aside. "Those taste like salt-less saltinesess."

"I think they're supposed to cleanse the pallet," said Camry while inspecting the offending cracker.

"Here's the thing," I said, except I didn't know what the thing was. My head felt spiny-y. *Get a grip, Liv.*

I opened my eyes and mouth real wide.

This was me getting a grip.

"What is she doing?" I heard Hazel say.

"I think she's trying to sober up," said Oliver or Camry or maybe Sandy. Everyone sounded similar and happy.

Turned out if you really liked the wine, they'd pour you a

whole glass! I loved all the wine! I was happy, too. There was laughter. There was more sipping. There was more sniffing. There was more laughing. I had found my oomph and it was called Pinot de-blah-blah.

Something happened because we were suddenly outside. The cool air felt good against my skin. I swayed to the music, not that there was any music playing. It was the music in my heart. And I was fairly certain I was saying all this out loud.

"You are," said Camry. "You've been narrating us the whole time. World building."

"Have I really? I said. Camry stared at me with an incredulous look on her face. I think she's amused."

"I am."

The Suburban rolled up and we all piled in. I bonked my head on the door and rammed my knee into the center console. Oliver buckled my seatbelt for me. "You're such a nice person." I squished his cheeks together. "And cute, don't you think he's cute?" I asked the driver. "It's okay if I say so because we're not real cousins. We're fake cousins."

The driver didn't respond.

Well then.

We drove home. There was a bush. Some stairs. My pillow and...

EPISODE ELEVEN

Guest Parking

It felt like an elephant was sitting on my face.

"You, my dear sister, cannot hold your liquor." Camry placed two aspirin and a cup of water on my nightstand. "You were about ten sheets to the wind before we finished the white wines."

"Don't mention wine." I tossed the aspirin into my mouth and chugged the water. "Yuck. Is this supposed to make me feel better?"

"Yes. Don't you *ever* drink?"

I pulled the pillow over my head and fell back on the bed. "I got drunk on my twenty-first birthday and swore I'd never do it again." Now I could remember why. "What time is it?"

"It's almost noon."

"What!" I attempted to jolt out of bed but lacked the luster to do so. I *rolled* to a forty-five-degree angle and cradled my head. "Why didn't you wake me?"

"I tried three times." Camry pulled my hair back into a makeshift ponytail at the nape of my neck. This sparked a memory. She did this last night while I puked in the bushes.

"*Ugh.* I remember talking to Sandy, the first wine and...not much else," I groaned.

"Don't worry. You recorded everything."

Why, oh, *why* did I agree to go wine tasting? I didn't like wine. I didn't like drinking. I didn't like feeling like a fifteen-ton elephant was sitting on my head. I liked to read, and work, and listen to podcasts, and...and...gah!

Oh no!

I was struck with a horrifying thought. "What if someone took a video of me drunk and posts it to YouTube?"

"Don't worry. Oliver insisted we take you home when you became too loose."

I was scared to ask. "What was I doing?"

"Making out with him."

This was getting worse by the minute. "Ahhh! Where are my clothes?" I was in a bra and underwear. And not even my own underwear! These were red and said, "Kiss the Bride" on the front. And...*what the heck?* "Are these made of licorice?"

"Yep."

"Tell me I didn't get married."

"Oh please, you think I'd let that happen? There was a bachelorette party at the next table, and you were chatting it up with the bride-to-be. One thing led to another and you ended up with this underwear. You might also be a bridesmaid."

I didn't want to know what *one-thing-led-another* meant. What I want to know was, "Why am I naked?"

"Random fact about drunk Liv: she likes to strip."

Oh no.

"But don't worry, you didn't strip until we got in the house."

I covered my face with both hands. "Please, please, please tell me it was just you and me in here."

"Sure, we'll go with that." Camry dropped my hair and sat crisscross on her own bed. "Liv, you are a super fun drinking buddy. We should do it again."

"Never." I stood and spun in a small circle, looking for pants and found them under the bed with my underwear still inside of them. "We have so much to do." I wiggled into my clothes. "We need to try Janet again. Go to Amelia's old high school. Record Hazel. Find a park ranger."

"And meet Detective LeClare," Camry said.

"Huh?"

"She called while you were passed out. We're meeting her at three."

Detective LeClare called *me*. This was good. This was really good! "I'm so glad you answered my phone."

Camry twisted her hair up into a knot on the top of her head. "See, I can handle things when you're incapacitated like the good peon I am." Her right nostril flared with each word and a memory from last night crept into my sloshy brain.

Crap. Flaring nostrils meant she was lying.

"Camry, what did you do?"

"Nothing."

"Tell me."

"Don't be mad," Camry blurted out in a panic.

"Is this about the sponsorship?"

"Errr...no. You don't have to worry about the advertising agreement we made. Oliver told Sandy that it's against company policy to accept freebies from locals and went ahead and paid the tab. And it was a big tab. You drank a lot. That's when you made out with him."

This sparked another memory. A horrible one. I'd thrown myself on Oliver while he worked hard to get me off, insisting we shouldn't do this while his grandma was watching. That's when I asked for the edible underwear.

Oh hell.

This is the penance I pay for drinking on the job. That, and this monstrous headache. It felt like little construction workers were behind my eyeballs jackhammering my retinas.

I need to sit down.

So I did.

I took a seat on the floor and put my elbows on knees, and my head in hands.

Camry sat beside me. "I have something to tell you."

"It's going to make me mad, isn't it?" I muttered.

"Yes, but wait until I'm done before you blow up."

"No promises." Lucky for her, I didn't have the energy

required to blow up.

Camry rummaged around in Leon's box then placed the picture of Amelia's car on the ground between my legs for me to see. "There's a small green note on the dashboard. Do you see it?"

I squinted. "No."

"How about now?" She placed a magnify glass over the picture and I could see a citation from Santa Maria Way Apartments: *Guest parking is reserved for visitors only. Please park your vehicle in your assigned space or risk being towed.*

"Remember how close her parking spot was to her apartment?" asked Camry.

I let go of my head and grabbed the picture to get a better look. I went crossed-eyed until I could see the date. "This says October 10."

"Mmhmm. While you were passed out, I drove to Santa Maria Way Apartments and took a picture of where the guest parking is located. Liv, it's on the *other* side of the building. Amelia's spot was right next to her apartment. There's no reason she would park her car there unless her spot was filled. Right?"

"Where are you going with this?" My brain was still drunk.

"I spoke to the manager and he said tenants will park their cars in the guest spots early, and leave their assigned spots open for a guest to come later." Camry rose up to her knee, like she was about to propose to me. "Which means Amelia probably had a guest on October 10. And according to the manager, the spaces fill up quickly at night. So whoever visited her, probably did it *that* night!"

"Did you happen to bring my recorder with you?"

"Obviously."

"Camry, this is great why would I be mad?"

"Errr...'cause it's not the only thing I did this morning." She twisted a dark strand of hair between her fingers, stalling.

"What did you do?" I asked.

"You were out a really long time."

"What did you *do*?"

"Funny thing, really." She grabbed her iPad and hugged it to her chest. "I accidentally hacked into HJZoomers22 YouTube account, found his email, and hacked into it, too."

"How do you accidentally hack into someone's account?"

"It wasn't as hard as I thought it would be. His password was the same for both YouTube and Gmail."

"That isn't what I asked."

"And his recovery question was easy too. *What was your high school mascot?* There are only so many high schools in the area. And, honestly, what does it matter? He's dead. It's not like he's going to care who's reading his emails."

"But—"

She held her finger up to my mouth to shush me. "Hear me out before you get mad."

"Too late."

"So maybe Blake Kirkland took this video, but he didn't post it on YouTube. The account was created *on* October 3. The email linked to the account is also HJZoomer22, and it hasn't been used since October 4, but I was still able to get in." She smiled, proud of herself. "There was a lot of spam and notifications from YouTube. Someone created this fake email and a fake YouTube account to post the video."

"How do you know for sure it's fake?"

"I'm glad you asked." Camry turned her iPad around. On the screen was a Gmail inbox. "I found this email. Read it."

It was a long exchange. I started at the bottom and read to the top.

From: BKirkland@DirectDental
To: Scottydog00
Subject: You know her?

What up? I'm doing the audio and video for the Gala tonight and one of the SM employees just tripped and sucker punched the CFO during Mike Cromer's opening speech! Caught the whole thing on video. Remind me to show next time I see you. You coming up for Farmer's Market next week?

R.B. Kirkland
Media Relations
Direct Dental, Inc.

From: Scottydog00
To: BKirkland@DirectDental
Subject: Re: You know her?

OMG! No way. The only employee there is Millie Clark. Send the video to me now! I have to see this.

From: BKirkland@DirectDental
To: Scottydog00
Subject: Re: Re: You know her? <<Attachment>>

Here it is. But don't show anyone.

From: Scottydog00
To: BKirkland@DirectDental

Of course I won't!

From: Scottydog00
To: HJZommer22
Subject Fw: You know her? <<Attachment>>

"Blake Kirkland took the video but had no intention of posting it," I said, re-reading the emails over again. "He sent it to Scottydog00, and he sent it to HJZommer22. If HJZommer22 isn't Blake Kirkland, then who is?"

"Scottydog is! That's the recovery email address used to create HJZoomer22. So Scottydog00 worked for Direct Dental, knew Millie, and knew Blake Kirkland. He created the fake account so he could post it to YouTube just to humiliate Amelia."

I re-read the email over again. If I remembered correctly, Jeremy said Blake Kirkland apologized for *sharing* the video, *not* for posting it. He had no intention of uploading it to YouTube, and yet he blamed himself for the aftermath.

"There's more," Camry said. She opened another email. My gosh, she's productive when I'm inebriated. "Also in the trash I found an email sent to every employee at the Direct Dental Santa Maria Branch, including Amelia, the CFO, *and* CEO with the YouTube link."

"That's terrible. Who would do such a thing?"

"Liv, this wasn't about someone who posted a video because they thought it would be funny. This was sabotage."

It sure was.

I knew the video had been uploaded to YouTube, I had no idea it had been sent out to everyone Amelia worked with.

"Can you hack this Scottydog00 email account to see who he is?" I asked. "Hypothetically speaking, of course."

Camry's shoulders fell. "The email address has been deleted, and resurrecting dead emails is beyond my superpower."

EPISODE TWELVE

She

Every little movement, every little sound, every hint of light hurt my cranium. Of all days for Detective LeClare to schedule a meeting, she had to pick today. I used my hand as a visor to protect my eyes from the assaulting fluorescent lights in the police station's lobby. A lady in a muumuu was at the counter speaking to a policewoman behind the Plexiglas, claiming her ex-boyfriend was stalking her, and her ex-boyfriend was at the other counter, claiming she beat him with a spatula. He brought the spatula as evidence.

"Should we tell Detective LeClare about the email and Scottydogoo?" asked Camry, who was sitting beside me in a black pencil skirt, white collared shirt buttoned to the top and black blazer. The same outfit she wore to court when she was charged with a Class B misdemeanor for email hacking. She was lucky to walk away with only a fine.

"What you did is unethical and illegal," I said under my breath. "We can't let *anyone* know about it. And we can't use the information you found unless someone else gives it to us." As much as I wanted to find out what happened to Amelia, I wasn't about to risk Camry going to jail.

"So that's a no?"

I cringed at the sound of her voice. Not because I found it annoying, but because it was so damn loud.

"Do you think Detective LeClare will let us look at the surveillance video from October 10?" asked Camry.

"I don't know," I muttered.

"What about notes from Leon's interview with Carlos?"

"I don't know."

"I bet she doesn't know about the guest parking citation. Do you think she does?"

"I don't know."

"She probably does. Leon probably saw it," she said, drumming her hands on her kneecaps. "He probably talked to her apartment manager and nothing came of it."

Probably.

"But we could use that, right? It's a good find?" She bounced her right leg. Which made the bench bounce. Which made me vomit.

Good news: there was a potted plant close by to barf in.

Bad news: it was fake.

That's unfortunate.

"Um...you okay, Liv?"

"I don't know." I smoothed out the front of my blouse and swiped a stray hair behind my ear. It took three layers of concealer to hide the hangover on my face and one glass of Alka-Seltzer to get me out the door.

The back pocket of my jeans vibrated. I knew without looking that it was Oliver texting, again. He wanted to talk. There was no time for talking. Not when I had a job to do, a sister to keep out of jail, and I was too embarrassed to face him.

"Are you Liv Olsen?" came a smooth voice, and I gazed up at the tall, *tall*, woman I assumed to be Detective LeClare or a supermodel in detective clothing. Either way, she looked like Tyra Banks and was *great* with child. I almost rammed my head into her protruding belly.

I stood up slowly and extended a professional hand, each movement felt like a great achievement. "Thank you for meeting with us," I said with a forced smile.

LeClare slipped her hand into mine and gave it a hard shake, jiggling my intestines. *Ugh.* "My pleas..." She dropped my hand. "Oh no, not again," she said, eyeing the fake plant.

Oops.

"Johnson," she called to the officer behind the counter. "We got a mess out here."

Johnson, a young cop with a buzz cut, peeked out into the lobby. "Got it, boss," he said and disappeared.

"Sorry about that." LeClare rubbed her belly when she talked. "Why someone throws up in the plant when there's trashcans all around the room is beyond me."

I wanted to say it's hard to concentrate when you're hungover, but I decided to keep that comment in my brain. I followed the detective to a small windowless interrogation room that smelled like coffee and felt like a sauna. The three of us took a seat at the table.

"Thank you for coming in," said LeClare. "I know you're busy."

"I was happy to get your call." I pulled at the collar of my shirt. It was *hot* in there. "Can I set up my audio equipment?" I held up my bag.

"I thought you might ask," she said. "I've talked this over at length with the DA's office, and I can't record an interview at this time, nor can I give any case specifics to you."

Well, crap.

"Why are we here then?"

As it turned out, we were brought in to talk about the apple incident. I told her about Leon, our conversation with Richard, the threat Carlos made, and the post on Facebook. Camry and I both told her our theories of why the apple was thrown: to scare us off, a prank, or a failed attempt to get our attention.

LeClare slunk back in the chair to get more comfortable. "Santa Maria has a small-town feel to it, but there's almost 110,000 people living here. This includes the unincorporated area of Orcutt where your aunt lives."

This I knew. What I didn't know is why she was telling me.

"With Facebook algorithms, a post will get lost if no one has commented on it. Especially in a sizeable group like the Moms of Central Coast," she added.

"Oh!" Camry said, having an epiphany. "That's why we haven't had any responses. Sorry, I don't come from the Facebook generation. No offense," she said to LeClare.

"None taken."

"Don't worry I'll bump our post." Camry smacked the side of my leg.

I was not worried about anything being bumped. What I was worried about is why Detective LeClare was saying this.

Was it her way of telling us, without telling us, that news of our podcast and whereabouts was not as widespread as we thought? That someone we had interacted with that day likely threw the apple?

Which would leave us with Leon, Richard or Carlos.

Leon was not an option. Richard appeared genuinely surprised when we told him, and he didn't strike me as the athletic type. Someone had to have thrown that apple hard enough to break the window.

Which left us with Carlos.

But I had a hard time believing Carlos would throw an apple. He struck me more like a brick, or a rock, or a machete type of guy.

"Do you think it was Carlos Hermosa?" I asked her.

She cocked an eyebrow. "We honestly don't have a suspect on this one."

"Did you run the prints on the apple?" asked Camry. "You can do that. They're doing it in England."

"Well, we aren't in England, are we?"

I nudged Camry with my knee to get her to shut up. We needed LeClare on our side.

"Have you been able to identify the body found at Waller Park?" I asked.

"Not yet."

"Can you tell me if it was male or female?"

LeClare took a moment to decide if she should answer.

"Off the record." I held up my palms. "I'm not recording, and I won't repeat. I just want to know."

"The Medical Examiner says it's a female between the ages of twenty and thirty, either white or Hispanic," LeClare said. "We don't know if it's Amelia, we're waiting on dental records."

Oh.

Having to wait on dental records to identify the body made me wonder if the victim was so badly decomposed that she could have been dead longer than ten years. The worker said he saw clothing, if he'd found what Amelia was last seen in, then they should know if it was her or not.

Unless Amelia changed before she disappeared.

"Do you know why I'm so passionate about Millie's case file?" LeClare asked, interrupting my thoughts.

"Millie? Did you know her personally?" Only family and strangers called her Amelia.

"We went to high school together." Detective LeClare adjusted in her seat and cradled her belly with both hands. "After Detective Ramsey retired, the file was passed around and sat on the bottom of caseloads. There were no new leads. It sat in limbo. Is it homicide? Is it a missing-person case? When I was forced to sit at a desk—" She pointed to her stomach. "—I saw Millie's file and decided to take another look, and do you know what I found?"

"What?" I asked.

"Nothing new."

Well, crap.

"This is where you two come in. Forensics has improved greatly in the last ten years."

I thought she was going to continue, but she didn't. Instead she stared at me and I stared back. I realized she was sending me a surreptitious message. Something she couldn't say out loud.

Unfortunately, my hangover brain was not computing.

So we did this for a while.

LeClare staring at me.

Me staring at her.

Camry's eyes bouncing between the two of us.

"Running DNA samples again would be *expensive*," she added. "Even if the technology has improved greatly over the last decade."

Still not...*ah, got it.*

"Well." I sat up straight, crossed my ankles, and played it cool. "If the department isn't willing to spend the money, then perhaps a little pressure from the general public would help change their mind."

"Perhaps it will." Detective LeClare continued to rub her belly with big, deliberate sweeps of her hands.

Got it.

"When are you due?" I asked.

"Four weeks and I'm off for eight weeks afterwards. When I return I'll have to devote my time to active cases."

Right.

Got that message loud and clear.

LeClare believed, or so I assumed she believed since we were only conversing in code and I felt like death, that a new test would show more than Amelia's DNA in her vehicle—just as Jeremy suggested. The agency won't pay for it. I needed to get listeners invested enough in Amelia's story for them to demand the agency run the DNA again using more modern technology.

And I had four weeks to do it.

No pressure or anything.

But before I could go have a nervous breakdown, I had to ask about HJZoomer22 without revealing my stepsister was a cybercriminal. "Did you ever make contact with the poster of the video?"

"Are you talking about Blake Kirkland?"

"I'm talking about the person who *posted* it," I said and stared at LeClare. It didn't have the same effect when I did it.

At least I didn't think it did until the detective said, "We've spoken to that person, yes."

Darn. I'd hope she'd have a slip of the tongue and say, "We've spoken to *her* or *him*." But she was too sharp.

"Do you know about the contaminated soil in the Morning Knolls neighborhood?" I asked.

LeClare's head tilted slightly. "Sounds familiar, why do you ask?"

"Several people have commented that Amelia didn't look good the weeks leading up to her disappearance. I'm wondering if she was sick and maybe that played a part in her reaction at the gala. I spoke to someone last night that grew up in the house behind the Clark's, and she said several people on her street had developed a brain tumor, thyroid cancer, and her own brother died of leukemia."

LeClare nodded. "Interesting theory...off the record." She gave me a look of warning and I held up my palms again.

"Not a word," I promised.

"I saw Millie three days before she disappeared, and she didn't look good. When I read in her file that she'd recently gone through a breakup, I thought that might have been why she appeared so frail. But my original thought, at the time, was that she appeared emotionally beaten and even afraid."

"Why do you think she was afraid?" I asked. "Jeremy alluded to the same thing when we spoke to him."

"Yes, he mentioned that several times in his interview with Detective Ramsey." LeClare's eyes went distant, as if she were seeing things long ago. "I'm not going to pretend that I knew Millie well. We didn't spend much time together in high school, but we did have several classes together. The reaction in the video appeared out of character for her, though. When I last saw her, we were at Morning Knolls Park and she was getting ready to go on a run. I asked her how she was doing. She said fine, of course. I didn't ask about the video, but I'd seen it. She cut our conversation short and took off running. A little while later, as I was getting ready to leave, I passed the tennis courts and noticed Millie was sitting on the ground, crying, and staring at her phone."

Hold on. "She had her cell phone," I clarified.

"Yes."

"The one that was on the floor of her car when it was found?"

"Yes."

"And she had it with her when she went on a run?"

"Yes."

Aha!

I was right. She didn't disappear while on a run! She didn't go to Orcutt Hollow Trail. Either Amelia or someone else planted the car there to make it look like she'd gone for a run and had either took off from embarrassment or she was taken.

"Are you thinking Orcutt Hollow is not the primary crime scene?" I asked.

"I'm not allowed to give case specifics," she reminded me.

"When was the last time you spoke with Jeremy Wang?" I asked.

She didn't answer.

I bit my lip. "He said Detective Ramsey never checked to be sure he was in Arizona. Have you?"

Again, no answer.

Shoot.

Camry piped in. "And you're sure it was Amelia's blood on the steering wheel?"

"Yes, it was Amelia's blood mixed with her own saliva," LeClare said.

Saliva?

This was new.

EPISODE THIRTEEN

The Stains

Our meeting with Detective LeClare continued much the same. I asked a question. She didn't answer. We did this for another thirty minutes before it was time to go.

Three important tidbits of information extracted from our meeting:

First, the body found at Waller Park was a young female, and she was not wearing the outfit Amelia was last seen in.

Second, Amelia's saliva was mixed in with her blood.

Third, HJZoomer was a woman.

Now I had to figure out how this new information fit into our case.

"What are you doing?" Camry asked.

We were sitting in my car, still in the parking lot of the police station. I gripped my steering wheel tightly, placing my fingertips exactly where the smudge of blood on Amelia's steering wheel was found.

Camry waved her hand in front of my face. "You there?"

"Where's the nearest fast food restaurant?" I asked.

Camry consulted her phone. "There's a Jack in the Box about a mile away. Why? Are you hungry?"

Heck no. I didn't want to think about food. Chances were Hazel had a seven-course meal prepared for us at home anyway.

But what I did need was free ketchup.

* * *

I watched Camry in my rearview mirror exit Jack in the Box with a grease-stained bag in her hand. "Got the best hangover meal for you," she said as she slid into the passenger seat.

"The whole point of coming here was to get *free* ketchup."

"They don't give out ketchup unless you buy something." She grabbed a curly fry from the bag. "What has this world come to?"

"I don't know. What did you get?" The aroma of deep-fried food trigged my appetite.

"Two tacos and fries. I love Jack in the Box when I'm drunk. It's the only time they taste good." She handed me a deep-fried taco still wet with grease. It was the most unappetizing thing I'd ever seen in my life. But I took a bite anyway.

"Wow, this is good."

"Told ya." She shoved a fry into her mouth. "I also got a handful of ketchup. They're stingy with the condiments."

"That will work." I wiped off my hands and grabbed the ketchup packets. "Can you take video of this and I'll do the audio."

"Aye, aye." Camry saluted me and got to work while I grabbed the picture of the bloodstains taken in Amelia's car.

Once we were recording, I applied a small amount of ketchup on my finger and grabbed the steering wheel tightly with both hands. The ketchup smudge didn't match the picture. Not even close. Of course, I was using tomatoes and not actual blood.

So there was that.

I heaved a sigh and looked at Camry, who was standing outside the car with her phone aimed at me. "Do you have anything in your bag that I can cut myself with?"

"Of course." She dug through her purse and produced a pocketknife.

"Why do you have that?"

"People are monsters."

Touché.

I used hand sanitizer to clean the knife and held it to the tip of my finger, giving myself a pep talk.

"Wait," Camry said. "Don't you think the blood came from her mouth since it was mixed with saliva?"

"Probably, but I'm not about to put this in my mouth." I was dedicated to the project. But I had to draw the line at gum mutilation.

"You can floss and make your gums bleed," Camry suggested.

"My gums don't bleed when I floss, if yours do, then it's time to see a dentist."

She rolled her eyes. "Just cut your finger and get it over with."

"Okay." I took a deep breath and counted to three. "Crap! That hurts." Instinctually, I shoved my finger into my mouth and...Wait a second! I stared down at my fingertip, now coated with a mixture of my saliva and blood. I wrapped my hand around the steering wheel. When I removed it, the smudge was faint, but there. I tried it again until I got it in the right spot.

"Amelia wasn't holding the steering wheel tightly," I said into the recorder. "Which makes me think she wasn't in any real distress when this happened."

"What about the seat?" Camry asked.

Right. The seat. I placed my hand on the bottom front of my seat, where the second stain was found. I was able to replicate the smudge by wiping my hand in an upward motion.

"I don't think this blood is from an attack at all," I said, going through the motions once more. "I think Amelia cut her finger, sucked on it, wiped it on the front of her seat, grabbed the steering wheel and drove away."

"Isn't the blood one of the main reasons they suspected foul play?" Camry asked.

"Not necessarily. She still left all her personal belongings in the car. Even if she did flee, it's likely she would have at least taken the three hundred dollars she withdrew from the ATM with her. But this is interesting, right?" I grabbed the picture and studied it with the magnifying glass, ignoring curious bystanders watching. Perhaps the Jack in the Box parking lot wasn't the best place to perform this experiment.

I squinted at the picture to get a better look, specifically studying the bag of Christmas decorations, pulling the magnifying glass further from my face. Hoping something would pop out at me, like a broken glass ornament or a sharp object she could have accidently cut herself with.

But there was nothing of consequence.

Only the same ole' Christmas decorations.

"What now, boss?" Camry asked.

I looked at my finger, then at Camry, then at the homeless man staring at us from behind the dumpster. "Do you have that list of CVS stores in the area?"

"Sure do."

"How many are there?"

"Two."

"Great. Let's go get me two boxes of Band-Aids."

EPISODE FOURTEEN

Efran Dym

I held on to Camry's arm to keep her from wandering over to the As Seen on TV aisle. She'd spent twenty minutes debating between an electrical nail file and a high-powered ear wax remover at the first CVS store we went to. The manager there had not heard of Amelia Clark. Nor was she working at that CVS location in 2008. She gave us the number for the previous manager—a number that rang busy every time we called. I gave a business card to the cashier, forgot the Band-Aids, and we went to the next store.

The chances of us recouping any information at this CVS were slim, but I actually did need the Band-Aid.

"Do you know what's kind of creepy?" Camry asked as we walked to the First Aid section.

"What?"

"That we could have met Amelia's killer already."

I'd thought about this, too. Especially when we were sitting across from Jeremy Wang. That is, "Assuming she's dead."

"It's been over ten years." Camry slowed to read the aisle descriptions hanging overhead. "Hype over the viral video has died down. What's the point of staying hidden?"

True.

What would be the point?

I'd laid in bed thinking this very question. Why would *I* run away and never come back?

And I'd come up with one answer: fear.

If I knew coming home or revealing my whereabouts would result in death (either my own or someone I loved), I'd stay hidden.

There were two other possibilities.

The first: Amelia took off with the intent of never returning, but ran into trouble along the way and was either locked away by some psychopath or she died.

The second: she was killed on the tenth.

For her sake, out of the two, I hoped it was the latter.

The fact Detective LeClare wanted to do more extensive DNA testing told me she believed Amelia was murdered. And she was privy to more information than I was.

But still.

I wasn't so sure about the blood in the car anymore.

What I was sure about was the blood on my finger.

"Grab the generic brand, please." I told Camry.

She plucked a package of bandages from the bottom rack. "Here. I got the jumbo pack. If your face is indicative of how the rest of the investigations is going to go, we're going to need them."

"Ha. Ha." I yanked the box from her grasp. "Let's go find the manager."

There weren't any employees walking around, so we got in line at the register and waited.

"Hey look," Camry pointed. "Isn't that Carlos?"

I turned around, and yep, it was Carlos. He was in—of all places—the holiday aisle. It was mostly Halloween decorations but there was a small section dedicated to Christmas.

"Should we go talk to him?" Camry asked.

"Seems rude not to at least say hi."

Carlos had a plastic Jack-o'-lantern in his cart along with fake spider webs and shaving cream.

"Hi there," I said as we approach.

"Hi," he said without looking up.

"It's Liv Olsen and Camry Lewis from *Missing or Murdered*," I said.

"Yeah, I know," he said, examining a box of fake tea light candles. "I saw you when I came in."

Oh.

And he didn't say hi?

"You're still doing that podcast thing?" he asked.

"Yes, we've had good interviews lately." I reached into my purse and grabbed my recorder. Never leave home without it. "One was with Jeremy Wang. Did Amelia ever talk about him?"

"Yes." Carlos put the tea lights back and grabbed a makeup kit.

"What did she say?" I asked, keeping my voice light and pleasant.

"I don't remember."

Sigh.

"Perhaps we could meet up this week and talk?"

"No."

"What about if we buy you lunch? Wherever you want to go."

"No."

"We found the parking citation from your old manager on Amelia's dash, and we were wondering why she parked in the guest parking space if her assigned spot was right by her apartment."

"No."

I blew out a breath. "That wasn't a yes or no question."

"I don't remember."

Carlos was acting as if the Halloween decorations were far more important than anything I had to say. He was clearly not going to give us information. No matter how pleasant I was.

Screw it.

"Did you throw an apple through our window," I asked.

Camry let out a faint gasp.

This grabbed Carlos' attention. He rose to full height and cocked his head. "What in the hell are you talking about?"

"Someone broke our window with an apple the night we spoke to you. You said we should stop the podcast before someone gets hurt. I'm wondering if it was you." I lost my resolve. Carlos' cheeks flushed with anger and a vein ticked along his temple.

"Are you crazy, woman?"

"Um...no?"

"I'm here to buy decorations for my kid's classroom. Why the hell are you coming at me with some stupid crap about a damn apple..." His voice trailed off. There was an undecipherable look in his eyes.

I took a tentative step back.

Carlos licked his lips and nodded, as if answering some internal question. "Like I said before, drop this stupid show and get the hell out of town. Got it, Red?" He shoved his cart into a candy display, sending it crashing to the ground and stormed out of the store.

Camry and I stood there like two statues carved of flesh, surrounded by hundreds of chocolate candy skeletons.

"Was that a warning?" Camry finally asked.

"Yep."

"Did he just call you, Red?"

"Yep."

"You hate being called Red."

"Yep."

"I think we just set off a ticking time bomb?"

"Yep."

"And we'll probably be the next to disappear."

I sure hoped not.

A woman with birdlike features and a gray ponytail cautiously approached us. Per her tag, this was Charlotte. "Are you two hurt?"

I shook my head, attempting to regain my composure, and look around. "We're fine. I'm sorry about the mess."

Camry and I both dropped to our knees and gathered the candy.

"Don't worry about it," said Charlotte and pressed a button on her earpiece. "We need clean-up on aisle four."

Camry stood and dusted off her hands. "Are you the manager?"

"I am, yes." Charlotte looked prepared for a verbal beating and

I wasn't sure why. It wasn't like the display attacked *us*.

I dumped a pile of candies on the shelf. "My name is Liv Olsen, and this is Camry Lewis. We're in town doing a podcast about the disappearance of Amelia Clark. We know she visited a CVS store right before her disappearance, and we were hoping to speak to someone who might have worked here during that time."

Charlotte blinked a few times. I guess that was a lot of information to throw at her at once.

"Have you ever heard of Amelia Clark?" I tried.

"Isn't that CinnaMann's daughter?"

"It is." We stepped aside as a young guy with sideburns and a CVS shirt appeared to put the display back together. "Were you the manager here in 2008 by chance?"

"No. I worked in Santa Barbara. Are you hoping for surveillance video or something?"

"Yes, actually that would be great. Or anyone who worked here at the time, we're also wondering if the police ever contacted the store."

"You sure Amelia came to *this* store?"

"No," I admitted. "It's a long shot, but a shot worth taking. Any idea who we can speak to?"

Charlotte ground her front teeth while she thought. "You'll want to talk to someone in loss prevention. They'd know all about the security footage. As far as someone who worked here, I wouldn't know. We have a pretty good turnover. Even our pharmacist is new. I wish I could help. That's a terrible thing to happen. I remember hearing about it."

"What's the name of the person in charge of loss prevention?" Camry asked.

"Todd Felderfen. If you have a card, I can give it to him and have him call you."

"That would be great." I dug around in my bag, but Camry had already produced one.

We thanked Charlotte for her time, apologized once again for the mess, bought the bandages, and headed back to the car.

*   *   *

We were a block away from Hazel's house when Todd Felderfen called. Turned out he was *at* CVS, in the back room, watching the entire thing on the security cameras. Also turned out he did not work at the company in 2008, but he knew someone who did—Shane Smith—and gave us the phone number. We called Shane Smith. Turned out Shane quit in June of 2008, but he knew who took the job after him. A man named Efran Dym, and gave us his phone number. We called Efran, he hung up on us before I could even get my name out. So we called Shane back, he told us to try a woman named Zahra. We call Zahra, who told us to call Chris. Chris told us to call Ben. Ben told us call Lee, who had us call Zack, and when Zack told us to call Efran we tried him again.

"I'm not interested," Efran said and hung up.

We were at Hazel's, sitting in the den with scraps of paper sprinkled around the room, scribbled with the phone numbers we'd been chasing all evening.

"He thinks you're a telemarketer," said Camry.

"Good point." I crossed my legs, rolled my shoulders, and composed a text message to Efran.

My name is Liv Olsen, I work for the podcast series Missing or Murdered. *We're doing a story on Amelia Clark, who went missing in 2008. I was told that you worked at CVS in October of that year. We think Amelia visited the store before she went missing and wanted to know if you knew anything. Thank you.*

"Okay...and...sent." I tossed my phone to the other side of the couch and massaged my temples. I had just spent two hours chasing CVS employees.

"This feels like a big fat waste of time," said Camry from a velvet armchair. "What are the odds this guy knows anything?"

"Low, but we might as well try. Have you boosted our Facebook post on the mom's group like LeClare said to?"

Camry covered her nose. "Yes."

I wanted to laugh, but lacked the energy to do so. "Can you

please do it now?"

"Aye, aye, captain."

Hazel entered with a tray of cookies, still steaming from the oven, and two glasses of milk.

"You girls find out anything?" Hazel slid the tray onto the coffee table. Camry helped herself to a cookie, juggling it around in her hand saying "hot, hot, hot," before she took a bite.

"Not really," I said with a sigh.

"We ran into Carlos," Camry said, and licked the chocolate off her fingertips. "He yelled. He told us to leave town. Basically, threatened to kill us. Knocked over a display case, and he called Liv, Red."

Hazel gave Camry a napkin. "Why would he do something like that?"

"Because she has red hair," Camry said.

"I meant, why would he threaten to kill you," said Hazel. "Did you call the police?"

"No. We talked to LeClare today, and I told her about our interaction with Carlos. We just need to be more vigilant going forward. Did Oliver ever install those security cameras?"

Hazel nodded. "Do you really think you're in danger?"

"Pffft. No, of course not. Carlos is all talk." That was a lie. Carlos Hermosa seemed like the type to keep his word. I was tempted to send Camry back home and check into a hotel. But I didn't think Camry would leave without me, and I was positive Hazel wouldn't allow us to go either. Making a big deal of it would only frighten them. I was hoping security cameras would work as a deterrent.

My heart hiccupped.

"You don't have to worry about us," Camry said. "Liv has pepper spray."

"I don't think that's going to help you in this case."

"She knows that," I said. "Camry thinks she's funny."

"I don't think." Camry shoved the last of the cookie into her mouth and smiled, showing her chocolatey teeth. "I know."

"You get that from your father." Hazel went to sit down on the other side of the sofa, moving my phone before she sat. "Have you texted Oliver?" Hazel asked me. "He's been trying to get a hold of you."

Ugh. I'd completely forgotten about that whole debacle.

"Not yet," I said.

"You can't call him. He won't answer." She folded her hands in her lap. "He can do anything else hearing people can, though." She looked at me, and I wasn't sure why.

"Okay," I said, unsure of how else to respond. I'd never questioned he couldn't.

"People don't realize how wonderful the deaf community is. Oliver was diagnosed right after his mom died." She stopped to cross herself. "We knew nothing about sign language or IEP's or interpreters or speech therapy or any of the resources available. But the deaf community helped us navigate. I made sure Oliver was fluent in ASL, was in speech four days a week, and had plenty of friends who were also fluent in ASL before he lost his hearing completely."

"When did that happen?" Camry asked.

"Shortly after my husband died. The two were very close. They'd go to baseball games together, camping, they were involved in Boy Scouts. We had three daughters, and Oliver's dad took off when he was five. Poor kid. I think the two filled a void in each other's lives. John was the father Oliver never had, and Oliver was the son John never had." We all paused to cross ourselves. "Perhaps the stress of John's death sped the hearing loss along. But before John died, Oliver had about 30 percent in his right ear and 20 percent in his left." She sighed. "Oliver has a hard life, but he's a *great* man." She looked directly at me again, and I had a feeling that I was missing something. "Women think just because he can't hear that he's a charity case. But he's not."

Okay, I was missing something.

"Did I offend you or Oliver?" I asked.

"Why haven't you texted him back? You were all over him at

the winery, but then you ignored him all day."

Oh.

Oops.

I massaged the back of my neck. "The reason I haven't texted him back is because I'm embarrassed by how I acted last night."

Hazel appeared shocked. "What are you talking about? You were a riot, Liv." She grabbed my hand. "You had us all laughing. Especially when you did the James Bond impression."

I can do a James Bond impression?

"Do you know what I think?" Hazel asked but didn't wait for a response. "I think you're too hard on yourself and too tightly wound. There's a fun girl in there." She pointed to my chest. "Let her out more. And text my grandson."

"Yes, ma'am." I grabbed my phone. "I'll do it right—Efran replied!"

Camry leapt over the coffee table and wedged herself between Hazel and me. "What did he say?"

"He said he knows all about Amelia and asked if we are available to talk right now."

"Aha! I told you it wasn't a waste of our time."

I gave her a look. "Sure you did."

"Stop staring at me and call him back!"

Will do.

Efran agreed to be recorded via Skype, and I worked quickly to set up the equipment. It was nearly nine p.m. in California, and he now lived in New York. The fact that he was willing to stay up past midnight to speak to us told me that he had something worth saying.

I sat in the closet, slid the door closed, put my headphones on, tested my mic, and made the call. I wasn't doing a video Skype— there was no point—I only needed the audio.

Efran had a younger voice than I imaged he would. Before we started, I asked him to talk so I could test the audio quality. He said the ABC's and we were good to go.

"Thank you for speaking to me so late. I really appreciate it," I said.

"I'm sorry for hanging up on you. I get way too many sales calls," he said. "But I do know about Amelia Clark and her disappearance. I followed it for a long time. As a matter of fact, last year I checked online to see if they'd ever found her."

"Did you know Amelia?"

"No, I never met her. I lived in Los Angeles, but I was all over the Central Coast and Southern California region for CVS. All stores from San Luis Obispo to San Diego."

Wow, that was a lot of stores. "Why were you so interested in Amelia's disappearance?"

"I had received a call from the Orcutt manager. She said the police asked for surveillance video from October 3 until October 12. I asked why and if they had a warrant. They did, and she told me it was for the Amelia Clark case, and went ahead and gave me a briefing of the viral video, the car, hiking trail, and that she had disappeared. We gave the police the video and I never heard from them again."

"Did they ask for surveillance from the other stores in the area?"

"No, just that one. They found a bag in her car and inside was a receipt from the Orcutt store."

That was the first CVS Camry and I went to.

"There's more, though," Efran said. "It just so happens that I was at that store on October 9, and I remember watching Amelia on the cameras when she was there."

I was confused. "You must look at a lot of surveillance, how do you remember Amelia?"

"Do you have an email address?"

"Yes," I said slowly and give it to him. "Why?"

"Check your email then call me back." The line went silent.

Okay, guess I'll wait.

It took several painful minutes for Efran's email to show up in my inbox. By the time it did, Camry was hovering over my shoulder, breathing down my neck. We could have probably exited the closet, but I didn't want to reset everything up.

From: Efran Dym

To: Missing or Murdered *tips*

My heart jumped into my throat when I read the subject line.

Subject: Surveillance Video from October 9, 2008

"Holy hell." Camry smacked my shoulders. "Open it. Open it. Open it. Open it. Open it!"

"I am, calm down." I clicked on the video and it took an excruciating amount of time to download. The cynic in me expected it to be a virus, but the optimist in me was shivering in excitement.

Finally, the video popped up. It was in black and white, with the time and date stamped in the corner, and *Video Camera One* along the bottom. The quality wasn't great. It looked like Efran took a video of a video. At first, all we could see was an empty feminine hygiene and family planning aisle. Then at exactly 1730 (5:30 p.m.), Amelia walked into the picture. She had on a baby doll dress, sandals, her hair in a ponytail, with a handcart swinging at her side. It was surreal seeing actual footage of her. It was surreal to think that one day later she'd be gone. It was surreal that Efran has this footage. Actually, it was *strange* that Efran had this footage.

Amelia stopped at the end of the aisle. The angle switched to *Video Camera Three*, and we could only see Amelia's back and I nearly choked on my own spit.

"Is-is-is she…" Camry stuttered out.

I nodded. "Sure looks like it."

"What the frog."

My sentiments exactly.

Amelia was looking at pregnancy tests.

EPISODE FIFTEEN

Mysterious Blonde

"It would have to be Jeremy's baby, right?" Camry asked.

I paused the video. "But she hooked up with Jeremy the week before. There's no way to find out your pregnant that fast."

"Maybe she hooked up with someone else? Like Carlos."

"But everyone commented on how thin she was." My mind took a sharp right, and I remembered when my sister-in-law was pregnant. She lost a considerable amount of weight the first trimester from all day morning sickness.

Holy hell.

I resumed the video, chewing on my cuticles as I watched.

Amelia bent down and looked at the bottom shelf, picking up boxes and reading the back. We couldn't see what she was looking at and I paused the video. "A pregnancy test would have been on the receipt. Which means Leon saw it. I'm sure he would have mentioned she was pregnant."

"He didn't tell us about Jeremy," Camry said.

True. "But an ex-boyfriend is different than being pregnant."

"Meh. Hurry up and push play. You're killing me."

I resumed the video. Amelia spent another two minutes looking at boxes until she was startled by something off in the distance. She threw a box in her cart and slowly rose to her feet, still looking at something in the background, and clasped her hand over her mouth. The camera changed to *Video Camera Ten*, and all we could see were the registers and a long line of customers waiting to be rung up. I paused the video and searched for a familiar face, but I didn't find one. Neither could Camry.

Resumed.

Video Camera Twelve and it was the front door looking into the store. Two people walked in, a young guy and a short girl with long blonde hair. All we could see was their backs. The camera changed again, and we were back in the feminine hygiene aisle. Amelia was gone, and the guy and girl walked hand-in-hand and stopped at the family planning section. I paused the video.

"Who is that?" I asked.

"It's hard to tell, but the guy has dark hair and looks about the same height as Jeremy. We need to see his face."

I resumed the video and, as if on cue, the camera changed so we can see their faces. It was Jeremy. He was younger and thinner and his hair was longer—but it was him.

"Who is the girl, though?" Camry asked.

"I have no idea, but whoever it is, he's about to hook up with her." Jeremy grabbed a box of condoms and the two laughed at something the girl said.

Camry reached over and paused the video. "Didn't Jeremy say he hooked up with someone who turned out to be crazy right before he went to Austin?"

"You're right. This is probably her."

"Unless he hooked up with another chick."

"It's a possibility. We need to find *this* girl, though."

"Absolutely. Now push play."

The video continued with Jeremy and the mystery girl chatting. The camera changed to the Halloween aisle. Amelia was crouched down with her hand over her mouth, shaking her head. She peeked up to see if Jeremy was still there and immediately dropped back down. In her basket was a rectangle box. It could have easily been a pregnancy test, or it could have been an ovulation kit, or yeast infection medication. They all have similar packaging.

Amelia crawled on all fours down the aisle; a collection of Halloween decorations lit up as she passed and she opened her arms, looked up, and mouthed, "Why?" Which made me laugh. Here she was trying to sneak away, and instead she activated a whole collection of witches and pumpkins and skeletons with glowing eyes. There was no audio, but I imagined it was loud.

She quickly crawled to the next aisle and the camera changed. Camry and I both leaned closer. It was the Christmas decorations!

Amelia grabbed several items off the shelves without looking and shoved them into her basket, presumably to hide the box. Then she sat back on her knees and peered around the corner, watching and waiting. The camera didn't switch, but I assumed she was waiting for Jeremy and his date to leave.

"She doesn't look scared," I said to Camry. "She seems embarrassed."

"Agreed."

"So she wasn't scared of Jeremy."

"Agreed."

At the three-minute mark, Amelia jumped up and ran. The camera changed and she was at the register, urging the clerk to hurry up, still checking over her shoulder. A three-foot receipt printed out. Amelia shoved it into her bag and knocked into a man with dark skin wearing a white shirt. The two talked and she opened her bag to show the man what was inside. Then she opened her purse and the man used a flashlight to check her belongings. He nodded and stepped out of the way.

Then the screen went black.

I called Efran back. He answered on the first ring, "Did you watch it?"

"Did CVS let you have this?" I asked.

"No, I took the video with my camera. That was me at the end, checking Amelia's bag. That's why I remembered her, because she was crawling on the ground. It wasn't until after the cops asked for the footage, that I went back and watched the other cameras to see what she was looking at. You saw the guy with the blonde girl, right?"

"Yes, that's her ex-boyfriend."

There was silence on the other end. "It looks like she's trying to avoid them."

"Did you turn this over to the police?"

"I did, but they never asked for anything else."

"Do you remember what was in her bag?" I asked.

"Christmas decorations and—" He sighed. "—I want to say a box of medication. But I can't remember."

"Was it a pregnancy test?"

"No, no, no. That I would remember. Pregnancy tests and razors were stolen regularly from that store. It was something else. Some kind of ointment. Yeast infection, maybe. I don't recall exactly."

She wasn't pregnant.

What a sweet relief.

"Can I use this video?" I asked. "Do I need permission from CVS?"

"I'd say use it, honestly. It's been over ten years, and I doubt anyone will care."

"Do you still work there?"

"No, I work for a sporting store now. But I am curious about what happened to her."

"You and me both," I said. "Thank you so much for this."

"My pleasure."

We hung up and I re-watched the video ten more times before I fell asleep.

EPISODE SIXTEEN

North Carolina

Camry spent the next two days "bumping" our Facebook post on the mom's group and the results were staggering. Two hundred comments followed from friends, former classmates, neighbors, teachers, people who volunteered on the search, those who worked with her at CinnaMann's and Direct Dental.

We conducted a Skype interview with Kelly Barnard, Amelia's former boss. She offered no new information. When asked why Amelia was fired, Kelly got defensive. "She wasn't fired. Millie gave her two weeks' notice in the video. HR thought, under the circumstances, that it was best to pay her the two weeks and let her go that day."

"Did you agree with them?"

"I did. Truthfully, Amelia was distracted those last few months. I shouldn't have let her go to the gala, but my kid had a talent show that night."

"Anything else you can remember?"

"Just that she'd lost weight and appeared physically and emotionally beaten."

The word "beaten" stuck with me. It was the same verbiage Detective LeClare used.

As word of our podcast spread through the city, suddenly everyone wanted to talk. Whether they had something important to say or not.

Our Facebook messenger inbox filled with leads.

She ate at Melba's Diner the week she disappeared.

We visited Melba's. The owner recalled seeing Amelia but couldn't remember what day it was and now, neither could the original tipster.

Dead End.

One woman got a hold of my cell number and left a detailed message of the time she was abducted by aliens and Amelia Clark was her roommate on the spacecraft.

Dead End.

We were losing momentum.

Nothing that lead us to Scottydogoo. Nothing on Carlos. No ID of the woman in the video. No new breaks.

Until we got a message from Dr. Deb Naidoo on Facebook Messenger.

My name is Dr. Deb Naidoo. When I first moved to this country, I worked at my cousin's restaurant. This was in the end of 2008. That's how I knew Amelia Clark. She went by the name Millie then. She was very upset about a video posted on the Internet. I did not know she went missing until I saw your post on the Mom's Facebook group. I thought she had moved away. I would very much like to offer my help. She and I talked a lot about her problems, and now I am very concerned.

Deb had me at "Millie."

Deb worked at a free medical clinic off Price Street in Pismo Beach (a small beach town about thirty minutes north), and we arranged to meet outside of the popular tourist stop, The Splash Café. Their clam chowder must be made of gold because it wasn't even lunch yet and the line was out the door and around the corner.

We were early and passed the time by taking pictures of each other in front of the clam mural outside the building. Camry sent the pic to our parents to prove we hadn't killed each other yet.

They each replied with smiley faces.

Price Street was busy. People riding bikes, surfers carrying their boards to the beach, tourists taking pictures. A bum dressed like a pirate gave me a flyer proclaiming *The End is Near! Repent now!* And told me a spaceship would land tomorrow afternoon. Maybe it was the same spaceship Amelia was on. I shoved the flyer into my bag.

As soon as the clock struck twelve, I spotted Dr. Naidoo walking down the street. I recognized her from her Facebook profile.

Dr. Deb Naidoo had dark skin, short hair, big brown eyes, and a no-nonsense stride. She was in blue scrubs and pink Crocs.

She recognized us. "You're Liv from the podcast," she said. Her accent was thick.

"I am, and this is Camry Lewis. It's nice to meet you." I held out a hand.

Dr. Deb jerked her head to the right. "We should go to the candy store on the corner. It's quieter there."

I retracted my hand. "Lead the way."

The three of us stepped into an old-fashioned salt-water taffy store. Deb bought a bag of root beer taffy. Camry bought three pieces of peppermint taffy. I bought none. It took several shimmies to get my pants on this morning. New clothes were not in the budget.

We sat near the window. I clipped a microphone onto Deb, tested to be sure we were recording and started.

"Please tell us your name, a little bit about yourself and how you knew Amelia," I said.

"I'm on my lunch. No time for my life story. I worked at my cousin's restaurant in 2008. Millie, she came in late one night with rice in her hair and a silver dress on. She was watching a video on her computer. She was very upset. She said she was at a gala for work but had to leave."

"What's the name of the restaurant?" I asked.

"Sal's Diner. Went out of business in 2009," she said, annoyed that I had interrupted her. "That was on a Friday night. October 3. Millie came back three more times. Once was on a Monday, and she met a young man with tattoos down his arms."

"Was one a pineapple?" I asked.

"No pineapple, but he ordered a salad with pineapple and gave it to her. I remember 'cause she was waving the fork in front of his face with the pineapple on it. They were laughing. I thought they were a couple."

Interesting.

"Millie told the boy that she came to Sal's because it was a metaphor. She will build her life from the very place it was ruined. She came back the next two days. She told me she was thinking about moving. Then I saw her on a Wednesday night, which would have been the eighth of October, and never again."

"Did she say where she wanted to move?" I asked.

"She once said North Carolina. You can get an apartment there for under five hundred dollars is what I overheard her say to the man with tattoos. I knew Millie was on a tight budget. She only paid with cash and she only bought the cheapest thing on the menu, and she didn't tip well."

This was consistent with what Leon said about her not having a debit or credit card. Which gave validity to what she was saying. Which made Dr. Deb Naidoo my new favorite person. "What was her disposition Wednesday evening?"

"She thought someone was going to post another video because she had an incident at a cell store. But I don't know what she meant. She talked about running away and starting over. Then she didn't show up for a date on Friday night, and I thought she did move away like she said."

I wasn't sure I heard her right. "She had a date Friday night?"

"Yes. The boy who worked at the computer supply store next door came in. He said he was waiting for Millie. I felt very bad because he waited for an hour then he got a call on his phone and left in a hurry. I never saw him again either."

"Wait, wait. Are you sure it was the same Millie?"

"Yes. I saw them talking many times before," said Deb. "They talked on Wednesday outside of Sal's. He was waiting for Millie, I know it for certain."

"Are you sure it was Friday night?"

"Yes, very sure. It was October 10. The same day I got the letter saying I passed the first United States Medical Licensing Examination. Sal and the chef's made me a special meal that night."

"What was the guy's name?" I asked.

"Not sure."

"Can you give us a physical description?" Camry asked.

"He had hair that was dark and wavy. He ate meatball subs to go. He was very nice. Once when he came in to get his lunch, I thought he was going to pass out—he got very dizzy—so I had him sit down and wait for it to pass."

Dizzy. Dark wavy hair. Worked at a computer supply store. Very nice. Not a lot to go off of but a start.

"Is there anything else you can think of that could be helpful?" I asked.

"No." Deb unwrapped a taffy and put it in her mouth.

I consulted my list of questions. "As a doctor, what did you make of her physical and emotional state?"

Deb waited to swallow before she answered. "I didn't like her coloring and I thought she was too thin. I asked her about her health, and she said she had a yeast infection. I told her to buy over the counter medication. She was training for a marathon. I told her not to go for a run because it will make it worse, and she should go for a walk or a nice hike."

Crap.

"You told her not to run but to go for a hike?"

"I did. She told me she had to exercise to help with her stress, because she was having breakfast with her mother the next morning and her mother stressed her out."

I reached over and grabbed Deb's arm before she tossed

another taffy into her mouth. "She said she was meeting her mom the *next* morning? Are you sure she said next?"

"Positive. She said she was meeting her mother 'tomorrow morning.' She told me her mother was hard to handle. Listen to me. In South Africa I was a brilliant surgeon. I came to America and served meatballs. It was a very boring and depressing job for me, so I listened to people to keep my brain active."

I believed her. "Have you spoken to the police about any of this?"

"Why would I? I didn't know she was missing until I saw it on Facebook."

"A detective never came to Sal's?" I asked.

"I quit the day I passed the first part of the exam."

I grabbed a notebook from my bag and clicked my pen. "Can I get your phone number and address? You should be hearing from a Detective LeClare soon."

"Why a detective?"

"Because Amelia's mother claims to have been in San Francisco all week," said Camry.

EPISODE SEVENTEEN

A New Suspect

Deb hurried back to work. Camry bought another bag of taffy while I left a message for Detective LeClare with Dr. Naidoo's contact information. If Amelia planned to meet Janet on Thursday, it meant Janet Clark wasn't in San Francisco. Which meant she lied about her whereabouts the week of Amelia's disappearance. Which meant Richard Clark lied as well. If they lied about Janet being in San Francisco, what else did they lie about? And why?

On the other hand, Amelia could have been mistaken.

Dr. Naidoo wasn't the only one to mention Amelia's sickly appearance. Her boss, Kelly, mentioned it as well. Per her missing poster, Amelia weighed 105 lbs. I weighed 105 pounds (at least I did before I met Hazel). I was five foot (on a good hair day). Amelia was six inches taller than me. It would be one thing if she were naturally lean. But she wasn't. Based on pictures, she was of average build until the last few months when she dropped a significant amount of weight.

We knew her neighbors had contaminated soil.

I wasn't captain of the statistics club like Amelia was, but the odds seemed to favor the Clark's had contaminated soil as well.

Which meant the odds are higher than average that she was exposed. At twenty-three, that would put Amelia about the same age as the other young adults diagnosed with cancers and thyroid problems.

It was a stretch.

But a possibility.

If Amelia were feeling sick and tired, she could have mixed up the dates.

I was not sure what to do with this information just yet. If it were true, and Janet was in town, it would be amazing investigative journalism on my part.

If it were false, then it would ruin the Clarks.

I decided to keep it quiet for now.

Camry and I left the candy shop and walked back to the parking lot. It was overcast but warm. Surfers were loading and unloading surfboards. Families were loading and unloading sand toys from their minivans. Seagulls swooped over our heads and the waves crashed against the shore in the background. The ocean breeze felt good against my skin. Reminded me of home.

When we reached the car, I held out my keys for Camry.

"You're letting *me* drive *your* car?" she said. "Who are you and what have you done with my sister?"

I dropped the keys in her hand. "I'm going to answer emails and get work done while you drive."

"Now I'm your peon and personal chauffeur?"

"Yep."

Camry and I got in and buckled our seat belts. She started the car and revved the engine. "Listen to that single cylinder? So much power! I hope I can manage." She put it into reverse "Where are we going?"

"Where do you think?"

"Computer Supply Warehouse to ask about the wavy-haired dizzy boy?"

"Bingo."

EPISODE EIGHTEEN

A Complicated Discovery

Computer Supply Warehouse used to be the one-stop shop for all your technology needs. The last time I saw a CSW store was when I was in middle school, and my dad needed a new fax machine.

Who needs a warehouse when you have Amazon?

And who needs a Tech Nerd when you have YouTube?

Conversing in person was a dying art.

Across the street was the hotel where the Direct Dental gala was held. I had assumed Amelia went home after she ran away from the security guards—but that doesn't appear to be the case. According to Deb, the restaurant to the right of the Warehouse used to be Sal's Diner. It was now a pizza place.

Logistically, everything Deb said matched up perfectly.

Inside, Computer Supply Warehouse looked like your typical office supply store with soft rock blasting through the speakers. Camry and I both had microphones clipped to the inside of our shirts, and we walked around for a while until we found an employee sitting on the floor stocking ink cartridges.

"Excuse me?" I said.

She looked up. Her hair was streaked purple and her eyes were circled in thick liner. "Can I help you?"

"I hope so. We're looking for information on an employee who worked here in October of 2008."

"Huh?"

"Is there a manager I can talk to..." I searched for a nametag pinned to her red polo. No tag. "Sorry, what's your name?"

"Sheila, and *I* am the manager."

"You should wear nametags," said Camry.

"We're not allowed to, it's against company policy."

"Makes sense." Camry shrugged. "Keep it impersonal. Great for business."

Sheila stood and confronted Camry. "Who are you?"

I stepped between them. "We're podcasters doing a story on a local girl who disappeared in 2008. We think she may have been dating a former employee."

"Which employee?"

Good question. "He worked here in October of 2008 and had dark wavy hair. He was nice."

"And he was once dizzy," added Camry.

"He was *nice*?" Sheila snickered. "Then he ain't work here no more. No one here is nice." Sheila took her box of ink and moved to the next aisle.

We moved with her.

"I'm sure if we look through your employee files we could find him," I said.

Sheila stared at me as if I just suggested she change her name to BoBo and runoff to join the circus. "I can't let you look through confidential employee files. If you want that kind of information you're gonna have to call corporate."

"Maybe we could ask your other employees if they remember anyone here by that description?" I said. "Do you have senior staff?"

"Don't be bothering my employees, we're very busy today."

The store was empty. I could almost hear the crickets. On the other side of the warehouse I spotted an employee in his mid-thirties working the copier center. "What about that guy. Has he been here long?"

"I don't need you distracting my employees. I think it's time for you two to leave." Sheila lived on a short fuse. We should introduce her to Carlos, I thought.

Obviously we weren't going to get anywhere with Sheila. "You know what, you're right. I should call corporate," I said. "Thank you so much for your time, Sheila."

"Yeah, yeah, okay."

Camry and I walked toward the exit. When Sheila went back to stocking ink, we made a U-turn and headed straight for the copier counter. "How long have you worked here?" I asked the man in lieu of a hello.

"About a month, but I can assure you I know what I'm doing." Copier Guy looked like Bert—as in Bert and Ernie. The similarity was uncanny.

"Is there anyone in today who worked here in 2008?" I asked in a rush.

Camry elbowed me in the side. "Sheila spotted us."

Copier Guy turned around and yelled to the guy working the Tech Nerd counter. "You work here in 2008?"

"She looks pissed," said Camry. "Hurry up."

I dug around in my bag and pull out the *End is Near! Repent Now!* flyer. "I need fifty copies, card stock, pink, ASAP." I slapped the crinkled paper on the counter. Sheila couldn't kick out a paying customer.

The Tech Nerd walked over while Copier Guy read the flyer. "Fifty copies?" he asked. "Of this?"

"What's up?" Ironically, Tech Nerd sort of looked like Ernie.

"Hurry up," hissed Camry.

"Did you work here in October of 2008, and if you did, did you know a guy who had dark wavy hair, and was very nice, and dizzy?" I blurted out in a panic.

Tech Nerd/Ernie scratched his head while Copier Guy/Bert worked hard to iron out the wrinkled flyer by rubbing it with his forearm.

"Are you talking about Lewis?" asked Tech Nerd.

Camry turned around. "What?"

"Sure," I said. "Could be Lewis. What was his last name?"

Sheila was fast approaching.

"Lewis," said Tech Nerd.

Sheila tapped my shoulder. "I thought I told you to leave?"

"I'm a customer!"

"She's right," said Copier Guy. "I've got it right here." He showed her the flyer. I didn't notice the spaceship drawing on the bottom before.

Or that it looked like a penis.

Camry dropped to the floor. "I tripped!"

"On what?" Sheila demanded.

"The floor is wet, and there's no wet sign. My ankle!" She held her calf. "Liv, get my lawyer on the phone."

"That's it! I'm calling the cops." Sheila pulled her phone from her back pocket.

Which gave me enough time to ask Tech Nerd: "Hurry, what was the guy's name!"

He looked flustered. "I can't remember his first name. We called him Lewis."

"Yes, my name is Sheila, and I'm calling from Computer Supply Warehouse, we have two women who are possibly on drugs causing a disturbance."

Camry leapt off the ground and grabbed my arm. "Didn't work. Time to go."

"Wait." I turned to Tech Nerd. "Think, please. I need a first name."

"Um...shoot! We just called him Lewis. But I know his first name. It's on the tip of my tongue. I hate when that happens."

"Send enforcements now!" said Sheila.

Geez.

"Give me something. Anything," I pleaded. "Andrew, Byran, Connor, Bert, Ernie!"

"Damn, it's not coming to me." Tech Nerd's face turned red from thinking too hard. "But I heard he's a YouTuber now."

My heart skyrocketed into my throat, and I stumbled backwards. "Not, *Oliver* Lewis."

He snapped and pointed right at me. "That's it."

"Let's go!" Camry dragged me toward the exit. Sheila chased after us, still on the phone.

"You still want these copies!" Copier Guy called after us.

I was too stunned to respond.

We got to the car. Camry pushed me in, started the engine and peeled out of the parking lot. "Cutting it close there, Liv...Liv?"

I can't breathe.

"Liv?"

Camry pulled over to the side of the rode and grabbed me by the shoulders. "What's wrong?"

"He said Oliver Lewis. Oliver Lewis!" I freaked.

"Lewis and Oliver are both popular names. It doesn't mean it's the same one."

"He said Oliver Lewis who now has a YouTube channel!"

"My cousin?"

"Yeah."

"The one you made out with?"

"Yeah."

"The one you stripped for?"

"Yeah...wait, what?"

"This isn't good."

"No!"

"But Oliver is deaf. Dr. Naidoo would have said that. She's, like, a doctor."

"He wasn't always deaf. Remember? Hazel said he has an inner ear disease. Inner ear problems can cause dizziness. And Hazel said he lost his hearing completely the day his grandpa died. His grandpa died the same day Amelia went missing."

"This isn't good," she said.

"This is horrible! If Oliver had something to do with Amelia's disappearance and I made out with him, I discredit the entire project!"

"Yeah, and also he's my cousin."

"I know!"

"Let's call Hazel."

"Okay."

Camry had the sense to put the phone on speaker. "Did Oliver work at Computer Supply Warehouse?" she asked as soon as Hazel answered.

"When he was in college. Why do you ask?"

I broke out in a sob. "This is so bad. This is awful. This is terrible!"

"Is that Liv?" asked Hazel. "What is she saying?"

"Errr...nothing."

"Did she ever text Oliver back?"

"Errr...no."

"She really should. He wants to speak to her."

"Yeah, okay. I gotta go." Camry hung up.

"He lied to us! He lied to me! And I kissed a possible suspect," I said, blubbering. "This ruins the credibility of the entire podcast. Even if he had nothing to do with her disappearance, he's a witness. My career is ruined."

Camry had her phone out. "What are you doing now?" I asked.

"I'm texting Oliver, telling him to meet us ASAP."

"Don't do that."

"I already did and...he's typing...and typing...still typing...dots are dancing on the screen....typing...still typing...he must have a lot to say....*and* we have a response."

I wiped my nose with the sleeve of my shirt. "What did he say?"

"He said 'K.'"

EPISODE NINETEEN

The Date

Oliver was on a hike of all places. A trail called Pirates Cove in Avila Beach (about ten minutes from Pismo, we were blowing through a lot of gas). It took about forty minutes to get there, which was about how long it took for me to get a grip.

I was no longer sobbing. I was seething.

Oliver knew Amelia. Not only did he know her, he dated her. There was only one reason for Oliver to keep this a secret from us: a guilty conscience.

No wonder he wanted me to drop this podcast.

In over my head.

Pffft!

Pirates Cove runs along the coast with a breathtaking view of the waves crashing against the cliffs. Oliver was standing at the ledge with his video camera out, pointed toward the Pacific.

Camry tapped his shoulder. He turned and smiled. "Wave." He held up the camera for a group selfie shot. I pushed it down. "What's wrong?" he asked.

"You had a date with Amelia Clark," I signed.

"Yes, but she never showed up," he signed back. *"I told you this when we were wine tasting."*

"I was drunk, Oliver. I don't remember."

"Seriously?"

"Yes, seriously. You saw me, how did you not notice?"

"I thought you were faded not drunk," he said while signing. "You don't remember anything?"

Camry waved her hand to get Oliver's attention. "She vaguely remembers making out with you," she said, as if this tidbit of information helped the situation. "And I told her about the stripping."

Oh geez.

Oliver scrunched his face. *"Is that why you didn't text me back?"*

"Not important. The problem is you knew Amelia and didn't tell me."

"I did tell you."

"I was drunk!"

A woman carrying her Chihuahua in a Bjorn gave us a sideways glance before she entered the trail.

"You know wine only has 15 percent alcohol, right?" Oliver said and signed.

Camry got Oliver's attention. "She's a virgin," she said.

Two college-aged girls walked by and giggled.

"What did Camry say?" Oliver asked me.

"I'm a lightweight," I signed and, for the record, not a virgin. *"Why did you wait so long to tell me?"*

"I didn't know this was a serious thing you two were doing," he said and signed. "And I don't want to be recorded. I have no idea what my voice sounds like anymore."

"Then how do you do videos?" Camry asked.

"I don't speak. I type the instructions on the screen, and I have a guy who adds in the background music."

Oh.

Guess there were two reasons why Oliver would keep a secret from me.

I dropped my head in my hands, unsure of what to make of this. Oliver lifted my chin, so he could see my mouth. "Are you mic'd?" he asked.

"We both have microphones on," Camry says. "And Liv has

pepper spray in her pocket."

Oliver's eyes cut to me. "Did she say 'pepper spray'?"

"Damn straight. I heard you knew Amelia. Then you asked us to meet you at a hiking trail. I may be a lightweight but I'm not an idiot."

Oliver frowned. "I had nothing to do with Amelia. And I really don't want to be recorded." There was pain and vulnerability in his blue eyes. and I couldn't help but surrender.

"That's fine." I reached around and turned off the mic pack in my back pocket. "I won't record."

"Thank you."

"But you have to tell me what happened."

He looked around. "Right now?"

"Might as well."

Oliver cleared his throat then eyed me suspiciously and decided to sign only, which made it harder for me. But there was no chance I could secretly record him, so I got it, *"I saw Amelia at a place called Sal's a couple of times. We talked. She was pretty, had a good sense of humor, so I asked her out. We agreed to meet Friday night at Sal's. I showed up Friday night and she never did. While I was waiting, I got the call that my grandpa wasn't doing well, and I came straight home. I had no idea she went missing until a couple of weeks later when I saw her picture on the news. I called the police right away and told them what I knew. I haven't heard from them since. That's it."*

"What time were you supposed to meet her?" I asked.

"At seven o'clock."

Amelia was last seen at six fifteen p.m. wearing a denim skirt, black leggings, black wedges, a white shirt and vest. Sounded like date attire to me. If she never showed up to meet Oliver, then chances were something happened to Amelia shortly after she took money out of the ATM. Which meant the chances of her deciding to skip town were slim.

"What are you thinking?" Oliver asked.

"I think something happened to Amelia right after she left the bank. And I'm fairly certain that something is murder."

My cell buzzed in my back pocket. I didn't recognize the number. "Ugh, you answer it." I handed the phone to Camry. "If it's the alien lady tell her the ship should be here tomorrow."

"Hello, Liv Olsen's phone. This is her personal secretary speaking. How might I help you?" said Camry.

"Is there anything else?" I signed to Oliver.

"I told you all I know."

"Does your grandma know about this?"

"Yes. She called me the night you two got in town and told me to give you an interview. And I told her I didn't want to be involved."

I thought back to when Hazel gasped at the dinner table. I assumed it was because her Internet famous grandson could help us by using his Internet fame to spread the word of the podcast—*not* because he knew pertinent case information.

I could now put together a timeline. Amelia disappeared sometime between six fifteen p.m. and seven p.m. It would have been dusk at that point, making it difficult for someone to grab her without being seen. Which made me wonder if she went willingly with someone she knew?

Oliver grabbed my attention and pointed to Camry. Her face was sheet white.

"What's wrong?" I asked.

"It was a reporter from the Channel Two news." Camry handed the phone to me. "A forensic team is back at Waller Park right now collecting more samples, and the body has been identified as Amelia."

EPISODE TWENTY

Waller Park

We spotted the yellow tape and unmarked police vehicles near the duck pond and pulled over. Oliver, Camry and I jumped out of the car and ran to the scene where two news crews were already packing up.

"The forensic team is at work. Taking pictures, measuring the distance from the pond to where the body was found, three men with gloves are on their knees, digging around in the dirt. I can't see much from my spot behind the police tape, but another person in a blue jacket is taking pictures. While another is gathering the ducks to keep them away," I said into the recorder. "It appears to be the same pond that the picture of Amelia hanging in her parent's entryway was taken at."

"I can't believe this," said Oliver.

"What exactly did the reporter say on the phone?" I asked Camry. After she said the Waller Park body was Amelia, nothing else mattered. The three of us ran to my car, jumped in and said no more than two words the entire ride.

"The reporter said the forensic team was back on the scene today to collect more information, and that they had identified the body as Amelia Clark," said Camry.

I craned my neck to look into the hole but could only see people doing their job. It was frustrating. "What more information do they need?" I asked out loud.

"I-I can answer that."

I spun around so fast my recorder flew out of my hand. Oliver caught it mid-air and returned it to me without taking his eyes off the crime scene.

Wow.

I turned more carefully this time, holding tight to the five-hundred-dollar piece of equipment in my hand.

Standing behind me was a twenty-something aged guy. He was tall, thin, blond hair, freckles and had an under bite. He had a knit hat on despite the fact it was almost eighty degrees outside. In his hand was a recorder. The type used for dictation not for sound quality.

"Who are you?" I asked.

"My name is A-Austin Mallor. I write for *The Santa Maria Tribune.*" He pulled a business card from his shirt pocket that stated his name was Austin Mallor, and he wrote for *The Santa Maria Tribune.* "I'm doing an article o-on your podcast for Sunday's addition. Leon Ramsey told me about it. H-he was m-my godfather."

I gave Austin the once over. Leon never mentioned he had a godson who worked for the paper.

He also never mentioned that he was dying.

I guess it was fair to say I didn't know much about Leon Ramsey.

"I'm Liv Olsen, nice to meet you. I'm sorry about Leon. He seemed like a nice man."

"Th-thank y-you."

"Do know what they're doing here?"

"Th-they're taking soil samples."

"And they identified the body as Amelia today?"

"N-no they didn't identify a-anyone. It's a rumor I-I started."

Camry decided to step in. "What is wrong with you?"

If Austin were a cartoon character, he would have had hearts protruding from his eyeballs. Camry poked him in the chest with her finger and he stumbled backwards.

I was interpreting the exchange for Oliver. He rolled his eyes.

"H-hold on, I can explain," said Austin.

"Then spit it out," Camry said with a warning glare.

Austin stuttered through the specifics.

Here's what happened: Austin had been covering the decomposed body in the park story. According to Austin's contact, they were able to decipher from initial inspections that the remains belonged to a female, late teens/early twenties and had been there at least ten years. Which, of course, I already knew. Austin posted to Twitter that he thought the body at Waller Park was Amelia Clark. Mistaking it as fact, Channel Two re-tweeted his tweet, and thus the rumor was born.

"Th-this will only help generate buzz for your podcast," said Austin, as if he did us a favor.

"He's an idiot," signed Oliver.

"W-what did he just say?" Austin asked me. "Sorry, I don't speak deaf."

Camry slapped her forehead.

"It was irresponsible for you to post speculation on Twitter when you write for the paper," I said to Austin. "What if her family read it?"

"H-hear me out. A-Amelia Clark is the only missing person from the area to fit the description. It-it's a strong possibility this is her."

"Yes, we already know that." We drove all the way here just to get information we already had. I hadn't been to the crime scene yet because I wanted to wait until we knew for sure it was Amelia. Seeing the forensic team felt too real. Too gruesome. Too finite. Too awful. I was furious.

"When will we know the identity?" Oliver asked.

"O-oh wow, *dude*, sorry, I didn't know you could...*talk* English," Austin said.

"He's an idiot," signed Oliver.

Austin asked me to translate.

"It's called interpret not translate," I said. "When will they release the identity?"

"M-my source said they should know in a few days. And he is telling m-me exclusively."

"Oh yeah?" Camry had her finger pointed, ready to stab. "Who is your source?"

"I c-can't give you that."

"Then I can't believe you." Camry waved him away. "Shoo. Shoo."

"Hold on, let's not be too hasty," I said, mostly to Camry. Ten seconds ago, I wanted to nut-punch Austin, but it would be beneficial to have a contact at the newspaper. Especially a contact who *had* a contact because, as it stood, I was contact-less.

"Did you want to interview me for your article?" I asked. "We could do it now, since we're already here."

"O-o-o-okay."

EPISODE TWENTY-ONE

Who is Janet Clark?

"What's this round metal thing for?" Hazel tapped the round metal thing over the microphone, otherwise known as a pop filter.

"It prevents plosives," I said. "Normally when you speak into the microphone we can hear breathing from the nose or mouth and the 'b' and 'p' sounds spike in the waveform."

"Well, aren't you fancy." Hazel shifted around in her chair to address the group. "You all need anything else?"

"No" was the collective answer. Everyone was gathered around the dining table eating berry pie while I set up for the interview. And by all, I meant Hazel, Oliver, Camry, and Austin—he'd been following Camry around since we left the park two days ago.

What we knew about Austin Mallor:

-He had a master's degree in journalism from USC.

-He was twenty-six.

-He grew up in Santa Maria.

-He was bullied as a child for his stutter and now mentors children at the Boys & Girls Club.

-He only stuttered when he was nervous.

-Camry made him nervous.

-He owned a beanie in every color.

-He didn't know Amelia, but he'd been to CinnaMann's.

-He lived in his parent's guesthouse.

-Both of his parents worked for the police department.

Which made Austin Mallor my new best friend. He got bonus points for being fun and knowledgeable. And he liked berry pie, which saved Camry and I from having to eat two slices each.

It felt good having everyone here. When I started this journey, I knew it would be hard. At the time, I thought the biggest stress would be possible career suicide and financial ruin. Now, I had the added pleasure of worrying about our safety. More specifically, Hazel and Camry's safety. Getting involved in Amelia's case wasn't their idea. It was mine. Having Austin and Oliver around eased my mind a bit. Not because they were big strong men there to protect us (Camry could easily take Austin), but because there was safety in numbers.

I hoped.

Hazel slipped the headphones over her ears, careful not to disturb her hair. "Do you want me to speak in my normal voice?"

"Yes, and speak directly into the microphone." I sat behind my laptop. "Pretend we're having a conversation."

"If you want, I can speak in my sexy voice," she said.

The room fell silent and we all stared at Hazel.

"Did she say sexy voice?" Oliver signed to me.

I nodded.

He grimaced.

"Oh, this I've got to hear." Camry put her pie down and rubbed her hands together.

"What do you want me to say?" Hazel asked.

"Tell us your name, age and how long you've lived in Santa Maria." I clicked record. "Whenever you're ready." I bit my lip to keep from cracking a smile.

Hazel first rolled her shoulders, then leaned into the mic and said, "Hello, my name is Hazel Susana Lewis." Hazel was right. She did have a sexy voice. It was a low, lush, sultry sound. "I have lived in Santa Maria for fifty years." She sensually drawled out the "s" in years.

If I closed my eyes, I saw a mature woman with jet-black hair, crimson nails filed to a point and a low-cut dress. When I opened them, I saw Mrs. Claus.

"How was that?" Hazel asked.

I couldn't formulate a response.

Oliver screwed his face into a question mark.

"Your grandma has a sex phone operator voice," I signed to him.

"I'm okay not hearing that." Oliver licked his fork clean and went to the kitchen to put his plate in the sink.

"She would be good for n-narrative," said Austin. "You know how podcasts have a different person say, *'last time on Cold in America.'"*

"He's right," I said to Hazel. "You have a great speaking voice. Can you say, 'last time'...pause...'on *Missing or Murdered.'"*

She leaned into the microphone. "Last time...on *Missing or Murdered.*"

I had chills.

"Maybe a little less sexy. We don't want to give the impression this is a geriatric porno," Camry added.

Good point.

Hazel tried again and it was perfect.

Next she talked about the mood in Santa Maria after Amelia disappeared—using her normal voice. According to Hazel, the local consensus around town was that Amelia had taken off. Many thought she was either on drugs or suffered from depression. Some thought she'd runaway to kill herself.

This was before the car with all her personal belongings and traces of blood on the seat and steering wheel were found. That's when people began to worry she'd been hurt. After a few weeks, the chatter dissipated, press coverage stopped, and people concentrated on surviving in a city hit hard by a bad economy.

Hazel went on to tell the story of when she asked Janet Clark about the parade committee.

"Had you ever seen Janet Clark at the bakery?" I asked.

"I've never seen Janet Clark anywhere. Not the grocery store. Not the mall. Not at any restaurants. If I hadn't seen her with my own two eyes that day, I'd swear she didn't exist."

"Would you say she's shy?" I'd yet to hear from Detective LeClare, and I didn't know if I'd use the information about Janet possibly being in Santa Maria. Austin said I'd need at least one more source to confirm this before I could use it. But Austin was a journalist.

I was not.

Hazel crinkled her nose. "I'd say she's more odd than shy."

"Have you ever had any other interactions with her aside from that one time?"

"Yes, I stopped by after Amelia went missing to see how she was doing. I normally don't show up empty handed, but John had just died." She stopped to cross herself. "And she owns a bakery, so it's not as if she needed more sweets. I thought what she could use was a friend, someone to talk to, someone to keep her company. She actually allowed me into her entryway that time, and she told me they were dealing with things the best they could but asked me to please respect their privacy."

"So she wasn't as abrupt with you that time?"

"No, I guess not. She was nicer but...I don't know. There's something about Janet Clark that rubs me the wrong way. Their house was too clean."

"Did that strike you as odd?"

"When my daughter passed—" She crossed herself. "—I could barely get out of bed, let alone clean my house. Then again, grief looks different on every person."

I exchanged a look with Camry. When we stopped by the Clark's house, the piano in the entryway was dusty and the picture of Amelia had cobwebs on the corners. Maybe Janet cleaned when she was grieving.

Or maybe she cleaned when there was something to hide.

Once Hazel's interview was done, I twisted in my chair to work out a kink in my lower back. The sun had since set, and Hazel closed the blinds and flipped on the above light on her way to the kitchen. I could smell dinner simmering—a pot roast with veggies and mashed potatoes—and my stomach grumbled.

Austin walked in from the bathroom and pulled out a chair. "H-how many episodes do you have edited?"

"Episode one is done. Two is almost finished, three is outlined, but I'm waiting for them to identify the remains before I move on to episode three. If it's Amelia, we'll spend less time on where did Amelia go? And more time on who killed her and buried her in the park."

Austin jotted this down on a notepad. He was still working on the article set to release in the Sunday paper, which was perfect, because on Monday *Missing or Murdered* was set to go live.

I'd never been so:

Nervous

Excited

Happy

Freaked

Frightened

And nauseous in all my life.

I played the first full episode for the group, giving Oliver a script to read. Forty-three minutes and twenty-two seconds of my heart and soul.

I listened with one eye shut, scared to see everyone's reactions.

As the outro played Hazel gave my shoulders a squeeze and kissed the top of my head. She had a confection sugar and maple aroma that reminded me of my own grandma who passed when I was ten. "I'm so proud of you girls. This sounds like a real professional radio show," she said.

"Podcast," I said.

"It sounds good, right?" Camry was beaming. Just as she was the first three times she heard it.

Oliver peeked up from the script. "I'm impressed."

I couldn't help but blush at all the praise. Until Austin opened his mouth.

"I-it's decent," Austin said, his eyebrows pinched.

Smile gone.

Decent?

What an awful, awful word.

Camry went puce. I worried she'd leap over the table and mangle Austin, so I sat on her lap to keep her put.

"Why is it only decent?" I asked Austin, attempting to keep the hurt out of my voice.

"I-I think the editing is good, but you sound too stiff."

I fell to the ground as Camry jumped from the chair and pointed her finger at Austin's nose. "You can keep your negative comments to yourself. My sister has put all her money and time into this project, and yes maybe she sounds like she's got a stick stuck up her—"

"Hey now!" I stood up. "Don't talk about me like I'm not here. If there's a problem tell me. When this goes live listeners will not sugarcoat their reviews."

The room fell silent while everyone inspected the floor. I looked to Oliver. He lifted his palms. "I'm not the person to ask. It reads good."

I looked at Austin. "Why is it decent?"

"I-I like most of it. It's your interviews. You sound b-bland. Your narrative is good, though."

"It's because I'm trying to stay neutral not reactive," I said, feeling a bit on the defense. According to Mara Lancer and Wikipedia, that's how an interview should be done. Neutral.

Neutral is not bland.

Neutral is...is...well...*bland.*

Dammit.

He was right. The interview portion sounded stiff. Like I was reading from a script.

I could do one of two things with this realization. One: lump it. Or two: record my own reactions and insert them, almost like in a book when you're reading the character's inner thoughts.

That could work.

I slammed my laptop closed, yanked the cord from the wall, and wrapped it around my hand.

"You're not quitting are you?" Camry said. "It's really not that bad, Liv. It's only the interview part. I'm sure no one will notice."

"Of course I'm not quitting!" I shoved my laptop under my arm. "I'll be in my studio if anyone needs me."

Recording, editing, re-editing, polishing, and resubmitting the episode to my hosting site, Audio Ninja, wasn't as hard as I thought it would be.

It was harder.

But somehow I managed to do it without having an emotional breakdown. And when it was all said and done—episode one wasn't too bad. Which was one step above terrible.

Austin Mallor had a keen ear.

He was a keeper.

I'd been sitting crisscross for the last three hours and I couldn't feel my feet. Giving my toes a good wiggle, I unfolded my legs one at a time, and a tingling sensation traveled down my calves. The same creepy doll was in the corner smiling at me, her eyelids half closed like she'd just been wine tasting.

I used the top of a dollhouse to help me to my feet when there was a tap on the door, and I fell back down. "Come in," I said.

Another tap.

"Come in!"

Another tap and I realized it was Oliver. I slid the door open and there he was with a plate in hand and a lopsided grin on his face. "Grandma said you have to eat. Roast beef sandwich, garlic mashed potatoes and a butter casserole."

"*What the heck is a...*" I didn't know the sign for butter. "A butter casserole?"

"Lots of butter, sour cream, Ritz crackers, cheddar cheese, cream of celery soup, more butter, and green beans. It's the only way I'll eat green beans."

"That sounds good. I'm starving. My stomach wasn't used to going so long without food anymore." Oliver helped me to my feet. Except my feet weren't quite ready to bear weight and I face planted into Oliver's chest. *Ouch.*

I think I broke my forehead.

Oliver didn't flinch, instead he set the sandwich on the nightstand and ushered me to the bed. "Did you hurt your ankle?"

"I'm fine. My legs fell asleep, that's all," I signed.

He sat beside me. The mattress sunk under his weight and I slid closer until our arms touched.

"Did you make your show not boring?" he signed.

"You thought it was boring?" I asked out loud.

"I said, 'blah' not boring."

Oh. I didn't know there was a sign for blah. *"It's not blah anymore."*

"You look like you know what you're doing." He winked.

"Not too bad for an amateur?"

"Not bad at all," he said without signing and lifted my chin until I looked straight at him. Without any warning he leaned in and kissed me. His lips were sweet and firm and his breath was hot and salty.

Holy crap.

I'm kissing Oliver!

His mouth opened mine. His hand was on my face, in my hair, he gently maneuvered my head to deepen the kiss. My breath caught in my throat as his arm creeped around my waist and pulled me closer. I reached under his shirt, feeling the ridges of muscle under my fingertips. In one swift motion, I was on my back, his mouth still on mine. He reached under—

"Well don't mind me," came a voice from the door.

I froze. *Oh please no! No. No. No. Please, please, when I open my eyes don't let it be Hazel standing at the door, watching me make out with her grandson, in her guest suite, on her guest bed, where her little grandchildren sleep.*

Oliver moved his lips to my neck and I dared to open an eye.

Yep, it was Hazel.

And now I may die.

I pushed Oliver off and he fell to the floor. "Hazel, um..." I smoothed down my hair and pulled my shirt down. "I'm...I'm..." at a loss for words.

Oliver stared at me, bewilderment dancing in his eyes, until I pointed to Hazel and then he looked like a teenager caught sneaking Victoria's Secret catalogues. "Grandma," he said as he adjusts errr...*things*.

I knew without looking that my cheeks were as red as the hair on my head.

Hazel pointed to the lock on the door. "Please use it."

"Yes, ma'am," I said, still looking at the ground, feeling like a sheepish sixteen-year-old.

"And if things get serious, there are condoms in the bathroom."

Oh dear.

Oliver bit his bottom lip and nodded. "Thanks, Grandma."

"Good. Now, I came up to tell you that Austin is on the phone with his contact at the police station. They've confirmed the identity of the body in the park."

I was off the ground and out the door before Hazel finished her statement. I flew down the stairs, sliding down three at a time (on accident) and ran into the dining room where Austin was sitting at the table on his phone. Camry was standing over him, with her hand covering her mouth like she was either going to scream or puke.

"R-right. O-okay." Austin looked stricken. "Y-you sure...Oh...Okay."

Oliver came running in behind me. The two of us grabbed hold of the back of a chair, staring at Austin, catching our breath, and waiting.

Austin finally hung up and lowered the phone to his chest. "N-not sure if this is good news or bad."

EPISODE TWENTY-TWO

Two Lies and a Dog

The body recovered in the park had been identified as eighteen-year-old, Brinkley Douglas. A UC Santa Barbara student last seen April 10, 2001.

I didn't know how to take the news.

Was I relieved that it wasn't Amelia?

Relieved she was not murdered and buried near a duck pond? Relieved because this meant she could still be alive?

Or was I disappointed it wasn't Amelia?

It had been over a decade, chances were she was dead, which meant her body was somewhere. Unless her remains were found, there would be no justice.

I was sad another young girl was gone. I was happy it wasn't Amelia...too many emotions.

When I don't know how to feel, I work.

Which was good, because there was still that whole career suicide and financial ruin aspect to deal with.

"There's too much to do." I paced the length of Hazel's dining room, signing as I talked. "We still haven't found out who the real HJZoomer22 is. The first episode comes out Monday and I don't have the second one finished. We have hundreds of messages in our inbox and not enough time to read them all. There's so much promotion to do—"

Camry blocked my pacing path. "Stop and take a breath." She

sucked air in through her nose and pushed it out through her mouth to show me how it was done.

I took a breath. Didn't help. So I went back to pacing.

"D-delegate," said Austin. "What can we do?"

"Sure. I'll do whatever I can," Oliver offered.

"Oh I bet you will." Hazel walked in from the kitchen holding a teakettle and a tray of scones. "I caught these two going to third base upstairs in the bedroom. The door was wide open for all to see."

Camry choked on her scone.

"Or was it home base?" Hazel said with a musing tilt of her head. "I get my bases mixed up. It's been too long since I played baseball."

I'm dying.

"Home *plate* is sex," Camry choked out and pounded on her chest. "Third is like...*almost* sex."

"I-I've never been past second," said Austin.

Hazel brought a hand to her heart. "Oh you sweet thing, that's so sad."

"Y-you're telling me."

Camry was still working the chunk of scone out of her throat.

"What base is heavy petting?" Hazel addressed the table.

"How about them Dodgers?" said and signed Oliver.

"You would talk baseball," said Camry, still coughing.

"Drink something, dear." Hazel poured Camry a cup of tea. "We don't need you dying on us. I think you're Austin's only hope at getting to third."

"Okay." I clapped my hands together. "No more baseball talk. If you need clarification on bases, please use Google. Now about episode two—"

"Got it." Austin held up his phone. "S-says here second base is kissing and above the shirt petting."

Oh my gosh.

"A-and th-third base is petting below the—"

"Hey now!" I interrupted before he got any further. "And for the record, no one went to third."

"And there's no chance we are either." Camry pointed to Austin. "So don't be getting any ideas."

Oh geez.

"Did you all still want to help?" I asked, desperate to change the subject. Not that there's anything wrong with two grown adults consensually playing baseball, but having this conversation in front of Oliver's grandma was about three levels outside my comfort zone.

"Don't be so uptight, Liv." Camry gave me a hug from behind. "We're only joking."

"Sh-she'd be less uptight if she went to home plate," added Austin.

Hazel doubled over in laughter and gave Austin a high five.

"Are you all done?" asked Oliver.

"One more. One more." Hazel flattened out the front of her apron. "Dang it, I forgot. It'll come to me. Go on." She lowered herself into a seat, still smiling.

"Anyway, if you want to help I would be honored and touched, but I can't pay you. I can't pay any of you. Not even a dollar," I said.

"I can do whatever you need," said Oliver.

"A-a-and he means *whatever*," added Austin.

Camry gave him an air high five.

"Aren't you all hilarious." I sat down with a cup of tea and took a sip when I realized it wasn't tea at all. It was hot apple cider. I loved cinnamon and apple together...*huh?*

Camry interrupted my train of thought. "Interesting podcast posse we've got here."

Austin laughed. "Y-yeah, we're like a podcasting posse of misfits. We got the old lady, the deaf guy, a-and the pretty one, a red head for a boss, and I'm s-socially awkward."

"That's not fair, Austin," said Camry. "Liv is socially awkward, too."

*   *   *

The hours flew by. We were closing in on midnight, and I had my headphones on, listening to the interview with Jeremy, taking note of when to insert reactive commentary. Camry was on the computer, doing what? I was afraid to ask. The less I knew the better so I couldn't be forced to testify. Austin was combing through Leon's notebooks, looking for new information. Hazel kept us fed. Oliver was updating our social media and filtering through leads sent in. He'd even added a forum to our website for listeners to discuss episodes.

A nice feature.

Now all we needed was listeners.

I removed my headphones and massaged the back of my neck. "How's everyone doing?"

Oliver stretched his arms above his head. "I scheduled a tweet to go out Monday, and I added the link to your site to the bottom of my YouTube bio."

"Th-that's right. You're the local YouTuber. We ran an article on you l-last year."

"He's an Internet star." Hazel placed another tray of cookies on the table. "And real smart. Did I tell you he installed Wi-Fi in my bathrooms?"

"Yes," we all said.

"Well then." She pursed her lips and scooted back to the kitchen.

It suddenly dawned on me that I'd yet to look up the famous Internet star grandson. The one I went to second base with. I minimized Adobe and clicked on YouTube and searched "Oliver Lewis."

Holy hell!

Hazel was right.

Oliver *was* Internet famous.

Five million subscribers.

Million!

My first thought: good for him!

My second thought: that's a lot of potential listeners.

Oliver shrugged it off like it was no big deal, but I was impressed.

Hazel came from behind and took the plate where my avocado toast used to be. "Are you all about ready to call it a night? I can't keep these eyes of mine open for another minute."

"Just about." I closed my laptop.

"H-hold on." Austin sat up straighter with Leon's notebook in hand. "D-didn't you say that you got an anonymous tip that HJZommer22 was really Scottydog00?"

Camry and I shared a look.

"Yeah, an anonymous tip." I traced the natural wood swirls on the table, refusing to make eye contact. He couldn't know about Camry.

"Why? Did you find the email address in there?" Camry asked.

"No, but L-leon had a discussion with Penny *Scott* who worked at Direct Dental. Could she b-be Scottydog00?"

"To be honest, I feel stupid for not asking that question earlier," I said. "Her last name used to be Scott."

"And Jeremy said the last time he saw Amelia she was crawling on the ground to hide from Penny," Camry added.

"The last time *we* saw Amelia was on the surveillance video, crawling on the ground."

I had an epiphany. My brain worked through epiphanies better when my feet were moving, so I got up and paced. "Penny Scott, *Scotty*dog00. Zero, zero. Does it say how old Penny was when Leon interviewed her?"

Austin scanned down the page. "Says here she was w-was twenty-five."

Twenty-five in 2008. Twenty-five minus eighteen, carry the three...

"Why are you making that weird face?" asked Camry. "You look constipated. Are you constipated? 'Cause you look it?"

"Did someone say constipated?" Hazel poked her head around

the corner. "I'll get the prunes."

"I'm not constipated," I said in a huff. "I'm trying to do math."

Oliver handed me his phone, which was opened to the calculator app, and I crunched the numbers.

"Aha!" I turned to show everyone the final sum, 2000. "She was Penny Scott age twenty-five in 2008, which meant she was eighteen in 2000, which means she likely graduated in 2000, which means it's highly possible her email could have been Scottydog00."

I dropped the cell like it was a mic and walked away, except I rammed my shin into a hutch and remembered that was Oliver's phone not mine. Oops.

"Smooth," said Camry. "And if you're done, I'd like to point out that on Penny's Facebook page it says she graduated in 2000 and her public bio says she loves dogs more than people. Doesn't seem like a stretch that her email address would be Scottydog00."

"W-why would she post the video?" asked Austin. "What's the motive?"

"You know who we should ask?" said Camry.

"Penny," I said.

"No, Jeremy. Let's send him a message." Camry's fingers flew around the keyboard. "Whoa...whoa...whoa...hold the phone. Look!"

We all gathered around and stared over her shoulder. Listed under Jeremy's friends was a familiar picture. Camry clicked on it.

It was Carlos standing at the beach, holding the hands of his little girl.

Carlos and Jeremy were friends?

"They live in the same city," said Oliver. "They both knew Amelia. Why wouldn't they be friends?"

"Because Jeremy said he didn't know Carlos," I said. "I'm pretty sure that I asked him multiple times."

I slipped on my headphones and pulled up my interview with Jeremy.

Me: "Do you know Carlos Hermosa?"

Jeremy: "No."

Me: "Detective Ramsey didn't ask about him?"

Jeremy: "No."

Me: "The name doesn't sound familiar at all?"

Jeremy: "No."

Me: "Amelia never mentioned him?"

Jeremy: "She lived with her parents during the time we were dating."

How did I not catch that the first time around? If Jeremy had no idea who Carlos was, then how would he know he was Amelia's neighbor?

In short: Jeremy Wang lied to me.

EPISODE TWENTY-THREE

The Motive

I had no idea what time it was exactly, but the sky had turned a metallic grey with a blush hue and I knew we were closing in on morning. We were still occupying the dining room, running on pure adrenaline. Hazel went to bed hours ago, leaving us to feed ourselves.

We ordered pizza.

"Y-you need to come at this from a different angle." Austin said from the ground. Sometime after midnight, he announced that he thought better when he was vertical and laid down with his hands clasped over his chest, like he was occupying a coffin. "Th-the police have tried the same narrative for the last ten years and we still don't know what happened."

Good point.

Camry grabbed a slice of cold pepperoni. "What if I disappeared tomorrow and all you had to go off of was what I had done this past week. What if you knew I went to Pirates Cove, but you didn't know why I went there, you'd assume I went there to hike."

Oliver sat up straighter. "I know where you're going with this. We should take what we know and assume the opposite of what's natural, just to see what we come up with."

Camry blinked. "That's actually not what I was saying."

"Assume the opposite of what makes sense?" I stepped over

Austin. "That's brilliant."

"Oh...you're welcome," Camry sang.

I erased the daily menu board Hazel had hung in the dining room. "Let's make a list of facts. Here." I handed the chalk to Camry. "You write while I talk and sign."

Facts:

-Amelia Clark is gone.

-There was saliva mixed with her blood.

-Blake Kirkland took the video.

-Scottydogoo posted the video to YouTube.

-Blake Kirkland is dead (we'd found his obituary online).

-Amelia left her job on October 6.

-Amelia and Oliver had a date October 10, but she never showed up.

-Jeremy Wang was in Austin.

-Jeremy Wang lied about knowing Carlos.

-Amelia parked in the visitor parking spot on October 10.

-The last reported sighting was October 10 at six fifteen p.m. Amelia withdrew one hundred dollars from a bank in Orcutt.

"I think we can assume she was on her way to meet Oliver," I said and signed. "She was dressed up."

"W-what about the apple?" asked Austin from the floor. "H-how does that factor in?"

"We have no idea," I said. "I confronted Carlos and he threw a cart at a candy display. It could have been him or not."

Oliver helped himself to a slice of cheese pizza, wiped the grease from his hands and signed. "If we're going against the obvious. What if it was Jeremy?"

"We hadn't talked to Jeremy before the apple," I said.

"He sure didn't seem surprised when we told him about the podcast, though," said Camry. "If your ex-girlfriend went missing and suddenly these two *hotties* show up in your office and want to interview you, wouldn't you be at least taken aback?"

Good point.

I drummed my fingers on the table. We had made a mess in

Hazel's dining room. Scraps of paper on the floor, two pizza boxes strewn across the table, paper plates and greasy wadded up napkins. It reminded me a little bit of what a mess Jeremy's office was when we visited him, which gave me a thought. "What if the girl with Jeremy at CVS was Penny?"

"Oooh," Camry said. "And the plot thickens!"

"Pull up the video."

"Aye, aye." She sat behind the computer and opened the video, while I found Penny's LinkedIn account on my computer. We all gathered around and compared the girl in the video to Penny's profile.

The surveillance video only gave us two good shots of the blonde's face, while the LinkedIn picture was of Penny ten years and many husbands ago. We needed another defining feature to be able to say the blonde was in fact Penny.

Aha!

Weight and hair length may fluctuate through the years, but height will remain the same. I rose to my toes, giving myself another two inches, and held up a hand to about where Jeremy stood in comparison to me when I had on my Converse Wedges. My head came to the bottom of his breast pocket. When standing next to Penny, she was barely taller than me *with* the extra two inches. Which would put her about five foot two or five foot three.

Which coincidently, thanks to the height measurement by the entrance of CVS, made Penny the same height as the mystery blonde. This coupled with Amelia crawling on the floor gave me reason to believe: "That girl is a young Penny."

"Th-that's a big accusation," said Austin.

Camry squinted at the screen. "Now that you point it out, I can see it."

I started pacing again, turning this information around in my mind again and again and again until it all clicked into place. "Jeremy said he'd hooked up with a girl who turned out to be crazy, that's why he went on a business trip. If this video is the day before he left, and he was buying condoms with Penny, then *she's* our crazy girl. Think about it!" My mouth was moving faster than my hands, and I couldn't keep up. I stopped to face Oliver so he could read my lips. "Amelia and Jeremy hooked up the week before the gala. If Penny *Scott* had a crush on Jeremy then she'd have the motive to post the video. She was jealous of Amelia. She wanted to humiliate her and get her out of the picture so she could move in on Jeremy."

I went to the chalkboard and wrote *suspects* in big blocky lettering under our facts list. "We have Jeremy, Carlos, Janet, Penny, *and* Richard, since he lied about Janet's whereabouts that week."

EPISODE TWENTY-FOUR

Penny Scott

We parked behind Target and waited for Penny to show up to work. I knew she was coming in today. Austin's cousin's girlfriend worked part-time at Target, and she looked at the daily schedule to confirm when Penny would be in next.

Austin had an arsenal of good contacts.

Penny arrived at 9:50 a.m. in a maroon minivan with stick figures stuck to the back window. The big one was Penny. The three smaller ones must have been her children. All that was left of Mr. McDonald (or Lin or Green) was half a leg.

Camry and I jumped out of the car like cops about to catch a perp and caught Penny before she walked in. "Can we ask you a few follow-up questions before you start work?" I said in lieu of a hello.

Penny clutched her chest. "You scared me. My gosh. Where did you come from?"

"I'm parked over there." I cocked a thumb.

"Oh. Okay. Is this about the aloe vera rub? I promise you I didn't know anything about the class action lawsuit until after I gave you samples,"

"What lawsuit?" Camry pushed past me. "I rubbed that stuff all over my face!"

Penny's eyes grew about an inch in diameter. "It's a foot and hand rub. Why would you put it on your face?"

"Because I couldn't remember where it went." Camry clawed

at her neck. "Is that why my skin has been burning all morning?"

"The reaction only lasts a few months." She pulled out a tub of lotion out of her bag. "Here. This should help."

"A few months!"

I nudged Camry out of the way. We were not there to talk about aloe rub—although that was unfortunate. I watched Camry lather her face in that green goo this morning. "I'm here to talk about the email address Scottydog00. Does it sound familiar?" I held up the recorder.

Penny looked from Camry to me. "I can't talk." She turned to leave and Camry jumped in front of her to block the entrance, even though I had specifically told her on the car ride over that we were not going to bombard Penny, nor were we going to do anything crazy like block the entrance to Target, prohibiting her from getting away.

Clearly, she and I had to work on our communication skills.

"This is your chance to share your side of the story," I said with as much compassion as I could muster.

Penny looked around to be sure no one was listening then heaved a sigh, sagging her shoulders. "It wasn't supposed to go that far," she said barely above a whisper. "It was just a stupid prank."

"Then why did you send the video to all the employees of Direct Dental?"

Penny began to cry. It had less effect this time around. "I was immature and jealous. How was I supposed to know she'd go missing one week later?"

"Why were you jealous?" I asked.

She ran a finger under her eyes to save the mascara from spilling down her cheeks. "It's stupid. She was with Jeremy and, like, she didn't even appreciate what she had."

"What about Blake Kirkland?"

"He moved away and stopped talking to me. He was mad I posted the video and then, like, he died." She paused to sniff up a snot bubble. "But *he's* the one who took it and sent it to me. He's the one who shared it first. It's not my fault."

Camry thunked her forehead with the heel of her hand. "You post a humiliating video for millions to see without permission from the person *in* the video, or from the person who *took* the video, and now one person is dead and another is likely dead and it's not your fault? You think it's all some crazy coincidence?"

"It was just a joke!" Penny blurted out. "How was I supposed to know so many people would watch it?"

Camry turned around and gave me a she's-nuts look then walked back to the car.

"It's not my fault," Penny said to me, pleading with her eyes. "I'm sure Blake would have died anyway, and Millie obviously had problems."

"Perhaps, but if Amelia so obviously had problems, then why not reach out to her and ask if you could help instead?"

Penny faltered. "I...I...I mean, it was just a stupid joke."

"What were you hoping to accomplish by posting it?"

"I don't know." She played with the hoop earrings dangling from her ears. "I thought maybe Jeremy would see how crazy Millie was, or maybe she'd lose her job. Look, if I could take it back I would."

"Then why haven't you removed the video?"

Penny threw her hands up. "That's the problem. I can't! My account has been hacked."

I could hear Camry whistling behind me, I imagined she was inspecting the sky.

"You *could* have taken it down as soon as you heard about her disappearance," I said.

"No! That's the thing. I couldn't!" Penny's breathing quickened. "The day I heard they found her car I went to take the video down and someone had hacked the account and I couldn't get in!"

Camry stopped whistling and returned to the conversation. "Did you try the recovery questions? Contact YouTube?"

Penny shrugged her shoulders. "I didn't know what to do. It just said that my password no longer worked."

"So you did nothing?" Camry said.

"It's not my—"

"Fault," Camry finished for her. "Right, got it." She turned around and gave me another she's-nuts look.

Nuts or not, if she were telling the truth then there was someone else out there who didn't want that video to go away.

But who and why?

"Do the police know it was you who posted the video?" I asked Penny.

"Aren't they the ones who told you? Detective LeClare? She's the one who figured it out."

"No. We had an anonymous tip," I said. "Very anonymous."

Camry went back to whistling.

"Does Jeremy know?" I asked.

"Not that I'm aware of." She paused to suck in a shaky breath. She was trembling and I felt a tinge of sadness for Penny. She made a bad judgment call. Even if she wouldn't admit it, she blamed herself. It was written all over her face.

Penny Scott/Green/Lin/McDonald felt guilty.

Hopefully someone listening to this story would learn from her mistake.

"When was the last time you spoke to Jeremy?" I asked.

"We hooked up before he went to Texas. He stopped talking to me after he got back."

"Do you remember going to CVS with him right before he left?"

She blew out a breath. "That sounds familiar."

I'll be damned.

"Wait, that's not right." Penny wrapped an escaped tendril of hair behind her ear. "I did actually talk to Jeremy the day after you interviewed me. I saw him at Melba's Diner eating breakfast. I said hi. He said hi. That's the first time we had spoken to each other since Millie disappeared."

Jeremy was at Melba's Diner the morning we were waiting for him. That explained why he wasn't in the office. Not ground breaking news, but something.

"When was the last time you spoke to Carlos Hermosa?" I asked.

"This morning," she said to my surprise. "Our daughters are in the same class." She readjusted her purse on her shoulder. "That's actually who Jeremy was having breakfast with that morning at Melba's Diner. I thought it was funny since we'd just talked about the both of them the day before."

Hold on. Jeremy and Carlos together. I guess Jeremy did know about the podcast before we met him.

EPISODE TWENTY-FOUR

Amelia's Cell Phone

We were back at Hazel's before noon. While we were gone, Oliver read a message sent to the *Missing or Murdered* Facebook page from Todd Erickson, a former classmate of Amelia who had a "strange encounter" with her the week she disappeared. Oliver thought the story checked out, and I set up a Skype interview with Todd for later.

But first, nap.

It had been an emotionally taxing day and I was working on very little sleep. My head was a fog, my limbs felt like Jell-O, and my eyelids were heavy. I walked up the stairs and flung open the door.

"Ugh." I kicked a pile of Camry's dirty clothes out of the way and maneuvered through her mess, which had managed to creep over to my side of the room.

Normally, this would have driven me insane, but I didn't have the energy to care.

I face planted into bed and didn't move for the next twenty minutes.

It was called a power nap.

Studies showed a quick snooze midday could revitalize the body. Twenty minutes later and I didn't feel particularly revitalized. More so like a drunken zombie. But if I didn't get up then, I may have slept until Tuesday.

When I walked downstairs, Oliver was sprawled out on the couch, asleep. Camry was curled up on the chair, asleep. Austin had his head on the table in the dining room, asleep. Hazel was sitting on the sofa in the den with a book on her lap, asleep.

Careful not to wake anyone, I took my laptop to the upstairs closet, set up my recording equipment and called the number Todd provided. On the third ring he answered. We exchanged pleasantries. *Hi, my name is Liv. I'm Todd. How are you? Good and you?* I asked him to say a few things to test the sound quality and he recited the alphabet—as most people did. Todd had a nasally voice. I pictured him with glasses, slicked hair, and a pocket protector.

I started with my go-to first question. "Tell me your name, a little bit about yourself, and how you knew Amelia Clark."

"My name is Todd Erickson. I grew up in Santa Maria, and I now live in Thousand Oaks, California and work as a biochemist at a pharmaceutical company here. Millie and I went to high school together. We had all the same classes for almost four years, and we even went to Homecoming Junior and Senior year."

This was the first person I'd talked to who actually interacted with Amelia in high school. "What was she like back then?" I asked.

"She was nice. Really smart. Really pretty. I had a massive crush on her, but she wasn't interested in a relationship. Millie played soccer, basketball, and she was on the tennis team for a couple of years. She wore her letterman's jacket every day, no matter how hot it was. She didn't like chickens, and she was good at math. That's about all I remember. Truth is, I didn't know her that well. She was pretty shy."

Well, shoot. I'd hoped for more insight. Seemed no one *knew* Amelia, aside from Jeremy. But he lied to us, so I have no idea if his account of her was true or not.

I glanced over the notes Oliver wrote down. He had impeccable penmanship. As if he used a ruler to trace each letter. "You had an encounter with Millie the week she disappeared," I read. "Can you tell me more about that?"

"Sure. I managed The Cellular Store in the mall while I was in college, and she came in. She'd lost a lot of weight and I almost didn't recognize her. When I approached her she immediately started talking about wearing foil. To be honest, I didn't see the video until yesterday. So I had no idea what she was talking about. The entire interaction had me uneasy."

"Why?"

"I didn't know what to make of the way she was acting. She was on edge from the minute she got there. I thought she might be on drugs. She wanted to cancel her cell plan and give back the phone. When I told her she couldn't cancel, she punched the counter, threw a display case, and accused one of the customers of taking video of her. It was really bizarre. If I didn't know Millie, I would have called the police."

This was the first I'd heard of Amelia lashing out. But, of course, there's the gala video so it wasn't a far-fetched idea she would "go mad" in public. Dr. Deb Naidoo said Amelia had an incident at a cell store. Her story had been spot on. Which had me asking the question: Was Janet home the week Amelia went missing?

"Did she say why she wanted to cancel her cell plan?" I asked him.

"That's the weird part. She said that she had found herself in a relationship with an egotistical maniac who was paying for her phone. I couldn't cancel the line because she wasn't the main account holder."

"Please, please tell me she gave you the name of the egotistical maniac." I crossed my fingers.

"No she didn't."

Dang it.

"*But,* after she ran out I did a search and couldn't find her name on any account."

I rose to my knees. "Did you ever tell the police? They should have been able to find out who paid for her phone. I'm almost positive they pulled her cell records."

"I never talked to the cops. When I heard she had disappeared, I figured she was strung out and left. My sister, who lives in Santa Maria, is down here visiting me for the weekend and she told me about the Aluminum Woman video and the podcast. So that's why I contacted you."

"Are you sure there were no accounts with her name on it?"

"I'm positive, but that doesn't mean anything. A lot of people add lines without saying whom the line belongs to."

I decided to play devil's advocate. "Do you think she was on her parent's account?" Up until a year ago, I was still on my dad's cell plan. Not a far-fetched idea.

"Have you ever met Richard Clark?" he asked with a laugh. "He's one of the nicest guys in town. There's no way she was talking about her father. I think it was an ex-boyfriend."

"Why ex-boyfriend?"

"Because she said she *found* herself in a relationship with an egotistical maniac. Seemed like something you'd say about a boyfriend not a father."

True.

The only ex-boyfriend we knew of was Jeremy Wang. But why would Amelia refuse to let her employer know she was dating Jeremy *but* be okay with entering into a cell plan together? Sure, they were together for a year, but they'd been broken up for three months at the time.

"Todd, do you remember the make and model of the cell phone Amelia had?"

"It was an older flip phone if I remember correctly."

"Do you mean older like six months? A year? Two years? Something straight out of the nineties? Can you be more definitive?"

"I'd say it was five or six years old. It wasn't a model that we carried anymore. You've got to remember, 2008 was the year the iPhone came out."

No, I didn't remember. It felt like the iPhone had been around forever. "When you start a new plan do you get a new phone?"

"Typically, yes."

"If Amelia's ex-boyfriend had added her to his line, would she have gotten a new number and phone?"

"Not necessarily. If she were with the same carrier, she could have kept both her phone and her number and be added to a different account."

I felt like I was on the cusp of pertinent information here, if I could only ask the right question. "And you said that you searched the accounts and didn't find Amelia Clark anywhere?" I confirmed.

"Yes, that's correct."

"Would she have shown up in the system if she'd cancelled her account recently?"

"Yes, it would have shown up, but it would have said cancelled. They kept account information in case customers wanted to come back."

"So..." I was thinking out loud. "If Amelia was added to an account, but she had a different cell provider before, could she have kept her phone and number?"

Todd paused. "*No*," he said with little confidence. "I think she would have gotten a new phone, just because we had our own SIM cards."

"And Amelia wanted you to take the phone."

"Yes, she was manic about it, too. She acted like the phone was holding her back. Like she was afraid of it. It's weird to say it out loud, but that's what I was thinking at the time."

"Do you think it's safe to say that Amelia was on someone's plan and, based on the age of her phone, that she'd been on the plan for a long time?"

"I'd say that would be a safe assumption," he said. "Yes."

Which begged the question: Was there an egotistical maniac we had yet to learn about?

Or had we already met him?

EPISODE TWENTY-FIVE

The Verge of Discovery

"I need to speak to Richard and Janet because this is getting out of hand," I said to Hazel. We were in the kitchen doing the dishes. She was washing. I was drying. Everyone else was in the living room watching the news coverage of Brinkley Douglas—the body they found in the park. They had a suspect, but I could only concentrate on one dead person at a time.

Hazel gave me a clean dish to dry. "Why don't you go over there and tell them the stories you've heard?"

"I would, but I don't have any real facts, just theories. I don't want to come across as if I'm accusing them." I added the dried dish to the pile and grabbed another from Hazel. "I don't have the tact for that, and Camry sure as hell doesn't."

"I haven't known you for long, Liv Olsen, but what I do know for sure is that you've got plenty of tact. You've got plenty of oomph, too. Whatever oomph means."

"It means...*oomph*. I'm not sure. I'd never used the term before Mara told me I didn't have it, now I use it all the time." I took a clean cup from Hazel, dried it off and added it to the stack. "I think it means drive, gumption...*balls*."

"I never understood why people say 'balls' like it's a good thing." She handed me a pot. "Who wants balls? A swift kick to the gonads and you're down. Balls make you vulnerable. Weak. When John used to complain I'd tell him to grow a vagina and suck it up."

I laughed. "Fine, I guess you could say I'm vagina-less then."

Errrr, that doesn't sound right.

Hazel emptied the sink water, dried her hands, and leaned against the counter. "Now you listen here, young lady." She shook a damp dishtowel at me. "Would a person without oomph quit their job and drive four and a half hours to stay with a stranger? Would an oomph-less person dump all their money into a missing-person case? A missing person they never met? Would an oomph-less person drive around town, stalking people at Target or CPA offices, spend their nights locked in a closet, working on a radio show?"

"Podcast," I said.

"Podcast, radio show. It doesn't matter. You my dear have more vagina than anyone I've ever met."

This was the sweetest compliment I'd ever received.

"And trust me," she continued. "Janet Clark is a weird cookie. I wouldn't discount any stories heard about that woman."

I removed the soaked apron tied around my waist. "I know you said that you don't see Janet around town, and that she stays inside her house. But, honestly, when was the last time anyone actually *saw* Janet Clark in the last year?"

Hazel filled the teakettle and put it on the burner. "I can't say. Why?"

"Curious that's all. She feels like an enigma."

"She's a crazy enigma is what she is."

I pulled a chair up to the counter and used it as a stepstool to reach the mugs in the cabinet. Short person problems. Hazel poured hot water into my cup and I dropped a chamomile bag in. I watched as the water turned to a murky orange. "People said the same thing about Amelia."

"Say what? That she was a weird cookie or a crazy enigma?"

"That she was crazy." I wrapped my hands around my mug to get warm. "And maybe she was. Maybe she was sick and skipped town. Maybe she was a little crazy. Maybe we're all a little crazy." I took a sip. The warm chamomile soothed my throat. I'd done a lot of talking in the last twenty-four hours. "But for both women to be weird cookies makes you wonder."

"Makes you wonder what?" Hazel asked.

"Makes you wonder if they were living with an egotistical maniac..."

Holy crap.

That's it!

I set my mug on the counter and walked out to the living room.

"What's wrong?" Hazel followed me.

Oliver was stretched out in a chair. Camry was curled up on the couch, wrapped in a crochet blanket. Austin was sitting on the floor in front of the coffee table. Everyone's eyes were glued to the television. Maybe we'd have to look at Brinkley Douglas for season two.

I stood at the front of the room. "I'm going to the Clark's house right now."

Camry checked her watch. "It's almost eight?"

"I want to talk to them." I pounded my fist into my palm. "And I've got enough vagina to do it!" I grabbed my keys, my bag, my recorder and the pepper spray. I'm ready.

"Did she say 'vagina'?" I heard Oliver ask as I closed the front door behind me.

"Was it necessary for *all* of us to come?" Camry asked from the backseat, squished between Oliver and Austin.

I looked in the rearview mirror. "All I said was that I'm going to the Clark's house and you all piled in the car."

"This is all rather invigorating," said Hazel from the front passenger seat.

"The black jumpsuit wasn't necessary though," I said to her. "I'm going to talk to them not rob them."

Hazel flattened out her black velvet suit, the one she changed into before we left. "It's important to dress for any occasion, dear."

I parked in front of the vacant lot at the end of the street. Camry and I left the podcasting posse in the car and knocked on the

Clark's door. The lights were off. The blinds were drawn. We could see the glow of the television through the front door window but there was no answer. Just like last time.

We went back to the car and waited. Someone would have to come home eventually.

The windows fogged enough for Austin to scribe his name. I turned on the defroster. "Can we all breathe a little less?"

"I can hold my breath for almost a minute," said Camry.

Austin stared at her in wonder. "Th-that's amazing."

"When I was a girl, I could hold my breath for two minutes," said Hazel.

Before I knew it, we were all holding our breath.

Oliver won with two minutes and ten seconds.

"I want a re-match," said Camry. "Austin messed me up."

"H-How did I mess you up?"

"You kept looking at me."

"S-s-sorry."

"Car lights!" Oliver said and we all ducked down.

A silver Chevy truck zoomed past us and pulled into the Clark's garage, right beside an old station wagon with wooden side panels.

I grabbed the recorder and turned to Camry. "Let's do this."

CHAPTER TWENTY-SIX

The Damaged Footage

Camry and I stood at the Clark's front door. We could still see the glow of the television, but for the first time, we could hear the accompanied audio. It sounded like a basketball game. Camry knocked.

No answer.

We waited for a while, knocked once more, and just as we were about to give up, the door opened.

It was Richard. He had on shorts, a faded Dodgers shirt, and tube socks. His eyes were tired and his smile flat. "What can I do for you two this late at night?"

"Sorry to bother you at home." I had the recorder at my waist, pointed at Richard. "There are a few details which have surfaced that we wanted to discuss with you."

He was not amused, and I felt a bit panicky. "Right now?"

You've got this, I told myself for the zillionth time. Calm down. "Was Amelia on your cell plan?"

"She was, why?"

Oh crap!

This, of course, proved nothing. But it sure did cast a shadow of doubt on the Clark's character, because I was 90 percent positive Richard Clark was the egotistical maniac Amelia was referring to.

Richard eyed the recorder. "I told you I'm not doing an interview for your show."

"Yes, you did." I didn't move. If I hid the recorder or counted on my lavalier mic to pick up his voice, the audio could be distorted, and this was important. "Was your soil ever tested for contamination?" These were the little questions I wanted answered before I could get into his or Janet's alleged mistruths. I had a sinking suspicion he wouldn't be happy once I asked.

"No. People are overly dramatic about everything," he said with a roll of his eyes. "The soil is *fine* around here; the whole thing was blown out of proportion."

"Did the oil company offer to test your soil?"

For an instant, his gaze darkened. "No."

Why would they offer to test everyone's soil but his? Is what I was thinking, but what I asked was, "Did you know Jeremy Wang and Amelia were dating?"

"Yes."

"Did Amelia ever introduce you to him?" It dawned on me that I never asked Jeremy if Amelia had ever brought him home. A year was a long time to date someone and not have them meet your parents.

"Put the recorder away," he said, instead of answering the question. "You said you'd be respectful of our family if we let you do this."

"Did you know Carlos and Jeremy were friends?" I asked.

"I don't know, but I'm not answering anything else until you put that recorder away!" Richard caught himself and took a breath. "You're not allowed to use any of my audio without my permission," he said more even toned.

"Actually, I can." Especially now that I suspected Richard Clark played a role in his daughter's disappearance. "But as promised, I will continue to be respectful of all parties involved."

Richard's jaws tightened. "How is recording me against my will respectful?"

"What hotel did you and Janet stay at in San Francisco?" I asked.

"Why is that important? The police already checked."

"Is Janet here? We'd like to speak to her."

"I told you she doesn't want to speak to anyone about anything."

"The problem is we've been told that Janet was in town the week of Amelia's disappearance, and we were also told that Amelia attempted to cancel her cell plan the week she disappeared. She said the reason for cancelling was because the person paying for it was an egotistical maniac. Would you like to speak to that?"

Richard closed his eyes, sucked in a breath through his nose and pushed it out of his mouth. He did this a few times before his eyes snapped open. They'd gone from brown to black. Like I was staring at the devil himself, and all I wanted to do is run. But I couldn't. I wasn't here for me. I was here for Amelia. I was here for Leon. I was here for the truth.

"We're done! No more podcast!" yelled Richard.

"With all due respect, I don't need your permission to continue," I said.

Camry tugged on my sleeve. "Maybe we should go?"

"No." I stood my ground. "I want to speak to Janet, please? It's only fair she has an opportunity to give her side." And I wanted to make sure she was still alive.

"Get off my property before I call the police!"

I rose to my toes. "I want to speak to Janet!"

He slammed the door shut and I stood there in shock.

Well that didn't exactly go as I planned.

Camry pulled me down the driveway by my arm. My heart was slamming against my chest and I felt agitated and icky. Like I needed a bath. Like I'd been hugged by a demon. It was an odd, terrible, uneasy sensation.

"Well, he's nuts," said Camry as we neared the street. "Screw cadaver dogs we need an exorcist."

I stopped at the end of the driveway. "Something isn't right."

"Ya think?"

"No, I mean it. When was the last time anyone saw Janet Clark? She could be dead for all we know. She could be locked inside. She could be locked inside *with* Amelia."

I turned around and glanced at the house. The rhythmic glow of the television played against the drawn blinds and...*what in the world?*

Between a blind slat was a pair of eyes gazing out at us. At *me.* They were too small and feminine to be Richard's. I cut across the grass to get a closer look. The eyes were blue, empty, old, and unblinking. They looked almost fake.

"Janet?" I mouthed.

The blinds shut and the eyes disappeared.

"What is happening around here?" I whispered to myself. Demon dad and mannequin mom. Perhaps Amelia really did run away.

In my periphery, something caught my eye. A blooming lemon tree branch was hanging over the backyard fence.

"Liv," Camry hissed, "I don't feel like dying tonight. Let's get off crazy dad's property."

"Hold on." I picked a lemon from the tree. It was an ugly lemon. Small, squishy, covered in yellow warts and...*morphed.* I run my thumb along the bumpy skin and thought about the contaminated soil and the ugly apple thrown through the window. Wondering what other fruit trees they had back there.

I jumped, catching a fleeting glimpse of the backyard. Trees lined the fence, but I couldn't tell what kind. Another jump and it was still not clear.

Why do I have to be so short!

"Liv," Camry was at my ear, "we need to leave."

No, I needed to see what was over the fence, but to do so I needed at least another foot or... "Go get Oliver."

"No," she said in a furious whisper, red-faced and shaking. I had the sinking suspicion that I may have missed something.

"What's wrong with you?" I whispered.

"You're so quick to replace me with your new boyfriend. Who gives a crap about the stupid *step*sister." She air quoted "step." "Have you noticed that I introduce you as my sister and you make sure everyone knows that I'm your 'step' sister." She air quoted "step" again, and I didn't know why. She *was* my stepsister. "You really think the only reason I asked to help with the podcast was because I *like* podcasts? I don't give a crap about stupid podcasts. I only started listening to them because the big sister I always wanted but never paid attention to me did. You know Austin for ten minutes and now he's working on the show. So is Oliver. You'll make them producers and I'll still be the stepsister." She blinked away a tear. "You don't care about me and you never have. So, fine, replace me with your stupid boyfriend."

I was shocked by her outburst.

But I could only deal with one family drama at a time—and right then, Amelia's egotistical maniac father appeared more pressing. "We can discuss this later," I whispered. "I don't want Oliver to replace you, I want him because he's tall and he can easily see what's on the other side of this fence."

Camry wiped away a tear. "Oh." She sucked in her bottom lip.

Crap. I felt terrible. I grabbed Camry by the hand, about to tell her how much I appreciated her, but the front door opened. Instead of giving my kid *sister* a heart-to-heart, I slapped my hand over her mouth, threw her behind a giant bush and jumped on top of her.

Heart-to-hearts would have to wait for a time when we weren't trespassing.

I watched Richard through the branches, my hand still over Camry's mouth. He was in Birkenstocks and socks, yawning as he watered the grass, acting as if there were nothing amiss in his world. Like it was perfectly normal to water your lawn by hand at nine thirty at night.

Once the grass was soaked, he watered the flowers under the window. Each plant got a good soaking and I could see where this was going. I shoved the recorder into my pants and waited for it.

Water sprayed down on us. I closed my eyes and took it, saying a silent prayer of thanks that my phone was in the car, and made a plea for the safety of the recorder currently shoved in my underwear. Five minutes later, Richard deemed the bush sufficiently soaked. He wrapped the hose around his arm, set it near the garage, and went back inside, slamming the door shut behind him.

The coast was clear.

Or so I hoped.

Camry and I cut through the neighbor's yard. My shoes filled with water and sloshed with each step.

"You're soaked," said Hazel as I slid into the car.

I pulled the recorder from inside my pants. Water dripped out of the speakers. "No! No! No!"

"...and then he went demonic and told us to get off his property..." Camry gave the play-by-play of what happened to Austin. "The door opened and it was Richard. He watered the entire yard, like he was taunting us, daring us to come out, then he hosed us down but we didn't move."

Austin leaned over the seat. "I-is the recorder okay?"

I was holding down the power button and the speakers frizzed and sparked and the light wouldn't come on. I felt faint. "It's broken. Richard Clark went nuts on us. Confirmed Amelia was on his cell plan. And now that footage is gone."

"What did she say?" Oliver asked Camry.

She wrung out her hair. "The recorder won't work, and Richard Clark is a whack-o."

"Give it to me." Oliver snatched the recorder from my tight grasp. I watched with hope, thinking he'd do some kind of Tech Genius voodoo, but all he did was push the power button. "It won't turn on."

"I know!"

"Drive back to the house right now," he said. "I think if I disassembled the whole thing, drain the water, and let it air dry overnight, it might work again. But we need to do it fast."

I was halfway down the street before he even finished. Driving like a mad woman. It was an emergency! The lemon fell off my lap and rolled across the center console over to Hazel's seat. I'd completely forgotten about it.

"Well that's one ugly lemon," Hazel said, holding it up for inspection.

"Liv stole it form the Clark's backyard," said Camry.

"Now why would you go and do something like that?"

I turned right on University Drive and passed The Santa Maria Way Apartments.

"Someone was staring at us through the window," I said. "Then I saw the lemon tree and wondered if they had ugly apples back there. If they did, maybe Richard broke your window." I stopped at a red light and watched the green bulb, willing it to turn on.

"Richard Clark would never do such a thing," Hazel said. "He's such a nice man."

Camry leaned forward so her head was between our seats. "If you saw the Richard Clark we did, you'd have a different opinion. That man is crazy and guilty of something."

"If-if he was guilty why would he throw an apple from his *own* backyard through your w-window?" Austin asked.

Good point.

I turned on Bradly Ave and thought about the eyes in the window. I thought about Richard's outburst. I thought about Amelia's outburst at the cell store. I thought about Jeremy's lies. I thought about Penny's lies. I thought about the look on Carlos' face when we told him about the apple. I thought about Austin's advice to look at things from a different angle.

What if the apple through the window wasn't a warning?

What if it was a clue?

Detective LeClare said it was likely someone we had talked to.

Carlos or Richard.

We thought Carlos told Jeremy.

Richard likely told Janet.

Carlos, Jeremy, Richard, or Janet.

I slammed on the breaks. Austin crashed into the back of my seat.

"Dude, wear your seatbelt," said Oliver.

Hazel touched my arm. "Liv, what is it?"

"We need to look in the backyard right now." I made a U-turn and Austin slammed against the back window.

"Seatbelt," said Camry.

"The sooner I can take this recorder apart the better chance you have at saving it," said Oliver.

Crap. He was right. I slammed on the breaks. Austin crashed against the seat.

"Why do you need to look in the backyard?" Hazel asked.

I pulled over and switched on my hazard lights. "What if the apple is a clue and not a warning? What if the apple was meant to lead us to the backyard?"

Austin rubbed his head. "B-but what are you going to do? Go up to the front door and ask to l-look in the backyard?"

Camry wrung out her socks. "That'll work. I'm sure he'll invite us right in. Bake us cookies. Give us a tour. Brutally beat us with a butcher knife. It'll be fun. Great idea. Let's do it."

"H-how would he beat you w-with a butcher knife?"

"Did he say butcher knife?" Oliver asked me.

"Whatever!" Camry threw her soaked socks onto the floor. "*Stab* us with a butcher knife. Honestly, you people are too literal."

The most awful thought crept into my mind, a theory so horrendous that I couldn't quite vocalize it. At least not yet.

"He's such a nice man." Hazel was still stuck on this. If my recorder weren't waterlogged, she'd think differently.

Oliver got my attention. *"If you think there's something in the backyard then you need to check it out before Richard Clark has a chance to get rid of any incriminating evidence,"* he signed, which made me think Oliver too had a horrendous theory about what or *who* was in the backyard.

Camry pointed to Oliver. "What'd he say?"

"He said we're going back to the Clark's house." I shoved the car into drive. "Buckle up, Austin."

EPISODE TWENTY-SEVEN

Heart

I parked in front of the vacant lot, unbuckled my seatbelt, shoved the pepper spray in my back pocket, grabbed my phone and turned to address the backseat crew. "I shouldn't be more than a minute, I'm going sneak into the Clark's next-door neighbor's backyard—it's vacant—and look over the fence."

"If Richard catches you he'll call the police," said Camry. "Or behead you. Man's crazy. Also, you can't see over the fence, shorty."

"I'll jump," I said.

Austin shot me an incredulous look. "J-jumping is your idea of being sneaky?"

Oliver placed a hand on my soaked shoulder. "I have no idea what anyone is saying, but I'm coming with you." He unbuckled his seatbelt and opened the door.

"Me too." Camry climbed out after him.

"I-I'm in."

Hazel slid into the driver's seat and clutched the wheel with both hands. "I'll stay here and drive the getaway car."

"We're not doing anything illegal," I said. "But just in case, keep it running."

The four of us huddled in front of the headlights. A shiver ran down my damp back and Oliver gave me his sweatshirt. It was about twelve sizes too big, but I appreciated the gesture and rolled the sleeves up to my wrists.

"We're not all going up to his door," I said and signed. "Richard is already on edge and the four of us showing up will only make it worse. Camry and I will go. Oliver and Austin, you two peek into the backyard and take video and pictures. See if there's a honey crisp apple tree. If there is, grab an apple, but don't go in the yard. We have nothing factual to give the police if they ask why we trespassed. Just reach over the fence and grab it."

"No," Oliver interrupted. "I'm going with you. You two," he pointed to Camry and Austin. "You go look in the backyard."

"But—" I started to protest.

"Trust me, I've got an idea," he signed.

I could hear the basketball game playing in the background and turned on the recording app on my phone. The sound quality would suck but it was better than nothing. Oliver knocked and I hid my phone in the sleeve of his sweatshirt.

"Follow my lead," he signed.

His lead?

Richard opened the door. His eyes were no longer black. His demeanor calmer. I liked this Richard better.

"Hello, how are you doing tonight?" he asked in a tone that implied he was happy to see us.

This man gave me whiplash.

Oliver started signing. *"I am going to sign really fast. This makes people uncomfortable."*

"Okay…good evening…" I said, pretending to interpret. "This is Oliver—" I faltered. What if Leon told Richard about Amelia's date with Oliver *Lewis*? "Um…Oliver…House…He's Oliver House." *Good one, Liv.* Before Oliver came up with this grand plan he should have ran it by me. I was a horrible liar. "He is…"

Oliver was signing so fast I had no idea what he was saying.

Richard huffed a sigh, growing impatient.

"He's…he's the…um… he's the executive producer. He's here to apologize for…for…what happened earlier."

Richard wasn't buying it. "You got a deaf guy working on a podcast?"

"Deaf people can do anything hearing people can do," I said. "He's an Internet star, a famous YouTuber with over five million subscribers."

Oliver grabbed my attention. *"They're at the backyard fence."*

Right.

"Anyway, Oliver House says...that he's sorry for the trouble and to please extend our apologies to Mrs. Clark."

"Who is at the door?" came a voice from inside. A woman appeared from the hallway. Her hair was long and gray. Her face crinkled and pale. She was wrapped in a paisley robe with slippers on her feet. I recognized her from the photograph. I recognized her eyes.

It was Janet Clark.

"Is this about the podcast?" she asked.

Oliver stopped signing.

"Hi, Mrs. Clark," I said after a moment. "I'm Liv Olsen, one of the executive producers on *Missing or Murdered*."

"I gathered that." Janet pulled the belt around her waist tighter. "What I don't understand is why you are at my doorstep this late. Didn't my husband tell you we want nothing to do with this silly radio show?"

"It's a podcast, and it's only going to help shed more light on Amelia's case."

"Nothing you're doing will help find my daughter." She stood behind her husband.

"She's right." Richard draped a protective arm around his wife. "We'd like you to leave."

Janet glared at me. "Please leave," she said.

I gulped, unsure of what to make of Janet Clark and looked to Oliver for help. He *did* have the super human ability to read facial expressions after all.

"They're back at the car," he signed, with no mention of Janet.

Not sure of what else to say or do, I lowered my phone. "We'll leave. I'm sorry to bother you."

"I think we all can agree tonight got a little heated," Richard said.

A little heated?

That's like saying the sun is a little hot.

"We miss our daughter." Richard pulled Janet closer and she leaned into her husband. "It's a hard situation and I hope you can understand."

"Of course," I said. "Good night."

"Good night."

Oliver and I walked back to the car without a word. Hazel was behind the wheel. Austin and Camry were in the backseat. I got in the passenger side and turned around.

"Well?" I asked.

Austin held up a honey crisp apple that looked *exactly* like the one thrown through the window. Which wasn't *exactly* incriminating but it was something.

"Did you see anything else?" I asked.

Camry showed me a picture she'd taken on her phone of pebbles formed in the shape of a heart on the ground. "Where was this?" I asked.

Camry looked as if she's about to be cry. "It's at the base of the apple tree. Looks an awful lot like a makeshift gravestone."

"Also," said and signed Oliver. "Both Janet and Richard are lying."

EPISODE TWENTY-EIGHT

What To Do Now?

Facts:

-We have a picture of pebbles in the shape of a heart.

-We have a deaf guy claiming to have a super-human ability to read body language.

-We have a guy who is stuttering through the story of the time he broke into a vacant house's backyard. With my step—I mean, *little*—sister talking over him.

-We have a twenty-seven-year-old woman, who looks twelve, wearing a sweatshirt that goes to her knees, and has a theory.

-And we have an apple.

It was no wonder Detective LeClare would only speak to us through the one-inch gap between her door and frame. "How did you know my home address?" she asked.

We all looked at each other.

"It's a matter of public record," said Camry. She stood behind me with an emergency blanket wrapped around her shoulders—the one from my roadside kit. "I'm freezing and my shirt is see-through. That's an emergency!" is what she'd said when she ripped open the kit with her teeth.

"Did you ever talk to Dr. Deb Naidoo?" I asked LeClare, to change the subject.

With a sigh of defeat, LeClare stepped outside and closed the door behind her. She had on a Fullerton State University shirt stretched over her belly, a pair of gray sweatpants on and she still looked like she could grace the cover of *Sports Illustrated*. "I've left two messages and sent a colleague to the clinic you said she worked at. She wasn't there,"

Dang it.

"Look, Liv," LeClare said in a way that meant bad news is to follow. "Between you and me and..." she looked around at Hazel, Austin, Oliver, and Camry. "Are you recording this?"

"No," I said. "This is beyond the podcast."

LeClare rocked from side to side. "I don't discount anything you're saying. Richard Clark has always felt too accommodating to me. *Too* nice. *Too* manipulative. I just don't have enough proof to do anything about it."

"What about the cell phone?" I asked.

"Hearsay."

"What about Janet? Have you spoken to her?"

"Many times. She came to the station by herself last week when I asked to speak with her. She's quiet. But from my understanding she's always kept to herself."

"Was it ever verified that she was in San Francisco with Richard?"

"Her name was on the reservations."

"That doesn't mean anything. Did you ever check surveillance footage from the hotel?"

"There wasn't surveillance requested at the time, no."

No? What a major oversight.

"And what about the apple?" Camry held it up by the stem.

"It's a piece of fruit. This proves nothing. My parents have an apple tree. My neighbor has an apple tree. Hell, I might have an apple tree in the backyard for all I know," she said. "Don't you see? I have no *body*. I have no DNA. I have no confession. Without at least two of the three, nothing will happen. *Ever*."

Camry raised her hand. "But you can—"

"I can't run prints on fruit," LeClare cut her off. "The *best* thing you can do for Amelia Clark is what you're doing. This is why

Leon contacted you. Someone here knows something. And that someone has been tightlipped for over a decade. Get the public to care about Amelia. This will force people to start talking. This will pressure the agency to run more DNA tests. I can't do anything with hearsay. Honestly, I really can't do anything without a body."

Then I guess there was no other option than to make sure this podcast was a hit.

EPISODE TWENTY-NINE

An Overnight Failure

On Monday, episode one, "Gone Cold," went live. Within the first twenty-four hours we had a whopping 200 downloads. I reminded myself this was not *Cold in America*, and I was not Mara Lancer, and building an audience took time.

The second episode, "The Suspect," released a week later. Within twenty-four hours we had a grand total of 135 downloads.

I wasn't great at math, but I did know that 135 is less than 200. Downloads should go up each week not down. This was a bad sign. And I made a conscience decision to ignore numbers and trudge forward. Which would be easier if I had interviews scheduled. Leads coming in. Even bogus leads. Where was my spaceship lady?

It was complete radio silence.

On the day before episode three's release, I went to the closet and sat in solitude. I cried. I prayed. I cursed. I crumbled up the show notes and threw them against the wall. I lamented my frustrations to the creepy doll. The podcast was a complete flop. I'd failed Amelia. I'd failed Leon. I'd failed Camry. I'd failed my podcast posse. I'd failed myself.

I was a complete and total failure.

Mad, I kicked Leon's box and it fell to its side. I couldn't help but wonder what our investigation would have been like if he hadn't died, if he'd been around to translate these stupid notes.

I yanked a book and flipped it open.

For example, on December 18, 2009, he wrote:

*Thiwlimg bach I...If? Riwanl pluwdmmu lile a fulle...*and a long paragraph of the same gibberish.

What does this mean?

"What does this mean?" I yelled to the ceiling, holding the notebook open.

It didn't answer back. Instead, the closet door opened and Oliver poked his head in.

"You've been in here for a while," he said.

I checked the time. It had been about four hours.

"I'm pouting."

"Would you like company?"

"Not really." This misery didn't want company, but Oliver took a seat anyway, wedging himself between an old dollhouse and me.

"Find anything new?" He pointed to Leon's notebook on my lap.

"No. I can't read gibberish."

Oliver grabbed the notebook and ran his finger under the lines. "Thinking back...I wonder...if Richard played me like a fiddle?" he mumbled.

"Can you read this?"

"About every third letter then I fill in the rest." He returned his attention to the notebook. "Looks like Leon had the same feelings about Richard that Detective LeClare has."

I hugged my knees to my chest. "What can I do about it?"

"Honestly, I have no idea. Sucks to think that Richard Clark could be guilty and walk."

Sucks was a good word for it.

Injustice was another good word, too.

What a complete disaster this turned out to be.

"S-sorry to interrupt," said Austin appearing at the door. "But w-we've got a problem."

"We have lots of problems," I said. "Which one are you referring to?"

He showed me his iPad. It was open to the CinnaMann Bakery Facebook Page and a post dated October 9, the day before the first episode was released.

To My Loyal Customers,

As many of you know our beloved daughter, Amelia Clark went missing on October 10, 2008. Janet and I worked tirelessly with local law enforcement to find our Amelia and bring her home safely. Unfortunately, this still hasn't happened. Recently a group of amateur podcasters has taken interest in Amelia's case. Janet and I were supportive at first. We thought the exposure would bring us the answers we've been praying for. Sadly, these podcasters have taken Amelia's story and twisted it for their own financial gain. There is very little information in the case, and once the Missing or Murdered producers realized this, they filled in the gaps with conspiracies and manufactured "facts." They are using our tragedy to line their own pockets. They're making a mockery of our community. We ask you to please not support them. We are living every parent's worst nightmare and have been for many years. We appreciate your prayers.

Sincerely,
Your Local Baker, Richard Clark.

Below was a picture of Richard and Amelia at the bakery. She looked to be about sixteen. Both of them had on chef jackets and megawatt smiles. They looked happy, but knowing what I did, I wasn't sure Amelia was happy. Her body language was...was...*what the heck am I doing looking at this?* I handed the iPad to Oliver. "What do you make of Amelia's body language in this picture?"

"She's smiling but pulling away from him. There's no affection on her part and, *dang*, there's over six hundred comments and it's been shared almost seven hundred times."

"A-a-a-nd everyone is supportive of the Clarks," said Austin. "Y-you need to release a statement."

He was right.

I pulled up Facebook on my laptop and shared Richard's post to the *Missing or Murdered* page. Before I posted it, I wrote a six-paragraph response talking about our encounter at his home, his black eyes, the question on whether Janet was in town or not, about Leon and LeClare's reservations, and about Todd's encounter. I signed it with "Your Local Podcasters, Liv Olsen."

Then highlighted the entire thing and clicked *delete*.

Venting frustrations online wouldn't do anything but prove Richard right. Instead, I typed: *There's a reason the Clark's don't want you to listen, and it has nothing to do with manufactured facts*, I inserted the link to the first episode and posted it.

There. I dusted my hands off.

Guess we'd have to wait and see what happened next.

EPISODE THIRTY

Press Conference

I woke the next morning to Camry screaming. She flipped on the light and danced around the room. It was probably a spider, again. I twisted myself more deeply into the sheets and fell back asleep. She could kill this one herself.

"We're sexy?" Camry jumped on my bed. "Sexy! Sexy! Sexy!"

"Whaaa?" I shielded my eyes from the overhead light and peeked at the clock. It was three forty-five a.m.

"We're number sixty on the iTunes podcast chart." She shoved her phone up to my face. I blinked to focus and...

"We're number sixty!" I threw the covers off and jumped with her. "We're number sixty!"

Hazel appeared at the door in her nightgown and curlers. "What the frog is happening in here? It's not even four a.m."

"We're number sixty!" Camry and I screamed in unison.

"Not sure what that means but, yay!" We helped Hazel up to the bed and the three of us jumped, holding hands, chanting "sixty!"

We did this until Camry checked her phone and declared, "We're number fifty-nine!"

Then we jumped and chanted, "Fifty-nine!" laughing, and cheering, and crying tears of joy.

By the time the sun rose, we were number forty-five and climbing.

* * *

Missing or Murdered took off and made the New & Noteworthy section of iTunes. Because of this, Audio Ninja was able to land us a sponsor, an energy drink called *Force!*. Never heard of it before. Oliver drove to Wal-Mart and bought a case. The five of us toasted a can, took a sip and spewed it out almost immediately.

"Blah, this tastes like watered down Sunny Delight," Oliver said, wiping his tongue with a napkin.

"More like vegetable oil." I gulped water to erase the aftertaste. No such luck.

"This is offensive to my taste buds," said Hazel.

Austin ripped open a tin of mints and shoved a handful into his mouth.

"I don't mind it so much." Camry held the can to her nose. "Smells like puppies and winter."

"Ha, ha, you're hilarious," I said.

"D-did I miss something?"

"No!" I said before Camry could tell the story. "But since you like it so much, Camry, you record the fifteen-second pre-roll spot and sixty-second mid-episode spot. But don't describe it as puppies and winter."

"Hold on! You're going to let *me* touch a microphone? Me? Little ole' me?" Camry fanned her face and clutched the can like it was a trophy. "I can't believe this is happening. First, I want to thank Starbucks for scorching what's left of my taste buds allowing me to stomach this drink."

Austin gave Camry a round of applause.

"Don't encourage her," I said to him.

"...and I want to thank my parents..."

"Sh-shut up!" Austin said.

"Geez, I was just kidding." Camry sat down with her *Force!* and pouted.

"No-no not you." Austin was scrolling through his phone. "My s-source says—" We all knew his source was his dad, but played along. "—after they received an anonymous tip, the Santa Maria PD obtained a search warrant of the Clark's home."

Anonymous tip?

Camry smacked the table. "That's unbelievable, we give Detective *I could be a Victoria's Secret model* everything we have and she goes with an anonymous tip instead?"

"What did the tip say?" Oliver asked.

"H-he said that Amelia was buried in the backyard under the apple tree."

"Oh my gosh..." I sank down on a chair and buried my head in my hands. Deep down I knew Amelia was dead. But there was a part of me holding on to hope that she wasn't. I didn't realize how big that hope was until then. Between the rocks in a heart, and Richard's outburst, and the apple through our window matching the apples found in the Clark's backyard, and Richard refusing to have his soil tested, and then an anonymous tip stating what I thought to be true... "Amelia really is dead," I said in a whisper.

"Oh you sweet thing, we sort of already knew that. Right?" Hazel said.

"I guess so." It hurt to say it out loud.

"We need cake." Hazel declared and scooted off to the kitchen.

Oliver lifted my chin, forcing me to meet his gaze. "We don't know anything yet."

"Yes we do." Camry wrapped her arms around herself. "She's dead and her parents killed her, bastards."

Two days passed before I got a text from Detective LeClare, there was a press conference on Wednesday at nine a.m. Camry, Austin and I arrived early and found seats in the second row. The press conference was held at the Town Hall. There was a podium up front with an American flag, California Flag, and the Santa Maria City Flag hung respectfully behind it. *Missing or Murdered* had broken the top ten. The popularity had turned Amelia Clark into a national news story and by nine a.m., the room was beyond maximum capacity.

The side door opened and the chief of police and Detective LeClare walked in, followed by a dozen men and women dressed in suits. The chief spoke first and thanked everyone for coming. He talked about Amelia, saying she was well liked and well known. He said her disappearance had left a hole in the community for over ten years and the PD had been working tirelessly to find answers.

After his spiel, he turned the time over to Detective LeClare. She was in a gray pantsuit with a black shirt underneath. From the front, you could scarcely tell she was pregnant.

"Thank you again for coming today." LeClare grabbed hold of either side of the podium, ready to address the crowd. "Recently, a podcast investigation into the case file of Amelia Clark was created. This helped us tremendously as it brought Amelia's disappearance back to the forefront of everyone's minds and put pressure on those who had information. We received an anonymous tip on our hotline. Now, we take every tip seriously, and based on the information we were given, and the information we already had on file, we felt we had enough reason to search the Clark home. For the past two days, cadaver dogs and the forensic team conducted a thorough search of the property. In the backyard, under an apple tree, buried four feet under the ground was a blanket. The DNA recovered from the blanket does belong to Amelia Clark. We were unable to locate a body or any other incriminating evidence. No arrests have been made at the time. But we'd urge the public, if you have *any* information regarding the whereabouts of Amelia Clark, or have any information at all, no matter how insignificant it may seem, please contact us directly. We'll now take questions."

My hand automatically shot up.

"Yes, Ms. Olsen."

All eyes were now on me. I should have thought of a question before I raised my hand. My mind was in shock. I held my new recorder to my mouth and asked, "What kind of DNA was recovered?"

"Hair."

Hair?

Who buries a blanket?

The reporter behind me was called on. "Do the Clark's have an explanation as to why there was a blanket buried in the backyard?"

"Yes, they said it was a memorial for their daughter that they created on the tenth anniversary of her disappearance."

My hand shot up again.

"Ms. Olsen."

"Are Richard and Janet Clark officially people of interest?" I asked.

LeClare leaned into the microphone and said, "No."

My heart sank into my gut. Nothing about this made sense. A blanket with Amelia's DNA was buried in the backyard?

Then why did someone throw the apple?

And more importantly: Where the heck was Amelia?

EPISODE THIRTY-ONE

Anonymous

"I heard the news," Hazel said as soon as I walked in the door.

"Liv doesn't want to talk about it." Camry dropped into a chair in the den with a thud.

I face planted into the sofa.

"We need donuts." Hazel scooted to the kitchen and I could already hear her firing up the deep fryer. The last thing I wanted was food, but I had no doubt I'd eat whatever she made anyway.

The lights around the room flashed on and off.

"One, two, three, not it!" Camry yelled before I could get the words out.

"Dammit!" I rolled to the floor and forced myself up to answer the door. It was a woman with a hooked nose and bright eyes, wearing a black silk shirt that clung to her shoulders.

"Hi, can I help you?" I asked.

"Are you the one doing the podcast?"

I hesitated, scared she'd throw an apple in my face and run away. But I was too tired to think of a better response, so I said, "Yes."

"My name is Falina Vanderbilt, my family owns Grotto De'Vino. You met my sister Sandy."

Oh.

"Yes, Sandy. We met the night we came in to do a wine tasting. You have a lovely facility." From what I could remember.

Falina gulped loud enough for me to hear. "I have information for you about the Clarks and Amelia. Do you have a moment?"

"Of course." I stepped out onto the porch and closed the door behind me. "Can I record the conversation?"

"No. I don't want my name out there, but I've tried everything and no one is getting it."

"Have you contacted the police?"

Falina waved her hand, as if the idea was ridiculous. "I'm the one who called in the anonymous tip and look what happened. Nothing!"

"You're the one who said Amelia was buried under the apple tree?" I asked in shock.

"Yes. I'm also the one who—" she snapped her mouth shut.

"Who what?" I finally asked.

Falina refused to make eye contact and it dawned on me. "Did you throw the apple?"

"It wasn't supposed to go through the window!" She blurted out. "It was just supposed to get your attention."

Holy crap.

I need to sit down.

So I did.

"You threw the apple. But how'd you know about the podcast? Did you read it online?" I asked.

"No, Val told me."

Val?

Who the hell is Val?

Confusion must have been written all over my face because Falina said, "Val is my babysitter, and she also works at CinnaMann's. She was there the day you came in to speak to Richard."

Oh, *that* Val. The young girl who was cleaning the display case the first time we went to CinnaMann's. The one I accidently introduced myself as Amelia Clark to.

"Val said you worked on *Cold in America*, which I love. And I thought if you looked in the Clark's backyard, you'd figure out where Millie was."

"You could have slipped me a note," I said.

"I just really don't want Richard to know I'm the one who told. Please."

"I won't use your name, I promise. Now, what do you know?"

Falina sat down and cracked her knuckles one at a time. I could tell this was difficult for her. "We lived behind the Clarks for many years," she finally started. "Millie was at our house every day during the summer. She mostly played with Sandy, since they're the same age. They liked to play outside." A look of horror flashed through her gaze. "No one knew that our ground was poisonous at the time."

I remember what Sandy had said about her brother. "I'm sorry for your loss."

"Thank you," she said, studying her hands. "My parents never got along with the Clarks. My mom thought Richard was a hot head and that Janet was weird. Richard once filed a lawsuit against my parents because my brother broke the bottom of the fence, and he wanted us to pay to replace the entire thing, not just the one broken slat."

"In the mid-nineties," I said. "I remember seeing online that he had a civil suit, but it didn't say what it was for."

"It was dropped before it went to court. My parents ended up paying for a new fence just to get Richard off their case. Of course, it strained our relationship, and Millie never came over again."

This story proved nothing except that Richard was a big butthole.

But that I already knew.

"That's why Richard can't know it was me who told you, because he'll destroy my family."

"I promise you that I won't tell."

"Good, because there's more," Falina said. "That heart in the backyard, the one the Clark's said they put there as a memorial for Millie, that's been there since at least 2010. They're lying."

"Yes, but the heart doesn't really prove anything," I said.

Falina gave me a look. "You and I both know that they didn't bury a stupid blanket. The Clarks are the only ones in the neighborhood who didn't get their soil tested or have their yard cleaned up by the oil company. I peeked back there when the whole lawsuit was going on and saw the heart. I told my dad that there's a reason the Clarks don't want anyone digging up their backyard, and I thought the reason was Millie."

"And what did he say?"

"He told me to stay away from the Clarks and drop it. But I couldn't. It's been eating me up for the last however many years."

"What makes you think they'd hurt Amelia?"

"Nothing matters more to Richard Clark than his public image. *Nothing*," she said. "I visited Millie at her apartment the night she disappeared to make sure she was okay, and she told me that her dad was livid."

Wait, whaaa...I scooted to the end of my chair. "What time?"

"Around five thirty. She let me park in her spot because I'd just had knee surgery and couldn't walk too far. *That's* the kind of person Millie Clark was."

So that's why Amelia parked in the guest spot. This information about the guest parking spot hadn't been shared on the podcast yet, which gave credit to what Falina was saying.

I perked up. "Can you tell me about your visit?"

"It was short, because she was getting ready for a date. I helped her put together the outfit. She was going out with some guy she'd met at a diner. I was happy for her because she hadn't dated anyone since Jeremy."

"Was she excited?"

Falina twisted her mouth to the side. "I wouldn't say she was excited; I'd say she was jumbled."

Jumbled?

"Maybe frazzled is a better word," she said. "Her dad was mad about the video. Said it brought shame to the family, and it would ruin his business, and he was *really* pissed off. I was lying on the bed while she was doing her hair..." Falina's voice trailed off.

"What's wrong?"

"I just remembered something. Her hair was falling out, and she asked if that had ever happened to me before. I told her no, but that she should get her thyroid tested and to ask her mom what she thought. Janet used to be a nurse before she married Richard, but you probably already knew that."

Actually I didn't.

"While we were visiting, Richard called *again* and asked Millie to meet the oven repair guy at the bakery at six, but she said she couldn't because she had a date. He lost his temper and started screaming at her to the point she hung up on him."

"Hold on." I grabbed Falina's arm. "He asked her to go to the bakery that evening. She was last seen at the ATM next to CinnaMann's. Do you think she'd go there to meet the repairman?"

"I don't know," she said. "Probably. As much as she couldn't stand her dad, she was also compassionate to a fault."

I was already plotting what to do with this information. Starting with reporting it to Detective LeClare and looking into oven repair shops in the area. If this were true, and Amelia did meet a repairman at CinnaMann's that night, then that man would have been the last person to see her.

"Did she ever talk about Jeremy or Carlos?" I asked, still trying to figure out how they fit into the equation.

"Carlos was her neighbor and they were friends. I didn't talk to her much while she was dating Jeremy. She spent most of her time in Santa Barbara."

"Do you know if she introduced Jeremy to her parents?" I asked.

"She loved Jeremy too much to subject him to her crazy parents."

Made sense. But that wasn't exactly telling. There were a lot of people who had "crazy" parents. Doesn't make them killers, though.

"What do you think happened to her?" I asked.

"Richard killed her," she said without pause. "I don't think he'd do it on purpose, but I think he got mad about the video and lost his temper."

"But he wasn't in town, and if she'd gone to the bakery to meet the repairman, then that proves he wasn't here yet. And she didn't show up for her date that night."

Falina rocked in the chair and swept a strand of hair behind her ear, staring off into the distance. "I don't know how he did it, or when he did it, but I just know deep in my gut that he did it." I could feel the conviction in her words, which was admirable.

Unfortunately, there wasn't much I could do with a gut feeling.

Fortunately, we had a new suspect.

EPISODE THIRTY-TWO

The Repairman

"She should have told the police about the repairman back in 2008," Hazel said after I told everyone about my meeting with Falina. We were gathered around the dining table, about to go over episode five before it was released: the episode where the apple was thrown through the window.

"Why wouldn't *Richard* tell the police about the repairman at CinnaMann's?" I said.

Austin was flipping through Leon's notebooks. "I-I-I've never seen any mention o-o-of a repairman."

"Me either," said and signed Oliver.

I clutched the back of a chair. "Is it credible? Can we use it?"

"You have to use this story, Liv." Camry was practically shaking with excitement. "Everything she said lines up perfectly with our timeline from the guest parking space to the date with Oliver."

"But we need to be careful," I said. "There can't be that many repair shops around here, and I don't want to start putting blame on any of them until we have proof. And I have a feeling Richard will not give us the information we need."

"Not a chance," Oliver said and signed. "I do think the reason Richard didn't have his soil tested was because Amelia was back there. And he had time to move her before the police came."

"B-but w-why would he leave a blanket? That d-d-doesn't

make any sense."

"Because the cadaver dogs were going to pick up a scent anyway, and they could say it was the blanket," said and signed Oliver.

"But CSI would notice that the dirt had recently been disturbed, right?" I asked.

Everyone did a collective shrug.

Which was of no help.

Gah! This whole thing was maddening. I felt like we were on the brink of figuring out what really happened to Amelia, but there were too many moving parts. Too many white rabbits.

"I looked up the Vanderbilt family and," said Camry, "according to everything I've found online, they lived behind the Clarks in 2008 and Richard *did* file that lawsuit against them in the nineties."

"Th-Th-Then Falina has reason to be mad at Richard," said Austin.

"Do you think she's making this stuff up to get back at him?" I asked.

"I-it's a possibility."

I massaged my temples. "Let's at least see if we can figure out if there was a repairman there on Friday night."

"Aye, aye." Camry gave me a captain's salute and got to work.

Lucky for us there were only two oven repair shops on the Central Coast.

Unlucky for us there were four in 2008.

This could take forever.

We called the two who were still in business, and neither would confirm if CinnaMann's was one of their customers, nor would they answer any other questions.

So we turned to our most powerful tool instead: Facebook Mom's Group.

My name is Liv Olsen, I am the executive producer and host of Missing or Murdered. We're looking for anyone who worked for any of the following companies in 2008: Industrial Repair, Joe &

Son's Repair Shop, Allen's Industrial Repairs, Hobart Repairs.

It took exactly two minutes before the leads started pouring in, and exactly three days before one of those leads turned into an interview.

Sheri Nelson was the former office manager of Joe & Son's Repair Shop, which closed their doors in 2009.

Sheri lived on the north side of town. Up a long driveway sat a small home with off-white stucco, light wood fascia, a stone chimney, and a single addition on top of the garage, which made the house look off balanced. There was no grass, no fence, but a collection of succulents in brightly colored pots on the porch.

Camry and I walked up to the driveway, the gravel crunching under our shoes, and knocked on the door. A German Shepard raced from around the backside of the house, baring his teeth and barking like his life depended on it.

Yikes.

Camry jumped on my back and I fell over.

Lucky for me, there was a potted plant to break my fall.

Unlucky for me, it was a freaking cactus.

The dog was yanked back by the chain attached to his collar, and he continued to bark, and thrash, and growl, while I plucked the little spines out of the palms of my hand. The door opened and there stood a woman with short gray hair, round glasses, a red and white striped shirt, blue shorts that went to her knees, and a well-worn pair of sneakers.

"Calm down, Boris!" she yelled to the dog.

Boris didn't listen and continued to test the strength of the chain holding him back.

Speaking of back, Camry was still on mine.

"You the podcasting girls?" the woman, who I assumed to be Sheri, asked.

"Yes." I pushed Camry off and stood, about to offer my hand but then thought better of it. Good thing the package of bandages was still in the car, because my palm was a bloody mess.

Sheri invited us in. Her house was cluttered with stuffed

animals, unfinished crochet projects, and stacks of paper. I counted at least ten cats, all lounging on top of the furniture, which explained the litter box smell permeating the air.

We gathered around Sheri's round kitchen table and she agreed to switch off the exhaust fan to avoid competing noise. The sink was piled high with unwashed dishes, the stove was crusty, and the clock blinked with the wrong time. I set up my audio equipment while Sheri poured us each a cup of coffee.

I didn't drink coffee but appreciated the gesture.

I used my brand new recorder and slipped on a pair of headphones. "Can you tell us your name and where you worked in 2008?" I placed the mic into a stand and pushed it closer to Sheri.

"My name is Sheri and I was the office manager for Joe & Son's Repair Shop for thirty years."

Not to geek out, but Sheri's voice was crisp and clear and there was zero buzz, hiss, room reflections, or plosives. The sound quality was beautiful.

I could cry.

But I didn't

Because that would be awkward.

"Was CinnaMann one of your customers?" I asked.

"Yes, Richard called us for warranty work on his Vulcan ovens." A tabby cat jumped on Sheri's lap and curled up for a nap.

"Do you remember a work order placed for CinnaMann's on October 10 in 2008?"

"I didn't, but after my daughter called to tell me about the podcast, and that you were looking for someone who worked for Joe & Son's, I started going through old work orders." She reached over to a stack of papers on a nearby table and grabbed a spiral carbon copy notebook from the top. "I save everything, because you never know when you'll need it." Based on the condition of her home, I believed her—she saved *everything*.

In this case, hoarding could very well help us find out what happened to Amelia.

Sheri licked the tip of her finger and flipped the notebook open to a marked page. "On October 8, Richard called because one of his older ovens wasn't working. Typically, Richard could fix it himself, but he was out of town. The soonest I could get someone out there was the tenth."

"Was there a window of time given to Richard of when the repairman would be there?" I asked.

"We told him between six and seven, but my guys called when they were ten minutes out."

"Can I see the work order?"

Sheri passed over the notebook and Camry looked over my shoulder. "How do you know it was completed?"

"Typically, I stamped them complete. See." She pointed to the work order below and, yes, there is a big red COMPLETE stamped across the bottom.

"Why wasn't this stamped?"

"Dunno."

"What does this mean?" Camry pointed to the initials on the bottom right corner.

Sheri slide the book back to take a look. "Whenever the tech took an order, I had them initial it so I could keep track of who took what."

"Whose initials are these?" I asked. "It looks like RH?"

"That would be Raymond Hermosa; he worked at Joe's for a few years."

Camry dropped her mug and it crashed to the ground. The tabby cat jumped off of Sheri and lapped up the coffee.

I know exactly what Camry was thinking.

Sure, there could be many people with the last name Hermosa in Santa Maria.

But it was too much of a coincidence not to investigate further.

Camry searched the Internet and fifteen minutes after we sprinted to my car (to avoid getting eaten by Boris); we were parked in front of a single-story home with blue siding and a red door. In the driveway was a utility van. The large white ones with no windows that kidnappers drive. Industrial Repair was stamped on the driver's side door.

I knocked and looked around. The walkway was freshly swept, and the landscaping was simple and clean.

We heard steps approaching and the *click* of a lock. The door opened and a small man with dark features and a well-manicured beard answered.

"Hi, we're looking for Raymond Hermosa," I said.

"Never heard of him," replied the man.

Oh.

Camry consulted her phone. "Raymond Hermosa doesn't live here?"

"No."

"Has he ever lived here?" Camry tried.

"Not that I know of."

"Oh, sorry for bothering you." I turned around slowly and walked back to my car.

"That was anticlimactic," said Camry, sliding into the passenger seat.

"I'm not buying it," I said, holding the steering wheel with my scratched hands, gazing out the window at the van. "What are the odds that you found the address of a Raymond Hermosa and there's an Industrial Repair van parked in the driveway, but no Raymond Hermosa lives here?"

"I don't see any pictures of him online. There's no way for me to confirm what Raymond looks like."

I reclined my seat and crossed my arms. "Let's wait a few and see what happens."

"If I knew we were going back to stalking, I would have brought a snack."

We didn't have to wait long. The man walked out of his house, swinging his keys on his finger, and jumped in the van. We waited until he was at the end of the street before we followed. This could be nothing but a bearded white rabbit, but I owed it to Amelia to see it through.

"What if he's going to the grocery store?" Camry asked.

"Well, you did say you were hungry."

"Ha. Ha."

We followed the white van through town, past the mall, through a residential area, and onto Santa Maria Way where he flipped his blinker and pulled into the apartments. I parked at the gas station, and Camry and I hopped out of the car and raced over to the apartments, hoping not to be seen. The white van was in the guest parking space and we crept to the back of the building and peeked around the corner. Carlos and the man (who we assumed to be Raymond) were chatting candidly. Carlos even wrapped his bicep around Raymond's neck and gave him a noogie.

Whatever they were talking about, there didn't appear to be any concern or urgency.

Carlos retrieved a long-sleeved shirt and duffle bag from his apartment. Then the two walked to Raymond's van, still joking around. Carlos got in the passenger side. Raymond into the driver's side. And they were off.

"Ah!" Camry and I stumble over each other and ran to our car so we could catch them. I fumbled my keys out of my pocket while Camry smacked the hood of my car. "Hurry! Hurry! Hurry! Hurry!"

Which, for the record, did not help me move faster.

We were in the car and driving down Bradley road. "Where do you think they're going?" Liv asked.

"I have no idea." I passed a car going five below the speed limit, careful to maintain a safe distance behind the Hermosa boys.

"What if they know we're following them, and they're leading us to an empty lot somewhere so they can kill us?"

"Well, that's a lovely thought."

"Oh please, you were thinking the same thing."

Yep.

We turned right on Clark Ave. "They're in the parking lot," Camry said as we passed Jeremy's office. "They're in freaking Jeremy Wang's parking lot. Holy crap!"

Holy crap was right.

I made a U-turn and parked in the alleyway behind the shopping center. Camry and I jogged to the side of the building and peeked around the corner.

Raymond's van was parked backwards in the handicapped space with the hazard lights on. Carlos walked down the stairs holding two moving boxes. Jeremy followed, holding the chair I'd sat on when Camry and I visited.

"Jeremy's moving?" I realized out loud.

"No, he said he was redecorating," Camry whispered.

"Yeah, and that's a brand new chair. Remember? It was wrapped in plastic when we were there."

"Why would he move?"

"To get out of town before the episode about him airs."

"Should we confront him?"

"Of course not. We're going to stalk him." I returned my attention to Jeremy, who shoved the chair into the back of the van. He was wearing black basketball shorts and a black shirt with red Chinese characters on the front. He moved with urgency and was back up the stairs, taking two steps at a time, and returned shortly with a moving box. Raymond and Carlos followed, carrying the plastic wrapped couch.

After several more trips up and down the stairs, the van was loaded. The three men huddled around Jeremy's phone. He pointed north, then cocked his thumb west, and it appeared he was giving them directions. The three said goodbye to each other and Jeremy climbed into a white VW Rabbit with Nevada license plates and a teal, pink, and blue ribbon on the bumper.

Camry and I hustled back to my car and followed Jeremy and the Hermosa boys onto the 101 Freeway, going south.

"They could be going to Santa Barbara," I said.

"Or they could be heading for the Mexican border. How long are we going to follow them?"

"Until we find something, I guess."

"I'm going to text the crew and let them know what we're

doing in case we die."

"Good idea."

An hour later we were driving through Santa Barbara. To my right was the ocean. Surfers were floating together, straddling their boards, waiting for the next wave. To my left were mountains, brown from months—if not years—of improper watering. The MPH sign was leaning sideways, threatening to fall over, and the metal was charred and curled on the corners, indicating the area had recently been burned by a wildfire. It was an odd juxtaposition to look out Camry's window and see water, then look out my window and see drought. Almost like two different worlds separated by the 101 Freeway.

But that's California for ya.

The freeway was congested as we neared Ventura, which helped us keep a better eye on the van and white sedan. They were a car apart in the left lane, while we were six cars back in the right.

The traffic dissolved around Camarillo (two hours south of Santa Maria), and Camry smacked me on the backside of the head. "The Hermosa boys are getting off!"

"Yeah, I guessed that when he turned on his blinker. But Jeremy is going straight."

"Who do we follow, Liv?"

I had three seconds to make a decision as the van had already exited and Jeremy was still going south on the freeway.

Jeremy or Hermosa?

Jeremy or Hermosa?

The boyfriend or the neighbor?

The *ex*-boyfriend or the repairman?

EPISODE THIRTY-THREE

When Vun Meets Fun

I chose to follow Jeremy. Why? I didn't know. A decision had to be a made, and I went with the ex-boyfriend. Except I was dangerously low on gas and we'd been driving for four hours.

"Liv is about to freak out." Camry had Austin on speakerphone in one hand and the recorder in the other. "I can see the sweat on her forehead."

"W-why is she freaking out?" asked Austin,

"*No*, I'm not about to freak out," I said.

Actually, I am.

The little gas pump light on my dashboard gave me anxiety. I'd never gone below a quarter of a tank—ever.

"I-I-I think h-he's going to Vegas," said Austin.

"No duh, Sherlock. We figured that one out when we got on the 210 Freeway and there was a big fat sign saying, 'this way to Vegas, idiots!'"

I shot Camry a look.

"What?" she snapped. "I'm hangry. I need food. When are you pulling over?"

I checked the dash. "We have two miles left." *Hiccup.*

"I-I-I can find his address in case you lose him," said Austin.

"We're not seriously driving to Vegas," Camry said. "I don't even have my clothes with me. And what are we going to do when we get there? Confront him? Be like, 'hey, we've been following you for six hours, but we're not crazy stalker people, promise. Anyway, two-part question for you: Did you kill Amelia, and if you did, where is she?' We should have followed the Hermosa guys."

Maybe.

Truth was, I had no idea what we'd do when Jeremy stopped. I'd asked myself this a million times over the last four hours. Gas was expensive. I was still cheap. And we were literally chasing a white rabbit.

But it was too late now to back out.

"Find Jeremy's address for us, please?" I said to Austin.

"Ugh!" Camry threw her hands up in the air. "This is the most un-Vegas outfit I own." She tugged on her red shirt and jeans, shaking her head.

Which, actually, was the exact ensemble I wore the last time I went to Vegas.

I gave my car gas, Camry food, Austin texted us the address, and we were back on the road. We caught up to Jeremy somewhere in the Mojave Desert.

Camry tilted a bag of Doritos my way. "Want one?"

"No thanks, but can you please try not to make a mess?"

She pretended to wipe her cheese-covered hands on the dashboard.

"Aren't you hilarious," I said.

"I know." She rolled up her bag of chips and licked her fingers clean. "How are your hands doing?"

I checked my scraped-up palms. It seemed like a lifetime ago when I fell into the cactus, when in reality it was earlier today. "They're fine."

"My dad had a thing for cactuses. Or is it cacti?"

"Cactuses, I think."

"Sounds right." She shrugged. "We used to have a bunch in our backyard, but my mom got rid of them after he died. I think they reminded her too much of him." She propped her elbow up on the window and looked out at the vast landscape. "I wish I could remember him more. You're lucky you were older when your mom died."

"I don't know that I'd call me *lucky*. At least you don't remember your dad dying. I was holding my mom's hand when she passed. It was awful." I shook the memory out of my head, but it bounced right back. Her hand, thin, dry, cold, and lifeless, sandwiched between my own...

"Is that why you never gave me a chance?" Camry asked. "Because it was still too painful?" The vulnerability in her voice tugged at my heart and brought me back to the present.

"I'm sorry, Camry. I grew up with my mom, dad, brother and me all in that house. When you two moved in, it felt like a betrayal to my mother's memory." I was surprised by my words. I hadn't realized I felt that way. "Then I was busy with finishing up high school, going off to college, and doing it all without my mom. I know you were craving a sisterly relationship, and I'm sorry you didn't get that. But you have it now. Does that count?"

"Sure." Camry acted like it was no big deal, but I could see the smile creep across her face in the window's reflection.

Anyway...speaking of cancer. "Hey, do you remember what the ribbon is for leukemia?"

Camry puffed up her cheeks and thought for a moment. "It's orange," she sighed. "It was also my dad's favorite color. Why? What's ovarian cancer?"

"It's teal. But I have no idea what teal, pink and blue is."

"Ohhhh, the ribbon on the back of Jeremy's car. Gotcha. Hold on, let's ask Google." She consulted her phone. "So teal and pink represents infertility and...got it. Teal, pink, *and* blue is the symbol for thyroid cancer."

"But Jeremy grew up in Santa Barbara. Not in Morning Knolls."

"I'm not a doctor, but I'm pretty sure you can get thyroid cancer no matter where you live."

True. But, "What's the treatment for thyroid cancer?"

"Again, not a doctor. But there was a chick in my econ class at Stanford who had thyroid cancer. They just yanked it out of her neck and she was fine. For the most part. She gained weight. But that could also have been the freshman fifteen."

"I would notice a scar on his neck. He did have one on his eyebrow."

"You can't take the thyroid out from the eyebrow."

"Thanks, Dr. Lewis."

"You're welcome. Where you going with this anyway? Because you realize he's not driving his own car, so basically this ribbon could mean nothing."

"Not *nothing*, but nothing to this case. But it is a strange coincidence that several people in Amelia's neighborhood had thyroid cancer."

"It's a strange coincidence we both lost a parent to cancer. It's freaking everywhere. I hate cancer!"

Me too.

We crossed the California state line and were officially in Nevada. Jeremy exited to get gas and we waited across the street in a casino parking lot.

"If he catches us following him, he's going to call the cops," said Camry.

"Probably." I stretched my arms and rubbed my eyes. I hadn't driven this far in a long time.

"Austin wants to know if he should fly to Vegas and meet us."

"I hope you told him no."

"Um..."

"Camry!"

"What? I need clothes."

I shook my head. "This is a round trip. No strip."

"Well aren't you a regular ole' Dr. Seuss."

I didn't get the joke, but it didn't matter because Jeremy was on the road again and so were we.

We were fifteen minutes outside of Vegas when Hazel called. Camry answered and put her on speaker, holding the recorder up.

"I have Oliver here," Hazel said. "He wants to know if you've ever looked into Jeremy's wife?"

"Doris Fundoogle?" I looked at Camry and she shook her head. "No, we haven't. Why?"

"Oliver found information on Doris *V*undoogle."

"But it's not *V*un it's Fun," said Camry. "As in, Liv doesn't like to have *fun*."

I rolled my eyes.

"Yes, Camry, Oliver *can* read. It's only his ears that don't work," said Hazel. "But Doris Vundoogle was Carlos and Raymond Hermosa's grandmother."

"So Oliver thinks Jeremy married Carlos' grandma?" Camry made a face. "No offense, but...gross."

"No, he's not saying that. He's saying...what exactly are you saying, dear? Stop signing so fast, I can't keep up," Hazel said in the background. "He says Doris Vundoogle died in September of 2008, and coincidently, there is no record of Doris Fundoogle prior to October of 2008."

"Holy crap!" Camry blurted out.

"My sentiments exactly," I said.

"No! Like crap, crap, crap. Liv look behind us."

I checked the rearview mirror. "Holy crap!"

"Why does everyone keep saying crap?" Hazel asked. "What's wrong?"

"Richard Clark is right behind us," said Camry.

EPISODE THIRTY-THREE

What Happens in Vegas...

"Are you sure it's him?" Hazel asked.

I glanced in the rearview mirror again. "Yes, it's his truck and I can see his face."

"Slow down," said Camry. "See if he slows down too."

"Why? He's obviously following us."

"No, he could be following Jeremy."

Good point. I eased off the gas. Richard switched lanes and zoomed by. Camry and I crouched down and turned our heads as he passed. "You're right. He's following Jeremy."

"Hazel, we'll call you back." Camry hung up but kept the recorder going. "I wonder who else is following him." She turned around in her seat. "Holy crap!"

"What now?"

"Nothing," she said with a smile.

"This is no time for jokes. We're following Jeremy. Richard is following Jeremy. And now we've got this whole Doris thing to figure out."

Camry took a picture of Richard's car with her phone. "I don't understand the Doris thing."

"Think about it, Camry. Doris Fundoogle, Doris Vundoogle. She dies the month before Amelia disappeared, and Jeremy has a ribbon on his car for thyroid cancer and everyone said Amelia looked sick and thin and scared. Jeremy said he was in town to keep an eye on things. We assumed he meant *his* family."

Camry's eyes were bouncing. "You're not thinking."

"Yes! I am thinking Amelia Clark is alive. I'm thinking Carlos gave her a new identity and helped her escape and Jeremy is married to her. And what would be the reason she would run away and never return?"

"Fear."

"Exactly. Afraid that returning would either get herself killed or the people she loves."

"Who was she afraid of?"

"Richard!"

"Oh..." she took this in. "Oooh! This is bad."

"This is *so* bad."

"This is terrible. Liv, she's been successfully hiding for years, and now her dad is on his way to find her because of you!"

Geez.

I hadn't thought of it that way.

"Yeah, I guess you're right. Dammit. If I'd known there was a chance she was hiding, I wouldn't have taken on the case. "We have to do something. Do we have Jeremy's number?"

Turns out we didn't. Camry looked up Jeremy's office number, but it went straight to voicemail. "Dammit! Do CPA's have after hour emergency lines?"

"Probably not. Can you find his cell phone number?"

"Ah, yeah, I could spend the next fifteen minutes looking for it or you could just speed up, catch Jeremy, and tell him yourself."

She made a valid point.

I slammed on the gas. Except my car needed at least sixty seconds before it could accelerate. As I neared Richard he turned on the blinker and exited the freeway.

"Crap!" I swerved off the road.

"Why are we following him now?" Camry asked, holding tight to the grab handle.

"He poses more of a threat."

"Great, sure, let's follow the lunatic then. FYI, I don't feel like dying today."

"That's probably what Amelia said as well." Richard turned right at the light and took another right into a little neighborhood. I'd never seen the residential side of Vegas before. There were parks and elementary schools, and newly constructed homes with little yards and kids riding bikes on the sidewalk.

"Email Jeremy," I said, keeping a safe distance behind Richard. "Tell him we're in Vegas and so is Richard, and see what he says."

"I'm not cut out for these high-stress situations." She grabbed her phone. "Gah, I forgot to put deodorant on." She cut her eyes to me. "And you better edit that out, got it."

"Not a chance."

Camry emailed Jeremy and dropped her phone into her bag. The recorder was in the cup holder. "I have a bad feeling about this, Liv. Like a really bad feeling."

"It's going be okay," I said as convincingly as I could. Perhaps I should have pulled over and called the police. Or I should have driven away. Why put myself into the middle of a dangerous situation?

Then again, I inserted myself into Amelia's life when I created an entire podcast about her.

Richard turned left on a street called Twilight Lane. All the homes looked the same. Two story, peach stucco, white trim, desert landscape, single car garage, all spaced about three feet apart from each other. I stopped at the end of the road and watched. Richard slowed when he reached the only house with a For Sale sign out front.

"See, he's just looking for new real estate," Camry said. "Can we go now?"

"Hold on." I flipped the visor to protect my eyes from the glaring sun. Richard made a three-point turn and parked on the other side of the road, but he didn't exit the vehicle. I couldn't tell what he was doing from my lookout location, but whatever it was, it didn't take long. He started the car and drove in the opposite direction.

"What now?" she asked.

"You stay here while I go check out that house."

Camry started to protest, and I placed my finger over her mouth.

"I need you to drive the getaway car," I said. "Promise me you'll stay put."

She slowly raised her hand to her forehead and gave me a captain solute.

"Good girl."

According to a quick Zillow search, 5676 Twilight had a radiant floor plan and was offering three good-sized bedrooms, two-and-a-half bathrooms and a spacious master. The home also featured a sunken living room with a vaulted ceiling and a cozy fireplace.

I knocked on the door, but no one answered. I tried the bell, but the chimes were muted by the hum of a vacuum. There was a long rectangular window to the left of the door, and I cupped my hands and peeked in. A woman with short brown hair was pushing around a Dyson.

I used both fists to pound on the window until I got the woman's attention. She came to the door and I stepped back, suddenly realizing that I didn't have the recorder on me.

Not that it mattered. This was beyond the podcast.

The woman answered and I heaved a sigh of relief. It was not Amelia. Not even close. This woman had brown eyes, a cleft chin, and a perm.

"Can I help you?"

I tucked a strand of hair behind my ear, not exactly sure where to start. "Hi, my name is Liv Olsen, and I was wondering about your house."

"You can schedule a tour with my relator." She snatched a business card off the entryway table and handed it to me.

"Thanks." I slid it into my back pocket. "Do you happen to

know a man named Richard Clark?"

"Sounds familiar, why?"

"What about Janet Clark?"

The woman's face lit with recognition. "Janet and Richard Clark are Amelia Clark's parents."

"Yes! You know them?"

The next-door neighbor's dog let out a low growl followed by a high-pitched bark.

"No, but I've been listening to the *Missing or Murdered* podcast while I pack," she said. "Wait a second...did you say your name was Liv Olsen? As in the host of the show?"

Errr... "Yes."

"How fun! Can I take a picture with you?"

I had more important things to do than pose for pictures.

But then again, she *was* a fan.

She held up her phone and we smiled. I felt awkward. I'd never been recognized before. Nor had I ever taken a picture with a stranger. "Are you moving to Vegas?" she asked. "Because this is a great house, and it's priced to sell."

"No, I'm not actually. But are you sure you've never heard of Richard Clark before?"

"Just on the podcast. Let me ask you this, do you think it was Carlos?"

Oh geez.

I was going to have to release three episodes a week to get listeners caught up. Right now, they were still learning about the apple through the window. She didn't know about Jeremy, or Richard, or even Penny.

But there was no time to dwell on work. Not when Richard was driving around who knows where, doing who knows what, to who knows who.

Also, the dog next door wouldn't stop barking, and it was giving me a headache.

"Thank you for listening," I said to the woman. "Be sure to tune in on Monday." I cut across the lawn when I heard a window breaking. The dog rapid fired desperate barks and I stopped in my tracks. The neighboring house looked exactly like the house for sale, except for the blue welcome mat at the front door. I peeked in through the side window and could see the tip of an elbow poking out from behind a wall.

Needing a better view, I went around to the side of the house and looked in. I had a full view of the living room and kitchen. Standing near the refrigerator was Richard Clark, he was yelling at a person who was blocked by the refrigerator.

I used the plastic trash bins lined along the fence as a boost to climb over into the backyard. The dog didn't pay any attention to me. He was too busy barking at Richard, and I grabbed a potted tomato plant from the garden and tiptoed to the back of the house.

The sliding door had a fist-sized hole near the handle and I carefully pulled it open.

"I'm not scared of you anymore!" came a woman's voice from the inside the kitchen.

I continued to tiptoe through the dining room until I was directly behind Richard. I lifted the pot as high as I could and slammed it against his skull.

In the movies, a pot to the head would cause any grown man to fall to his knees.

In reality, not so much.

Richard spun around. "You?" he almost spit the words out. "You!" He lunged toward me. I grabbed the pepper spray out of my back pocket and sprayed his eyes. He fell back against a wall of pictures and slid down to the floor.

There was a moment when Richard was holding his face, and I was standing there with my pepper spray in hand, that I locked eyes with a brunette in a loose-fitting jersey dress.

I knew those blue eyes.

I knew that nose.

It was Amelia.

I never thought in a million years this podcast would end with Amelia standing before me alive, and married, and brunette. But before I could dwell too much on Amelia, I was on the ground. Richard Clark was on top of me, and he was a *big* man. I couldn't move. Amelia wrapped her arms around Richard's neck and he pushed her away with such ease you'd think she was a feather.

I couldn't take Richard Clark. He had at least two hundred pounds on me. His eyes were black and red-rimmed. The harder I struggled, the tighter his grasp. I could feel my bones succumbing to the pressure.

"Get off!" Amelia broke a picture frame over Richard's head. The man must have had a skull constructed of titanium because he didn't flinch. He grabbed the bottom of Amelia's dress and pulled her to the floor, still pinning me down with his body weight. She cracked her head against the tile floor and let out a moan.

I kicked my legs, frantic to break free. Richard cupped his left hand around my neck, and his right hand around Amelia's. It felt like I was breathing through a straw. Amelia clawed at Richard's arm while I fought to remain conscious.

Richard let go of my neck, keeping his other firmly around Amelia's. I gasped for air, my body still pinned under his. He reached into his back pocket and produced a gun. Crap!

He placed the barrel on my temple. *Oh no. Please no.* I knew my skull was not constructed of impenetrable material. This was not how I wanted to die. He cocked the gun. I kicked my legs, using the last bit of oxygen I had left in my body. His finger went to the trigger. I squeezed my eyes shut. There was a *click*. I opened my eyes.

"Dammit!" Richard stared down at the gun as if it had betrayed him.

"Get off of my sister!" Camry was standing in the living room holding a brick. She cocked her arm and threw it with terrible precision. The brick sailed over Richard's head and crashed into a lamp. It offered enough distraction where I was able to wiggle my right arm free. I reached for the pepper spray on the floor, using the tips of my fingers to edge it closer, and when Richard looked back down, I gave him another squirt right into the eyes.

He fell to his side, holding his face. Amelia and I crawled backwards on our elbows, gasping for air. Camry grabbed an empty vase from the side table and hurled it at Richard with better accuracy this time and it landed on his shoulder.

Richard let out a moan and clutched his arm. The vase didn't even break, but Richard was acting as if he'd been shot. He rolled to his stomach, still clutching his shoulder until he gasped one breath and...

Camry and I shared a look. Amelia struggled to her feet.

"Um..." Camry took a step forward. "Richard?" She poked him with the toe of her shoe, but he didn't move.

I pulled myself upright using the back of the couch and shuffled over to the large man lying motionless in the middle of the floor. If he was playing possum, he was a good actor because even the vein on his neck had stopped pulsing.

"I think he's dead," I said.

"What!" Camry freaked. "I didn't mean to kill him!"

"Bastard deserves it," I said, rubbing my sore next. "Maybe he had a heart attack? Did you call 911 already?"

Camry looked at me but said nothing.

"Call 911!" I barked at her.

"Yeah, okay." Her fingers flew across the screen of her phone, and she slammed it to her ear.

I stared down at Richard, knowing what I had to do.

Yes, if his gun had worked properly I would be dead right now.

But that's the thing. I was not Richard.

Oh hell.

I pushed him onto his back and straddled his stomach, placing my clasped fists on the center of his chest just below the sternum. "One, two, three, four..." I counted with each compression. Then I plugged his nose, opened his mouth, and closed my eyes.

"The operator says to only do chest compressions and not mouth-to-mouth," said Camry before I had a chance to make contact.

"Thank you, podcasting gods." I returned to chest

compressions until I could hear the sirens approaching. Camry unlocked the front door and two paramedics entered and took over for me.

I clutched on to Camry's arm to keep from falling over, as I did a quick scan of the room.

Amelia was gone.

"Go outside and wait for the police to arrive," I told Camry.

"But—" she started to protest.

"Make sure you tell them that Richard attacked first."

She gave a feeble nod of her head and did as asked. I took the opportunity to search the house, going from room to room. Parked in the garage was Jeremy's car. I should have asked the woman next door if she'd ever heard of Jeremy Wang or Doris Fundoogle instead of Richard.

Not that any of that mattered at this point.

Up the stairs I went, starting with the hall bathroom and what appeared to be a guest room. The master bedroom had double doors, and I grabbed both handles but they were locked.

"Amelia?" I called through the thin crack in the door. "Amelia are you in there? It's okay. You can come out." I wiggled the handles. "Hello."

It *was* Amelia.

Wasn't it?

I tromped back down the stairs and stopped at the last step. A picture of Jeremy and a girl who looked a lot like Amelia hung between two sconces. The girl had a fuller frame, a smile that reached her eyes, and brown hair that touched her shoulders. She was wearing a sleeveless white dress that fell to her feet. He was in a suit and tie with a single rose pinned to his lapel. They were standing on the steps of what looked like City Hall, holding hands.

Well, I'll be damned.

The police arrived just as Richard was rushed into the back of an ambulance. He had an oxygen mask over his face, but the paramedic was still performing chest compressions. Richard showed zero signs of life.

"I'll admit," Camry said, swinging an arm around my shoulders. "I did not see this ending coming."

"Me either." I snaked my arm around her waist. "Thanks for saving my life."

"Meh, I was in the neighborhood." She winked down at me.

And here I thought bringing her along would be more of a chore.

We were approached by a female police officer with slicked black hair and thin lips. "Can you tell me what happened?" she asked.

Camry and I shared a look.

"I'll go," Camry said. "So it all started when Liv's boss said she had no oomph..." Camry proceeds to tell the officer everything from the podcast to our impromptu trip to Vegas. "And when Liv didn't come back, I went looking for her and heard the commotion inside this house, saw Mr. CinnaMann choking Liv and another woman and sprung to action."

"And who is Mr. CinnaMann?" the officer asked.

"Sorry, that would be Richard Clark. He owns a bakery."

"Okay," she said and directed her attention to me. "Why were you in the house?"

"I heard a struggle and the dog was barking, when I looked inside I saw Richard about to attack his daughter."

Camry gasped. "You saw Amelia?"

"She's up in the master bedroom."

"You *saw* Amelia?" Camry repeated.

"There's a picture from her and Jeremy's wedding day in the stairwell."

"You *saw* Amelia?"

The white rabbit car screeched to a stop behind the police car. Jeremy got out and slid over the hood like they do in the movies. He ran toward us, worry creasing his brow. I cocked my thumb behind me. "She's safe inside your room, and Richard is at the hospital."

Jeremy opened his mouth, searching for words, when Camry

gave him a shove. "Get your butt inside and help your wife."

She didn't have to say it twice. Jeremy bolted up the stairs, taking two at a time, and passed a police officer walking our way, shaking his head.

"You're not going to believe this story," he said to his partner.

EPISODE THIRTY-FOUR

Dori

I closed the closet door and sat on the ground. Hazel moved all the toys and dress up clothes to a different room, allowing me enough space to work without creepy dolls staring at me. Camry and I constructed a small desk I'd ordered from Ikea, and we learned that we should never construct furniture together.

It nearly broke our relationship.

The door slid open and Camry poked her head in. "Are you nerv—"

"Shhh," I cut her off. "Stop asking me that."

"Sorry, geez. Are you...what are you?"

"Relieved." I plugged in the microphone and gave her a headset. "Do you want to listen in?"

"No. It's your podcast, and you're the one who found her, and you're the one who is the super famous host, and you're the one who put all the money in, you should do this last interview in peace."

"Take the headset, Camry."

"Okay." She snatched it from my grasp and sat on the floor.

I set up the mixer and got everything ready for the call. Then I switched over to Skype and used the email address provided. The screen turned blue and I slipped on my headset, listening to the ringing. Of course, I'd hoped Amelia would grant me an interview, but after all that she'd been through I didn't plan on asking her for at least two weeks, wanting to give her space. So you could imagine how surprised I was to receive her email the day after we returned home from Vegas.

"Hello?" Amelia answered.

I heaved a sigh of relief. There was a part of me that thought she'd change her mind. "Hi, it's Liv and Camry," I said. "How are you doing?"

"Good," she said. "And you?"

"We're doing good." I looked down at Camry and she gave me a thumbs up. "Before we get started can we test the microphone?"

"Sure. One, two, three, four..." she continued to count to twenty until I could adjust the sound quality. Amelia had a sweet, soft voice, which was charming, but made it harder to catch.

"Okay, we're recording. Thank you for speaking with us," I started. "I was surprised to get your email."

"Honestly, I was surprised I sent it. But it seems only right to give my side of things. I've listened to all the episodes up until now, and I don't want anyone's name unnecessarily dragged through the mud."

"Are you talking about Carlos?" I asked.

I could almost hear Amelia nodding her head. "He's a good friend. I know people automatically assume he's trouble just because he has a rough exterior. But he's a really good guy."

"I can see that now, and I'm certain listeners will see that, too," I said. I had to crank out the episodes, three a week, to get listeners caught up. "Can you tell us about the night you disappeared?"

"Sure," she said with a long exhale. "Well, you know about the video. And you know that *Richard* was not happy about it." His name fell out of her mouth like it was an offensive word. "Public perception was everything to that man. He put so much pressure on us to be perfect that it broke my mom. That night I had a date with Oliver." She lets out a little chuckle. "What are the odds, right?"

I assumed she's referring to the fact that she had a date with Oliver, and I was currently dating Oliver...well, if you called nights spent in eating pizza and "playing" baseball dating.

Which, for the record, I do.

"What happened after the ATM visit?" I asked.

"*Richard* asked me to meet the repairman at CinnaMann's that night. He was driving home from a conference and didn't think he'd make it in time. He'd been on my case all week about the stupid video and losing my job, and I sort of snapped. I told him I wouldn't go and hung up. But then when I was at the ATM, I remembered Carlos' brother worked for Joe and Son's, so I thought I'd at least let him in to the bakery. But when I got to there, *Richard* was there. He'd sent Raymond home, because it turned out to be an easy fix. We sort of got into it. He wasn't used to me standing up for myself, but I'd had with that man..." her voice trailed off and I waited for her continue without pressing for more details.

"Anyway," she finally said. "*Richard* wasn't a violent man. Words were his weapon of choice."

"What was he saying?" I asked, feeling a bit pushy, but I knew the listeners would want to know.

"The normal. What a disappointment I was, and how I was as crazy as my mother. How the video would hurt business...I was just done. So I threw a whisk at his head and knocked him over."

"A whisk?" I asked, to be sure I heard her right. "Like the little handheld thing you whisk stuff with?" I broke a pot on the man's head and he barely flinched.

"No. You've been in the bakery. Do you remember the standup mixers that are big enough to fit a person in?"

I thought back to our tour. "Yes, I do remember seeing one."

"Right, so the whisk attachment is what I threw at him."

Oh, yeah, that might hurt.

"He got really mad," Amelia said. "And he grabbed...honestly, I don't know what he grabbed, but he threw it at me and knocked me out. Next thing I remembered, I was in the backseat of the car. He took me home so my mom could look at me because she used to be a nurse. He didn't even care that he'd hurt me. He said it was my fault because I threw the first punch. I probably had a concussion, but then I tried to leave and he wouldn't let me. I told him that I was going to call the police and tell them that he'd assaulted me. That ticked him off and he got in my face. I think it was just a mixture of years of resentment, and everything that had happened with that stupid YouTube video, and I was going through the break-up with Jeremy, and I didn't know it at the time, but I was sick. So I, um, I kicked him."

"I hope it was in the balls," Camry blurted out.

"Yep," said Amelia. "But here's the thing about Richard Clark, he doesn't like to be kicked there. I paid for that mistake. He attacked me the same way he attacked you, Liv. I didn't know what else to do, so I played dead. He got off me, and I was on the floor conscious, but my mom put her fingers on my neck and told him I was dead. She was so convincing that I questioned if I was. That's when he freaked, he blamed her and blamed me, and then he was talking about how he couldn't go to jail."

Camry rolled her eyes.

As did I.

The man thought he killed his daughter and his first reaction was what was going to happen to him.

"What happened next?" I asked.

I could hear Amelia lick her lips. When she spoke, she did so somberly. "My dad went to the bakery to move my car, and my mom was in charge of disposing of me. He always made her do his dirty work, so that makes sense. After he left, she told me to run. So I did. I was hurt, but I didn't have my phone or wallet or anything else on me. I went through the Vanderbilt's backyard and hopped the wall over to The Santa Maria Way Apartments. I went straight to Carlos' place. I knew that if Richard found me, he'd kill me before I could tell anyone what he'd done. And I couldn't go to the police. Everyone loved Mr. CinnaMann, and everyone thought I was crazy. Richard doesn't think rationally when he gets mad. Carlos hooked me up with a new identification and I took a bus to Arizona."

"And Jeremy met you there?"

"Not right away. Carlos told him what happened and he found

me." I could hear the smile in her voice.

"What was it like reconnecting?"

"It was hard at first, but we managed."

"And now you're married," I said. "To be honest, I didn't think this story would have a happy ending."

"Me either."

There was a lull in the conversation and I checked my notes. "Is it okay if I ask your opinion on Richard now?"

"What am I supposed to say? He's gone."

She was right. Thanks to a lifetime of cinnamon rolls (and two blocked coronary arties), Richard Clark was in fact gone. He'd died of a heart attack before he reached the hospital.

"What did Richard say to you when he showed up at your house?" I asked.

"I don't want to talk about it."

"Understandable." I crossed my legs and leaned in closer to the microphone. "Can I ask what you thought when you first heard about the podcast? Because knowing what I do now, I'm surprised Jeremy ever agreed to speak to us."

Amelia laughed. It was a pleasant, freeing sound. "When Carlos called me, he said you were two kids who were trying to do a podcast. I didn't think it would turn into what it is today. And if Jeremy didn't talk to you, he'd look suspicious."

She made a good point.

"Is there anything you didn't know that you learned from the podcast?"

"Penny," she said with a sigh. "I didn't know Penny sent the video."

"Are you surprised?"

"No, not really. But there's no point on dwelling on that is there?"

No. I guess there wasn't.

"Is there anything we got wrong?" I asked.

Amelia clicked her tongue. "Carlos is the one who hacked Penny's YouTube account to make sure the video wasn't deleted."

"Why would he do that?"

"I asked him to. I figured if everyone thought I was crazy, people would stop looking for me," she said. "And there's one big piece you missed entirely."

Camry rose to her knees, with both hands holding her headphones to her ears.

"Leon," Amelia said. "Six months ago, Leon found me."

I nearly fell out of my chair. "Th...wh...ho..." I paused to collect my thoughts. "Detective Leon Ramsey found *you*?"

"I was at Jeremy's office here in Vegas, and one day Leon showed up looking for me."

"But...he never said anything? Why wouldn't he...I'm sorry, I am having a hard time processing this."

"He said I was his only case that hadn't been closed, and he had recently been diagnosed with stage four lung cancer. He asked me to press charges, but I refused. Even if Richard were found guilty, he would have served maybe eight years, if that. And I just wanted to stay hidden. There wasn't really anything he could do at that point. Then I guess he thought if my story was out there then perhaps Richard would suffer the consequence of a public jury. Honestly, at first I was mad when Carlos told me that Leon had contacted you, but it seems to have worked out, I guess."

"But he acted like he had no idea where you were. He acted like this case was baffling to him. It's part of the reason I wanted to tell the story."

"In his defense, there's no way you would have touched my case if you thought I was alive and hiding from an egotistical narcissist maniac."

Not with a ten-foot pole.

"So you're in Vegas," I said. "With your husband and your health is good?"

"My health is great, actually. And my mom is here with us."

This I knew. Hazel told me. She'd gone over to Janet's house to see how she was. Janet slammed the door in her face, but not before saying she was moving in with her daughter.

"I'm happy you're well," I said. "Thank you for allowing me to tell your story, Amelia."

"No, Liv. Thank *you*. And you can call me Dori."

BONUS EPISODE

True Crime Con

Three Months Later

We followed the producer to the stage. I could hear the audience chatting on the other side of the curtain and my stomach did a summersault.

Austin pulled at his collar and filled his cheeks with air. He had on a black suit and a black tie. When the event director invited us to speak, he told us to dress casual. Austin looked ready for his own funeral.

"Oh you sweet thing." Hazel rubbed his back.

"W-w-w-w-why did I agree to th-th-th-th-this?"

"You'll be fine. Just let us do all the talking." Hazel flipped open a compact mirror, applied a layer of red lipstick and smacked her lips together. She looked quite fabulous in a layered blouse and gaucho pants.

Camry looked ready to perform. She was in a sequenced short-sleeved shirt, shiny black pants and four-inch heels. She had fake lashes, fake hair, and enough makeup on to paint the room. Oliver looked quite dashing in dark jeans and a white dress shirt tucked in.

Me? I was in black pants and a sleeveless green jersey tee. My hair fell below my shoulders in red curls and I was wearing my Converse wedges. I had a pair in every color.

Today I was wearing black and I had found my oomph.

"I'm so excited!" Camry glanced at me. "Are you excited? 'Cause you look excited. Are you excited?"

"Heck yeah I'm excited!"

Who wouldn't be?

We were at True Crime Con! This was the biggest conference for true crime in the world. Held in Raleigh, North Carolina at the convention center, over 100,000 people flocked here every year to listen to their favorite true crime podcasters, television hosts, and meet their favorite authors.

I'd never been before, but Mara had been the keynote speaker for the last three years in a row. Her appearances were recorded, and I'd listened to them on playback during editing.

"How much longer until we start?" signed Austin. His face was stark white and his forehead glistened under the overhead lights.

"About ten minutes." signed Oliver.

"Take a breath and picture everyone in their underwear," Camry signed.

"B-but my m-mom is in the audience."

Camry made a face. "Ew, then don't do that."

A frazzled woman wearing a headset gathered us together. "You all look fabulous. Thank you again for coming. We've got a packed house."

Austin gulped loud enough for me to hear.

The woman consulted her clipboard. "You're on in five minutes. Did they tell you where you'd be sitting?"

"They did," I said. "And there's an interpreter, right?"

The woman gasped. "Sorry! I forgot one of you is deaf! We don't get many deaf people at these *con-ven-tions*! Yes! There is an interpreter out there!"

"You don't have to yell," Oliver said.

The woman nodded, then shouted the last of our instructions and hurried back down the stairs.

Yikes.

Now I'm nervous.

I'd never been a public speaker before.

"Liv Olsen is that you?"

I turned around and gazed up. I couldn't believe it. Mara Lancer. She looked every bit as fabulous as she did the last time I saw her with her signature red-rimmed glasses and blonde hair streaked in blue.

We hugged. It was good to see her again. In a way, she was the reason *Missing or Murdered* was the success that it had become.

"Look at you?" She held me at arm's length. "I feel like a proud Momma."

"Found my oomph."

"You sure did, kiddo. I had no doubt you would."

I didn't believe that for a second. If she genuinely thought I'd be a success, then she would have produced *Missing or Murdered.* But she didn't.

And now I was the keynote speaker.

With the number one podcast in the country.

Still, Mara's seal of approval was the cherry on top of what had been an emotionally taxing and exhilarating sundae. I introduced her to the rest of the podcast posse. And we chatted about the business, like most podcasters do when they got together, until the lights went down and the host took the stage.

Mara and I parted with plans to get together for lunch "one of these days."

Basically never, especially since I was living in Santa Maria and she was still in San Diego. But the sentiment was there.

"Ladies and Gentlemen," the host settled the crowd. It was Ken Mathers, the producer and host of *True Crime with Ken.* He talked like he was from Brooklyn and looked like he was from Texas with cowboy boots and Wranglers on. "Thank you to everyone who has made this conference a smashing success." The crowd erupted in applause and Ken playfully took a bow. I pulled back the curtain and peeked out. Dad, Camry's mom Elena, my brother David and his wife were in the front row. Dad had his camcorder out and I couldn't help but laugh.

I'd never been more grateful for that kindhearted, fun-loving, honorable man I got to call my father. Not everyone was so blessed in the parent department.

I called Camry over and showed her. "Is Dad seriously wearing socks with Crocs?" she asked.

After further examination I realized yes, yes he was. But I found his misguided fashion attempts endearing.

"And now, what you've all been waiting for," Ken said. "Please direct your attention to the screen." He waved his hand and the room went dark.

Amelia's face filled the back of the stage. Talking in the background was Hazel, in her *slightly* sultry voice, giving the details of Amelia's disappearance. The picture of Amelia at her high school graduation—the one I took at CinnaMann's—flashed across the screen along with photos of Amelia's apartment, her car, the Clark's apple tree, and footage from the press conference and the YouTube video. It ended with a photo of Leon, and a snippet from our interview, "the last case of mine still open..."

Watching it brought back so many conflicting emotions to the surface.

Sadness over the loss of Leon.

Happiness that Amelia was free.

I was *mad* Richard Clark never spent time in jail.

And I was proud. Proud of what I'd done. What *we* had done.

Most of all I felt grateful. Blessed to be part of something bigger than myself.

"Are you ready to meet the minds behind this masterpiece?" Ken asked the crowd.

Everyone cheered and clapped.

"The wait is over. Here they are! First we have editorial advisor, Austin Mallor."

Austin rushed across the stage and took the seat closest to us. Per our detailed instructions, that was my seat, but I dared not move Austin.

"Next we have director of operations and narrator, Hazel Lewis."

Hazel glided across the stage, waving her hand as if she'd just been crowned. She was met with stunned silence. This was the typical reaction she got when meeting fans. The voice didn't match the person. Eventually the crowd erupted in loud cheers for the sultry Mrs. Claus.

Ken helped her into the seat. "Next we have line producer, Oliver Lewis."

I told Oliver to go out and the crowd was on their feet, screams and whistles proceeded. That was the typical reaction he got when meeting fans—mostly female fans. He sat beside Hazel and waved to the crowd.

And then there were two.

I turned to Camry. "Let's do this."

She gave me a hug. "Let's do this!"

"Please welcome, executive producer, Camry Lewis!"

Camry stepped onto the stage and threw both hands in the air like she was running for office. She was in her element and the crowd loved her. As they should.

Crap.

It's my turn.

I took a deep breath.

"Now, the person you've all been waiting for. The genius creator of *Missing or Murdered*, executive producer and host, Liv Olsen!"

I stepped on to the stage and held my hand up to protect my eyes from the lights. The crowd was invisible, but I could hear their cheers and my dad's "whoop-whoop-whoop."

I may burst.

But before I did, I sat between Camry and Oliver.

For the next hour we talked about *Missing or Murdered*, how we went about recording, the equipment used, how I chose the case. Every time Richard was mentioned the crowd booed.

Then it was time for questions.

The lights above the audience turned on, and I could see for the first time just how many people were there.

Oh my...

There were thousands and thousands. More than I could ever count. I didn't have to look at Austin to know he was currently living his own personal nightmare.

People lined up behind the microphones placed in the aisles. The first question came from a man named Brooks from Tennessee. "My question is for the entire cast. Do you still talk to Amelia Clark?"

Camry started. "No, I think she's still processing everything that's happened, and we want to give her space."

The next question was from a woman who drove all the way from Oklahoma. This one was for Oliver and I cringed, waiting for the question I knew was coming.

"Oliver, are you single?" she asked and the interpreter standing stage right, signed for him.

Not the question I was afraid of.

"Yes, I am," he said and signed.

What can I say?

Camry changed my Facebook status to "it's complicated" because it was.

We were no longer playing baseball.

For now.

Next question: "Oliver, can you truly be an impartial participant if you knew Amelia Clark personally?"

That was the question I was waiting for.

"I met Millie briefly," Oliver said. "As explained in the podcast, I didn't know anything had happened until I saw the missing-person report."

Episode "A Complicated Discovery" was about Oliver's involvement. It was our highest downloaded episode. I had not included our night of wine tasting. That footage no longer existed.

"What ever happened to Dr. Deb Naidoo? And did you ever find out if Janet was in town the week of Amelia's disappearance?"

an audience member asked me.

I held the microphone close to my mouth. "That's a good question. Detective LeClare did eventually get a hold of Dr. Naidoo. But that was after we'd found Amelia and, yes, Janet was in town."

Next question: "What about season two?"

"We are busy working on it now," said Camry. "We're looking into the murder of Brinkley Douglas." Camry gave me a sideways glance. She was not happy about this. She wanted to find another Amelia, but we decided to focus our efforts in Santa Maria, and Brinkley Douglas was proving to be just as complicated as Amelia's. Even though there was no chance she was holed up in Vegas.

The one problem with Brinkley's case: there was no doubt that there was a murderer out there.

A murderer who had successfully remained hidden for almost twenty years.

And we were about to uncover who that murderer was.

The next question was for me: "What was the best part of doing this podcast, and what advice do you have for aspiring podcasters?"

"Best advice is to be open to change," I said. "What you hear is nothing like what I pictured in my head. And the best part is that I was able to do this with my *sister*."

The crowd did a collective "awe."

As did Camry.

Next question was for me again: "You said that the podcast didn't turn out like you imagined it would in your head. Are you upset that Amelia was found alive?"

Geez.

I readjusted in the chair and took a moment to think about my response. "No, I'm ecstatic she's alive. What I meant by that was, I didn't set out to solve this case. I'm not a detective. I have no sleuthing experience. I set out to tell her story. And I did that. What drew me to Amelia was the public shaming she underwent. What was the point of it? What I see when I watch the video is a woman who is experiencing very real, very raw pain. I don't see Aluminum

Woman. I don't see how this is entertaining either. Or how this is beneficial. It's easy to shame people with modern digital platforms. And I do believe an argument can be made that it is effective. But what was effective about Amelia's video? She didn't make a racial slur. She didn't take a grand political stand. She fell and had a panic attack. Her video was uploaded for the purpose of humiliation and look what ended up happening. I think what we can learn from Amelia is the need for empathy. If you see a person in distress, don't film them. Help them. Yes, this may have been a happy ending, per se. But I am one hundred percent positive that if that video had not been shared Amelia wouldn't have had to endure all that she has. She wouldn't have had to go into hiding. Richard Clark might still be alive. Who knows? Just think about that the next time you're tempted to snap a picture or share a video of someone without his or her knowledge. Think about Penny and the daily guilt she feels. Think about the job she lost, and think about the public bashing she's received. Think about Blake Kirkland, the guilt that ended his life. Think about Amelia and realize you have no idea what happens behind closed doors."

ERIN HUSS

Erin Huss is a blogger and a #1 Kindle bestselling author. She shares hilarious property management horror stories at *The Apartment Manager's Blog* and her own horror stories at erinhuss.com. Erin currently resides in Southern California with her husband and five children, where she complains daily about the cost of living but will never do anything about it.

The Podcasting Sisters Mystery Series
by Erin Huss

MICROPHONES AND MURDER (#1)

Henery Press Mystery Books

And finally, before you go...
Here are a few other mysteries
you might enjoy:

PUMPKINS IN PARADISE

Kathi Daley

A Tj Jensen Mystery (#1)

Between volunteering for the annual pumpkin festival and coaching her girls to the state soccer finals, high school teacher Tj Jensen finds her good friend Zachary Collins dead in his favorite chair.

When the handsome new deputy closes the case without so much as a "why" or "how," Tj turns her attention from chili cook-offs and pumpkin carving to complex puzzles, prophetic riddles, and a decades-old secret she seems destined to unravel.

Available at booksellers nationwide and online

Visit www.henerypress.com for details

FATAL BRUSHSTROKE

Sybil Johnson

An Aurora Anderson Mystery (#1)

A dead body in her garden and a homicide detective on her doorstep...Computer programmer and tole-painting enthusiast Aurora (Rory) Anderson doesn't envision finding either when she steps outside to investigate the frenzied yipping coming from her own back yard. After all, she lives in a quiet California beach community where violent crime is rare and murder even rarer.

Suspicion falls on Rory when the body buried in her flowerbed turns out to be someone she knows—her tole-painting teacher, Hester Bouquet. Just two weeks before, Rory attended one of Hester's weekend seminars, an unpleasant experience she vowed never to repeat. As evidence piles up against Rory, she embarks on a quest to identify the killer and clear her name. Can Rory unearth the truth before she encounters her own brush with death?

Available at booksellers nationwide and online

Visit www.henerypress.com for details

Made in the USA
Monee, IL
05 February 2020